THE ROOT

OF

MURDER

A LOVERS IN CRIME MYSTERY

BY
LAUREN CARR

THE ROOT OF MURDER

Designed by Acorn Book Services

Publication Managed by Acorn Book Services
www.acornbookservices.com
acornbookservices@gmail.com
304-995-1295

Edited by Jennifer Checketts
oceanswave15052@yahoo.com

Cover designed by Acorn Book Services
www.mysterylady.net/acorn-book-services

ISBN: 9781798920299

Published in the United States of America

THE ROOT

OF

MURDER

A LOVERS IN CRIME MYSTERY

CAST OF CHARACTERS

In Order of Appearance

Vera and Cliff Newhart: Elderly couple. They have lived a   quiet simple life on their small farm in Hookstown, Pennsylvania until the night they find a body.

Cameron Gates: Lieutenant with Pennsylvania State Police' homicide division. Married to Joshua Thornton. They have an adopted daughter Isadora Thornton.

Joshua Thornton: Hancock County Prosecuting Attorney. Retired after his first wife died suddenly to return to his home town of Chester, West Virginia, to raise their five children. Now he's remarried to Cameron. They share an adopted daughter.

Isadora Thornton (Izzy): Cameron and Joshua's fourteen-year-old daughter. The light of Irving's and Admiral's lives.

Irving: Thornton's twenty-five pound Maine Coon cat. Black with a white stripe down his back, he resembles a skunk.

Admiral: Thornton's enormous Great Dane-Irish Wolfhound mix.

Tony Seavers: Cameron's new partner. Newly promoted to detective in homicide. This case has him hitting the ground running.

Tracy Gardner: Joshua's elder daughter. She's a successful caterer and business woman. Married to Hunter. She'd won his heart through his stomach.

Poppy Ashburn: J.J. Thornton's fiance. Trains J.J.'s champion quarter horses.

Elizabeth Collins: Receptionist/office manager at Madison's Dance Studio. She took dance lessons with Tracy, Madison, and Heather when they were in school.

Madison Whitaker: Owner of Madison's Dance Studio. Daughter of Shawn and Sherry Whitaker. Took dance lessons with Tracy and Heather when they were in school. She dated J.J. Thornton in high school.

J.J. Thornton: Joshua Thornton's eldest son. Owns Russell Ridge Farm and Orchards, inherited from his first love. Young criminal lawyer. Engaged to Poppy Ashburn.

John Davis: Murder victim. Vice-president at nuclear power plant in Shippingport. Married to Kathleen Davis for over thirty years. They have four grown children. One of his daughters, Lindsay was killed in car accident three years ago. He and his wife have permanent custody of her young son, Luke.

Lindsay Ellison: John Davis's younger daughter. Got pregnant in high school. Dropped out and married Derek Ellison. Heavily addicted to alcohol and drugs. Killed three years ago in a car accident. She'd left behind Luke, her young son.

Heather Davis: John and Kathleen Davis's older daughter. Used to take dance lessons with Tracy and Madison. She dated J.J. Thornton in high school, too. Works in marketing.

Kathleen Davis: John Davis's wife. Heather Davis's mother. Has four grown children. Her younger daughter, Lindsay was killed in a car accident three years ago. She and her husband have permanent custody of Lindsay's young son, Luke.

Luke: John and Kathleen Davis's seven year old grandson, by their late daughter Lindsay. Derek Ellison's son. The Davises have legal custody of him.

Derek Ellison: John Davis's estranged son-in-law. Addicted to drugs and alcohol. Murder weapon found in his home.

Sheriff Curt Sawyer: Hancock County Sheriff.

Hunter Gardner: Tracy Gardner's husband. Hancock County Sheriff Deputy.

Sadie Ellison: Derek Ellison's suffering mother.

Ollie: J.J. Thornton's pet lamb. He thinks he's a dog.

Charley: J,.J. Thornton's watch rooster. He's got issues.

Pilgrim: Rescued pregnant horse.

Gulliver: Poppy's Appaloosa horse. He's a Houdini horse. Likes to open the stall door and roam around.

Comanche: Izzy's horse.

Sherry Whitaker: Madison's mother. Married to Shawn Whitaker, who is missing. Dog breeder and trainer.

Shawn Whitaker: Sherry Whitaker's missing husband. Madison's father. Truck driver. Went out on a long haul. No one has heard from him since.

Bishop Moore: Rents apartment in Calcutta, Ohio, where the police find the victim's car. His application says he's a travel agent.

Ross Bayles: Manages apartment complex where Bishop Moore resides.

Brenda Bayles: Ross's wife. Wheelchair bound. Nasty woman.

Bea Miller: Murder suspect. John Davis got a restraining order against her. Could she be mad enough to kill?

Aaron Collins: Elizabeth's husband.

Jessica Faraday Thornton: Joshua's daughter-in-law. Married to Murphy Thonrton, J.J.'s identical twin brother. One of Poppy's bridesmaids. She's an heiress.

Murphy Thornton: J.J.'s identical twin brother. Married to Jessica. He's J.J.'s best man. Can he get J.J. to the ceremony on time?

Tristan Faraday: Jessica's brother. He's dating Sarah Thornton, Joshua's daughter, which can be a dangerous thing to do.

Sarah Thornton: Joshua Thornton's younger daughter. Midshipman at the United States Naval Academy. Bridesmaid.

Donny Thornton: Joshua Thornton's youngest son. College student. Groomsman.

Jealousy is no more than feeling alone against smiling enemies.

Elizabeth Bowen

PROLOGUE

Hookstown, Pennsylvania

"Cliff, what's that smell?"

Tying the belt to her bathrobe, Vera descended the stairs to go into the living room where her husband was snoring through the last half of a late-night talk show. On the farm nestled deep in the woods between the West Virginia state line and Hookstown, Pennsylvania, the elderly couple were accustomed to smoke from neighbors burning leaves.

In mid-January, leaf burning season was very much over.

Not only that, but this smell was different.

Cliff responded to his wife's question with a snort.

Vera went into the kitchen and looked out of the window over the sink. Through the line of trees across the back yard, she saw the bright orange glow of flames in the pasture.

"Cliff," she called out, "there's a fire out in the field!"

The word "fire" shocked her husband into consciousness and propelled him out of the recliner.

"Are all the horses in?" She followed him out onto the back porch.

LAUREN CARR

Cliff saw that his wife wasn't imagining things. There was a fire. It was too far away to see if it was spreading across the field toward their house or not. With the brisk winter wind, it could reach their home in no time.

"Someone must have dumped off their trash and tried to burn it." Cliff grabbed his coat, a flashlight, and fire extinguisher and rushed out the door.

Shrugging into her coat, Vera followed him across the back yard and through the gate into the pasture. It was only when she stepped in the icy mud that she realized she was still in her bedroom slippers. "It doesn't smell like trash." She ran as fast as she could in her slippers and the dark to keep up with her husband.

"Smells like a dead animal."

"Why would someone dump a dead animal in our field and set it on fire?" Vera had to shout for him to hear her above the wind. The odor of gasoline reached her nostrils.

Luckily, the pasture was too soggy after three days of heavy rain for the fire to have enough fuel to spread.

Several yards ahead of his wife, Cliff reached the source of the fire first. It took only a couple of blasts from the fire extinguisher for him to douse the flames. He shone his flashlight on the figure to determine what someone wanted to get rid of so desperately. It was too small to be a cow or horse. Yet, too big to be a dog. His jaw dropped when Cliff was able to make out the shape of a man.

"What is it?" Vera came to a halt when her husband threw up his hand.

"Call the police."

"The police?"

"Yes, Vera," he sputtered out. "The police. Now!"

Vera ran out of her slippers in her haste to get back to the warmth and safety of their farmhouse.

CHAPTER ONE

Rock Springs Boulevard, Chester, West Virginia

Uttering a sigh filled with bliss, Joshua Thornton fell back onto the bed he shared with his wife. "Now that was something to wake up to."

Cameron Gates dropped to lie on top of him. The locks of her cinnamon colored hair tickled his nose. "Oh, yeah," she breathed. "Lucky for you, I had a really dirty dream and couldn't keep it to myself."

He could feel her heart's rapid beat against his chest. It was like they were beating in unison. In the dark bedroom, he was only able to see her silhouette when she sat up.

"Mad that I woke you up?"

He kissed her with a chuckle. "Sharing is good for a marriage."

"Any naughty dreams you want to share with me?"

He threw his arms around her and rolled her over to pin her onto the bed. "Remember," he whispered into her ear, "you asked for it."

Her giggles turned into shrieks when he proceeded to tickle her ribs and stomach. It took several rings of her cell phone to break through the ruckus. Realizing it was her phone, they stopped laughing and stared over at the night stand on her side of the bed.

It rang again.

She looked up into Joshua's eyes. With a sigh, he rolled over to his side of the bed. She snatched the phone from the night stand. "Detective Gates here."

"Lieutenant," Joshua said.

"I'm calling for Lieutenant Gates," the dispatch officer said into her ear.

"That would be me," she said with a roll of her eyes. "I'm *Lieutenant* Gates. Sorry."

Joshua chuckled next to her, to which she gave him a good-natured punch in the shoulder.

While she took down the address, Joshua pulled the blankets up to his chin, on which he wore an ultra-short beard.

Disconnecting the call, she turned to him. "Silver foxes do give out rain checks on dirty dreams, right?"

His blue eyes, which were striking even in normal light, shone in the moonlight. "Depends." He ran his fingers through her hair, which she wore in short layers.

"On what?"

"On how long you're gone. I can't promise that I'll wait for you. You've seen the hordes of women beating on our door." He kissed her softly on the lips. "Now I know how Valerie must have felt."

Stroking his wavy silver locks, she asked, "I'm not sure how to take that. We make love and minutes later you're thinking about your late wife. Should I be offended?"

"No," Joshua said. "What I mean is, when I was in the Navy—doing investigations—more than once I would get called out in the middle of the night for a mission and …

sometimes that call would come when we were in the middle of ..." He shrugged his shoulders.

"What not?"

"What not. Now the shoe is on the other foot. Now my police lieutenant wife is getting the phone call in the middle of the night and running off to Lord knows what, and I'm the one being left in bed alone."

"Yeah, well, this is not a matter of national security." Cameron kissed him quickly on the lips and climbed out of bed. "Nor am I jetting off to Naples or some undisclosed location someplace." She yanked open a dresser drawer and proceeded to get dressed. "I'll be back in the morning, or at the latest, in time for dinner ... unless you make tuna casserole. Then I may have to stake out a burger joint someplace."

"Where are you going?"

"A farmer in Hookstown found a dead body in his pasture," she said. "Someone tried to burn it."

"In a field?" Propping himself up on pillows against the headboard, he admired her slender body. For a woman in her mid-forties, she kept herself in good shape. Chasing down murderers helped.

"It's the Newhart farm. Back off one of the side roads this side of Hookstown," she said while pulling on a pair of black slacks. "The killer could have thought the farm was abandoned." Offering him one more kiss, she shrugged. "Whatever. I'll run out there, check out the scene, catch the killer, and come back to you to cash in my rain check for your fantasy—just like I always do."

Joshua grinned into her pretty face. "You make it sound so simple."

She strapped on her utility belt and tucked her service weapon into its holster. "I only make it look that way." She pecked him on the lips. "Love you."

"Love you more."

She stepped out into the upstairs hallway of the three-story stone house on Rock Springs Boulevard to discover that another member of the Thornton family was not in bed. Izzy, her and Joshua's fourteen-year-old daughter, was at the top of the stairs at the other end of the hallway.

Everyone called her Izzy because hated her proper name, which was Isadora.

Cameron had met Izzy during a murder investigation in which her mother had been the victim. There was an instant emotional attachment, and Joshua agreed to Cameron's request to adopt the orphan.

Since Izzy had never had a father, she found it easy to call Joshua "Dad." However, she called Cameron "Cam" out of respect for her late mother. Unsure of how the name "Mom" would sound when directed at her, Cameron was totally okay with that.

With a shriek, Izzy jumped high enough to cause her long nightdress to float up. Her head full of tight blond curls bounced. She thrust both hands behind her back. "You're up!"

Cameron regarded the young girl staring down the length of the hall at her with her big eyes.

Looking equally guilty, Irving, Cameron's twenty-five-pound Main Coon cat, circled around Izzy's skinny bare legs and feet while gazing up at the goodie behind her back. With his long black fur and white stripe from the top of his head to the tip of his tail, Irving was notorious for frightening their neighbors who regularly mistook him for a skunk.

Close to forty pounds heavier than Izzy, the Thornton's Great Dane-Irish Wolfhound Mix stood two steps behind the girl. Admiral's focus was also directed at the hidden treasure.

Cameron cocked an eyebrow in her direction. "Yes, I'm up." She sauntered down the hallway toward her. "I have to go to work. What's your excuse?"

"We wanted to tell you to be careful out there."

Placing a hand on the girl's bony shoulder, Cameron eased her around to peer behind her back. Discovering a bowl filled to the top with rocky road ice cream and slathered in hot fudge sauce, she let out a laugh.

"I couldn't sleep." Izzy bounced with a wide smile across her face. "I'm too excited about going shopping for bridal gowns tomorrow." Worry crossed her face. "You'll still be able to go with us, won't you?"

"I'm going to do everything I can to go," Cameron said. "Even if I can't make it, you're still going. You can't not go. Poppy can't pick out her bridesmaids' dresses without her maid of honor."

Izzy's curls shook. "I can't wait to pick out my dress. Poppy said we'll get to pick out whatever we want."

"But you and your sisters have to agree on what it is you want," Cameron said. "Sarah is talking about desert camouflage. Tracy is thinking more along the line of Jane Eyre." She lowered her voice. "It's your job to keep them in line. Even if Poppy is allowing all of you to decide what to wear, she is the bride. Don't let anyone ram something atrocious down her throat."

"Whatever the bride wants, the bride gets," Izzy said. "I've been reading all about that. I'm going to be the best maid of honor ever! I even downloaded an app on my phone to stay organized. I'm so glad Poppy isn't a bridezilla. She says her and J.J.'s wedding is a celebration for all of their friends and family. They want everyone to have fun and it's no fun when the bridesmaids have to wear ugly dresses."

"I think that's a fabulous attitude," Cameron said. "I'd hate for your brother's family and friends to attend his wedding only because they want to see the bride fall face first into the wedding cake."

"That's not going to happen with Poppy." Izzy was bouncing again. "I am so excited about Poppy becoming my sister." She put a spoonful of the ice cream in her mouth. "I thought a snack would help me sleep," she said between licks of the spoon.

Taking the ice cream dessert from her, Cameron held it up to admire the size of the treat. "Your father and I haven't been a bad influence on you, have we? This looks like something he would have concocted."

"Well …"

Cameron took the spoon and helped herself to one bite. "Be sure to go to bed as soon as you finish this and don't forget to take your dirty bowl down to the kitchen in the morning." Handing the spoon back to Izzy, she kissed her on the forehead.

"Thanks, Cam." Izzy gazed up at her in the dimly lit hallway. "I meant what I said."

"About what?"

"Being careful out there." Izzy hugged her.

It was cold, dark, and drizzly. The thought of a murder victim laying alone in a muddy field in such weather struck a morbid cord as Cameron pulled her white SUV up to the edge of the crime scene tape.

To say that Cameron Gates investigated homicides in Pennsylvania while making her home a state away in West Virginia was not as strange as it may seem. Tucked in the tip of West Virginia's northern panhandle, Chester was only a couple of miles from both the Ohio and Pennsylvania state lines. More often than not, Cameron found herself pursuing leads and suspects in the neighboring states.

An exceedingly slender man with a shiny new gold detective's shield clipped to his coat's lapel gingerly stepped over the muddy road to meet her when she threw open the driver's side door.

An exceedingly slender man with a shiny new gold detective's shield clipped to his coat's lapel gingerly made his way along the muddy road to meet her when she threw open the driver's side door. He stuck out his hand. "Lieutenant Gates, I'm Detective Tony Seavers. Just assigned to homicide. Captain Doyle told me that we were going to be working together."

Clasping his hand, Cameron took her time to look him up and down. The "working together" phrase was telling. The state police officer had gained a reputation of not playing well with his immediate supervisors. She had been given a heads up via the grapevine that Detective Seavers had filed a grievance against his previous boss after being reprimanded for using his cruiser to conduct personal business.

"Lieutenant Gates." She paused to remind herself of her promotion, which was still fresh. It had been due only to Joshua's prodding that she finally took the lieutenant's exam. "And yes, the captain did ask me to show you how things are done in homicide." She didn't miss the frown that crossed his face at the reminder that she was aware of her position over him. She leaned into the SUV to extract a pair of evidence gloves from her case. "Any ID on the vic?"

"Nothing in his pockets," Detective Seavers told her while leading her down the road to where the crime scene investigators had erected a tent over the body to preserve as much evidence as possible from washing away in the rain. "He seemed to be wearing dress shoes and slacks. Not a homeless guy."

Cameron stopped and looked at the field and woods surrounding the scene. The field was surrounded by thick woods and far from any main roads. "Did you find a car?" She shivered when a drop of icy water rolled down the back of her neck and between her shoulder blades.

"Still looking but can't find any so far."

She picked up the pace to the tent offering shelter. "How did he end up here in the middle of nowhere?"

"Someone dumped him." The detective followed her.

"Which means the primary crime scene is someplace else." She took a couple of steps before stopping. Tony slipped in the mud while trying not to collide with her.

"We've got tire tracks," Cameron followed the path of the tire tracks in the mud. "It looks like whoever dumped him turned onto the dirt road leading back to this farm and then turned off onto the access road and followed it back here." She squinted through the darkness into the thick woods. "That's a round-about way. Why not just pull over off the road and dump him in the ditch? If they were lucky, he'd decompose, and his body would be eaten by scavengers?"

"If they didn't want him found, they wouldn't have dumped him in a hayfield next to a farmhouse and set him on fire," he said.

"Exactly. The killer wanted him found." In the tent, Cameron knelt next to the medical examiner, a middle-aged woman, and tried to look over her shoulder at what appeared to be a charred mummy. The body had been wrapped in something before being set ablaze. "What have we got, Vivian?"

"A body wrapped in a comforter, which was soaked in gasoline and then lit." The medical examiner peeled back what was left of the blanket to reveal a charred body. She pointed to his arms, which were clutched close to his chest, with his fists under his chin. "We might be able to pull fingerprints. At the very least, we can get dental x-rays."

"Based on what I can see of what's left of his clothes, he's well dressed." Cameron tugged at the thick material under his arm that went up to his armpit. "My guess is that he has a family, or at least someone who will notice that he's missing. Tony, check with missing persons."

"Sure." He took out his computer tablet to make a note.

"Any idea of COD?" Cameron asked the medical examiner.

"Do you see the smoke coming off his charred corpse?" Vivian said with a smirk.

"Can you tell if he was dead before or after he was set on fire?" Cameron asked.

With a sigh, Vivian said, "I've got to get him back to the lab and—"

"—and open him up. I know. I know." Cameron patted her on the shoulder before standing up.

"Have the invitations gone out for the wedding yet?" Vivian asked.

"The wedding isn't for another two months," Cameron said.

"But I am on the list, right?"

"You're on the list." Cameron prepared to step from under the tent's shelter. "Tony, come with me to interview the witnesses who found the body."

Together, they trudged across the field toward the farmhouse.

"Are you getting married?" Tony asked her along the way.

Cameron laughed. "No, my stepson J.J. is getting married the last weekend of March. He owns Russell Ridge Farm and Orchards."

"Wow."

"He and his sister Tracy have decided to become partners. They're renovating the old Russell mansion to open a restaurant. He owns the mansion, and the dairy farm and orchards will provide most of the food that will go straight from the farm to the table. Tracy's a gourmet chef and caterer, so she'll provide the menu. They're planning the grand opening to be with J.J. and Poppy's outdoor wedding and reception."

"Fancy."

"It will be a reception to die for," she said. "My step-daughter is the best cook in the tri-state area. *That's* why everyone is fighting for invitations to this wedding."

Vera was waiting for them at the back door of the farm house. Surprise crossed her face upon seeing the slender woman in shaggy brown hair wiping her shoes on the worn doormat. "You're a homicide detective?"

"That's why they gave me this shiny gold badge." Cameron took her detective's shield from her jacket pocket and showed it to her. "Lieutenant Cameron Gates and Detective Tony Seavers with the state police. May we come in?"

The older woman opened the door and invited them inside. "I know. I know. Women are doing everything nowadays. It's just you're so pretty and it's so dangerous being a police officer." She backed up upon seeing the weapon Cameron wore on her hip. She turned to Tony. "And you're so young. How does your mother feel about you doing this?"

"She's not thrilled," Tony said. "She wanted me to be a lawyer."

She went on to introduce herself as Vera Newhart and her husband Cliff before rushing to the kitchen to make tea to warm them up.

The interior of the quaint farmhouse was decorated with knick knacks collected throughout many generations that had lived on the Newhart farm. Family pictures occupied the fireplace mantle, end tables, and shelves throughout the house. Many of the more current pictures were of a pretty blond-hair girl from childhood to adult. She was dressed in a variety of flowing, shimmery outfits. In most of the pictures, she held huge trophies.

"Do you know who he is?" Cliff asked.

"We came in to ask you that," Tony said. "It seemed like the killer went to a lot of trouble to dump him here."

Cameron paused in studying one of the pictures on the mantle to shoot a warning glance in Tony's direction. He was giving the witnesses more information than necessary.

"That's our granddaughter, Madison," Vera told Cameron in reference to one of the portraits upon returning to the living room with two mugs of tea. "She's a wonderful dancer."

"The best," Cliff said with a smile. "State champion three years in a row. All through high school."

"She owns Madison's Dance Studio in Beaver Falls," Vera said. "I'm sure you've heard of it."

"I'm not that much into dance." Cameron blew into the hot tea to cool it off.

"Do you have any children?" Vera asked them.

"I'm not married," Tony said.

"Well, you're so young." Vera turned to Cameron for her response.

"Six."

"Six?" Vera looked her up and down—admiring Cameron's slender, athletic build. "How do you keep your figure?"

A slim grin crossed Cameron's lips. "Chasing bad guys." She didn't go into explaining that she was stepmother to Joshua's five adult children and their daughter Izzy had been adopted.

"We have one—a daughter." Vera picked up a framed portrait of a young woman posing with a cocker spaniel. "Sherry's a dog groomer. She's groomed several champions."

After admiring the picture of the blonde, who appeared to be a slightly older version of Madison, Cameron returned it to the end table from where Vera had grabbed it. "Have you been living here long?"

"Three generations," Cliff said. "My father built this house for my mother. I grew up here with my brothers and sisters. I was the only one who wanted to stay after my parents passed. Why do you ask?"

"We're trying to figure out why someone would dump a dead body in your field," Cameron said. "Can you think of who he might be?"

"What does he look like?" Vera asked. "I didn't really see—"

"Middle-aged man," Cameron said. "You said you only have a daughter—"

"And one granddaughter," Cliff said.

"Any ex-husbands or boyfriends?" Tony asked.

Both Vera and Cliff shook their heads. "Sherry is happily married," Cliff said.

"Shawn isn't around that much on account he's a cross-country truck driver," Vera said. "But Sherry says that's why their marriage is such a success. They've been together twenty-eight years."

"Is Shawn out on the road now?" Cameron asked.

"He was here just yesterday to help me fix a broken door in the barn," Cliff said. "Him and Sherry stayed to have dinner with us."

"Shawn left early this morning to go pick up a load and head out on the road again," Vera said.

"I think he said he was going to Montana," Cliff said.

"They are very happily married," Vera said. "Everyone loves Shawn. No way that can be him."

"Is there anyone you can think of who would possibly want to send you a message by dumping a dead body practically in your back yard?" Cameron asked.

Vera placed her hands on her hips. ""Lieutenant Gates, what kind of people do you think we are? We're nothing but a couple of old goats. We work hard. We pay our taxes."

"We don't even drink," Cliff said.

"Do we look like the type of folks who'd know anyone who'd kill someone, dump him in a hayfield, and then set fire to him?"

"Well, maybe your brother Stan," Cliff muttered to his wife.

"Stan's much too lazy to go to that much trouble."

"That's true." Cliff told Cameron, "She's right. Her brother is one lazy son-of-a-gun."

Chapter Two

Beaver Falls had been a travelers' hub in western Pennsylvania's early days. Boasting multiple modes of transportation from railroad, river canal, highway, and even an intercity trolley, it had become a popular spot for residents to make their homes. Decades later, Beaver Falls remained a popular area for folks yearning for a more personal shopping experience in a quaint old-fashioned atmosphere.

With no identification on their victim, Cameron decided to resume her weekend while the medical examiner conducted the autopsy, and the crime scene investigators examined the physical evidence that had survived the rain and fire.

She had made it to Beaver Falls just in time to park next to stepdaughter Tracy Gardner's red SUV, which had placards on the side and rear panels reading, "Prime Event Catering."

Cameron smiled at the three ladies who waved enthusiastic greetings upon seeing her pull into the space next to theirs.

With a flawless figure, lush auburn hair, and her father's striking blue eyes, Tracy was every bit of Daddy's little girl—in that she had her daddy wrapped around her little finger. In the few years that Cameron had known her, Tracy had grown from a daddy's girl into one of the area's most success-ful businesswomen.

After her mother's sudden death when she was only a teenager, Tracy had taken over her mother's role in manag-ing the household—especially in the kitchen. Between her culinary gifts and experience cooking for a large family, she became a natural gourmet cook. After graduating from the CIA, that is the Culinary Institute of America, she returned to Chester, where she married her high school sweetheart, Hunter Gardner, a Hancock County sheriff's deputy.

In less than two years, Tracy was quickly outgrowing the caterer's kitchen she had installed in her home. It was while out on a trail ride at her brother's farm that she happened upon the abandoned century old mansion that had been the former main house at Russel Ridge Farms.

Her entrepreneur juices started flowing and a partnership was born.

"Cam! I knew you'd make it!" Izzy ran around the back of the cruiser to take Cameron into a hug.

"You missed breakfast at the café." Poppy Ashburn slipped an arm around her waist and gave her a hug. In contrast to Tracy's stylish dress with matching cloth coat and heels, the horse trainer, who many in the area called a "horse whisperer" was dressed in clean jeans, boots, and western hat. She wore her long, wavy red hair lose. While it was hard to miss her red hair, it was impossible to miss the multitude of freckles that kissed her face.

"No, I didn't miss breakfast," Cameron told her. "I had lukewarm coffee and donuts."

"Well, you didn't miss much," Tracy said with a wave of her hand before leading them across the street to the bridal shop. "The eggs were overcooked and dry. The bacon was greasy, and they'd put too much vanilla in the pancakes."

Cameron was halfway across the street before she noticed the sign over the storefront that read "Madison's Dance Studio." She almost stopped. *That must be the Newharts' granddaughter.* The tug of Izzy's hand on her arm urged her to join Tracy and Poppy on the sidewalk.

"You look like you just saw a ghost," Tracy told her as Poppy and Izzy trotted into the shop.

Cameron pointed at the store only two doors down from the bridal shop. "Madison's Dance Studio. I met Madison's grandparents last night. Cliff and Vera Newhart. They live on a farm in Hookstown. They're witnesses in the case I just caught."

"You mean they saw a murder go down?"

"No, a body was dumped on their farm."

"Anyone they know?"

Cameron shook her head. "They say it wasn't. Hard to say if that's for certain. The body was burnt beyond recognition."

"If they're who I think they are, then I took dance lessons with their granddaughter." Tracy looked through the glass front into the studio's waiting room. It was filled with parents waiting for their children to finish a lesson. "Maddie Whitaker. She went to New York to become a dancer on Broadway. I thought she was good enough. Guess she didn't make the cut. I'd heard rumors that she was back."

A young woman with bleached blond hair falling to her shoulders stepped into the waiting room. Her red leggings and black and white horizontal striped crop top made her curvaceous figure appear broader. Upon seeing Tracy and Cameron peering through the window she stopped.

Tracy waved to her.

A broad toothy smile crossed her face and she hurried through the door. "Tracy Thornton? Is that you?"

Tracy let out a gasp. "Elizabeth?"

With a squeal, they hugged each other.

"What are you doing here?" Tracy asked.

"I work here, of course." With a giggle, Elizabeth clutched a gold chain from which a heart-shaped pendant hung. She cast a glance at Cameron—noting the police shield and weapon on her belt. "I'm working with Madison. Running the office, keeping the website updated. Elizabeth of all trades. You know."

Through the window, Cameron saw a slender blonde in a purple leotard with a matching wrap-around skirt step into the waiting room.

"Isn't it fabulous?" Elizabeth gestured at the sign above the door. "We opened in August and some classes are already full."

The blonde threw open the door. "Tracy Thornton, are you causing trouble again?"

"It's Tracy Gardner now." Tracy took her into a hug. She introduced them to Cameron. "Maddie, what happened to Broadway?"

"Oh, New York is such a jungle," Madison said while bouncing on the balls of her feet, which were bare. "Back stabbing. Dog eat dog. I decided I'd rather be a big fish in a small pond. So I came back here. You?"

"Tracy owns Prime Event Catering," Cameron said with pride.

"That's you? One of my parents used your catering for her daughter's wedding. She recommended you for our year-end recital in May. Do you have a business card?"

Always prepared to promote her business, Tracy whipped out a card from her phone case. "But you need to get booked right away. My schedule is quite busy."

Madison handed the business card to Elizabeth. "Be sure to put this in the recital folder. Don't let me forget to call her early next week."

Elizabeth took the card and noted the reminder. "I can get the next class started with warm-ups if you want to catch up with Tracy for a minute."

Madison's eyes grew wide. Her mouth dropped open before she shook her head. "No, I'm coming in right now."

"Would you like me to run to the store for some aspirin after you start the next class?"

"That's okay. I'll tough it out,"

As Elizabeth ran inside, Madison rubbed her temple. "I woke up with an awful migraine this morning."

Cameron nodded her head. "I can't imagine anything worse than trying to teach dance to a class filled with children with a migraine."

"If I learned anything in New York, it was how to tough things out."

Seeing Izzy step out of the bridal shop to check on them, Cameron urged Tracy to say good-bye to her friend.

"How's J.J.?" Madison asked before they could step away.

"He's fine," Tracy said a low laugh. "As a matter of fact, we're here to pick out a bridal gown for his fiancé. He's getting married the last weekend of March."

Madison's face fell with disappointment. "Well, tell him I said hi." She went back into the studio.

"I take it she's one of J.J.'s old flames," Cameron said while they hurried back to the bridal shop.

"They dated off and on for about a year when we were in high school," Tracy said with a roll of her eyes.

They found the bridal shop's manager shaking her head at Poppy, who looked dejected.

"They don't have her gown," Izzy told Cameron and Tracy with a frown.

Taking note of the wall-to-wall dresses and gowns around them, Cameron asked, "Have they looked?"

"She should have ordered it two months ago for a March wedding," the manager said.

"What do you have?" Cameron asked.

"Nothing with gold lace," the manager snapped. "Nothing like what she is describing."

"Gold lace?" Cameron turned to Poppy.

"It's a mermaid gown, but has a huge detachable train," Poppy said. "It's my dream gown."

"Every woman has a dream gown," the manager said. "The thing is, when it comes to ordering their gown, they have to come back to reality."

"No." Poppy shook her head. "Ever since J.J. and I have gotten engaged I've been dreaming about my wedding. I can see everything like I'm there. It's always the same gown—one of a kind."

"Custom designed." The manager folded her arms across her chest. "That's impossible."

"Don't you have some puppies you need to go kick?" Cameron asked.

With a huff, the manager stormed away to find a more reasonable bride-to-be to deal with.

"Is it always the same gown that you dream about?" Izzy asked.

"Always," Poppy said. "Look, I'm not a big dream person, but this dream is so real. It's like I'm there. And before I go down the aisle, I look in the mirror—and I've never felt so beautiful before—I feel like a princess—there's this woman behind me in the mirror. In my dream, I know her. And I feel …" Tears came to her eyes. "I feel like she's my mother." She wiped a tear away. "But she's not. No way."

Cameron felt her heart skip.

They were Poppy's family. Before the Thorntons, Poppy had no one—except her Appaloosa horse Gulliver. Poppy's father had gone missing when she was a child and was presumed dead. Her stepfather had raped Poppy when she was a teenager. Poppy's mother disowned her after she killed her abuser in self-defense.

Since then, Poppy had been on her own—traveling across the country—just her and Gulliver—until she happened onto Russell Ridge, where J.J. hired her to breed and train his champion quarter horses.

"What does this woman look like?" Cameron asked.

"Long blond hair," Poppy said. "Blue eyes. Very pretty. She blows me a kiss before I go down the aisle … to marry J.J."

"Well, if that's the gown you're meant to wear, then we're going to keep on looking until we find it." Izzy pushed herself out of her seat.

Cameron felt her cell phone vibrate on her hip. While the bride-to-be and bridesmaids continued talking, she pulled the phone from its case. The caller ID read "Tony."

"Maybe Jessica can help," Tracy said in reference to her sister-in-law. An heiress, Jessica was married to Murphy, J.J.'s identical twin brother. "She knows loads of fashion designers. Maybe she'll know who designed that gown. Maybe you saw it in a magazine—"

Poppy was shaking her head. "No, I dreamed about it before I even looked at any bridal magazines." She clenched her fists. "I have to find it. It's important that I wear that gown."

"Then let's keep looking," Izzy said. "There's more than one bridal shop around. You're only getting married once. If that gown is the one you're meant to wear, then darn tootin' we're gonna find it. Right, Cam?"

They turned around to find that Cameron had slipped outside onto the sidewalk.

"They got a hit on the guy's fingerprints," Tony told Cameron. "He was a vice president at the nuclear power plant in Shippingport. His fingerprints were taken for his security clearance. Name is John Davis. Fifty-three years old. Lives in Chester with a wife, Kathleen Davis. Has four kids."

"John Davis from Chester, West Virginia," Cameron repeated as Tracy led Izzy and Poppy from the shop.

"John Davis?" Tracy asked. "What about him?"

Tony was still talking in Cameron's other ear. "Looks like he was dead before the fire. There was no smoke in his lungs. Vivian found stab wounds. She counted thirty-two times to the neck and chest. He had defensive wounds to his hands and arms, too."

"Stabbed thirty-two times," Cameron noted. "Defensive wounds. That points to a crime of passion and someone he knew." She told Tony to text her the address and she'd meet him there before disconnecting the call. "Do you know him?"

"Sure," Tracy said. "We know his family. He's a bigwig at the nuclear power plant. He travels a lot, so I don't know him that well. But, Kathleen Davis, his wife, is president of the Chamber of Commerce. She's the director of human resources at Mountaineer. I went to school with Heather, their daughter." Cringing, she looked at Poppy out of the corner of her eye. "J.J. dated her off and on for about a year."

"I thought Murphy was the Romeo twin," Cameron said.

"J.J. had his moments," Tracy said. "What about Heather's dad?"

"He's the murder victim whose case I caught this morning. I need to go tell the family."

Tracy reached into her purse. "Dad should go with you."

"Is that my phone or yours?" Joshua crooked his neck to look under his armpit down to his coat hanging on a hook in the foyer.

"Yours." Perched at the top of a second ladder, J.J. pressed the button on the nail gun to drive a nail into the new crown molding. The physical labor from renovating the house and doing chores at his horse farm had added muscles to his slender frame.

Positioned on ladders at opposite ends of the wall, the father and son wore thick jackets in the drafty house. Working almost every day on the renovations, J.J. would go for two or even three days without shaving. His auburn hair had grown shaggy to the top of his collar.

Joshua, on the other hand, had a more public career as Hancock County's prosecuting attorney. That meant court appearances and occasional interviews with the media. He could only escape the razor on the weekends. For that reason, he kept his silver hair and ultra-short beard and mustache neatly trimmed.

The original crown molding that encompassed the ceilings in the old mansion had elaborate wood carvings. Tracy had insisted on keeping them. Unfortunately, during the two decades since the house had been abandoned, the roof had sprung leaks that resulted in whole sections of the ceilings and walls needing to be replaced.

Envisioning a gorgeous spring wedding as a huge marketing event to show off the trendy, elegant farm-to-table restaurant, Tracy had talked J.J. and Poppy into setting their wedding date to double as the grand opening.

Tracy's proposal had been based on the mansion needing only a little "fixing-up." It wasn't until the siblings had committed to the venture that they discovered that their restaurant venue was a money pit. J.J. suspected this was the reason Suellen Russell, the partner who had left her estate to him, had built her home at the other end of the farm.

In the six months since forming their partnership, the Thornton men, including Tracy's husband, had spent every weekend, and many evenings, working on restoring the Russell mansion. A new roof, plumbing, electrical.

With two months left to the big day, they were racing the clock to complete the restoration and plan an elaborate wedding. It still needed to have a commercial kitchen installed and the dining rooms decorated and furnished.

This Saturday, father and son were replacing the intricate crown molding, which had been contaminated with mold, in the rooms on the ground floor. They could hear the winter wind whistling across the farm, through the huge century old trees, and the house.

After four hours of work, they were ready for a break and some lunch. The coffee maker they had plugged into the wall and rested on a folding table was empty.

Once J.J. had secured the molding, Joshua climbed down from his ladder and fetched the phone from his coat pocket. "Maybe Tracy is calling to get our lunch order so that she can bring us some food."

"I doubt it." J.J. leaned back while descending his ladder to check on the position of the molding. "More likely, she's decided to have us take out the wall between the sitting and living room to create a more open dining experience."

With a laugh, Joshua read the caller ID. The call had been from Tracy. Rather than checking the voice mail she had left, he hit the button to return her call.

"I'm serious," J.J. said. "She was talking about that last night. I told her, 'That time has now past.' She told me, 'We'll see about that.'"

"Hey, Dad, where are you?" Joshua could tell by the background noise that she was driving.

"J.J. and I just finished putting up your crown molding. Did you ladies pick out your dresses already?"

"No," she said. "John Davis was murdered last night."

"Davis? John Davis?"

"Kathleen Davis's husband. Heather's dad."

"Where—"

"Cameron just got the ID. She's on her way there. I'm taking Poppy and Izzy back to the farm and then going to their place. I thought you might want to go over, too, to help Cameron break the news."

Joshua looked down at his stained and torn jacket. His work boots were muddy. While he wasn't exactly presentable, he decided the Davis family wouldn't notice under the circumstances. He was aware of J.J. watching him with a slight grin when he hung up.

"Son—"

"You have to go." J.J. narrowed his blue eyes—identical to those of his father.

Joshua looked around the room at the work benches, tools, walls that needed painting, and hardwood floors that needed restored—and only one man left to do it all—alone.

"Hunter–"

"His shift isn't over until five o'clock." J.J. took a long drink of water from a thermos and wiped his mouth on his sleeve. "Don't worry about it, Dad. Go."

Joshua remembered why he was leaving while putting on his coat. "Heather Davis's father was killed last night."

The news hit J.J. "Are you serious? Why would anyone kill him? The guy's a workaholic at Shippingport."

"Cameron is the lead investigator." Joshua zipped up his coat. "Tracy is going over to their house now to meet Cam. She thinks I should be there. I've worked pretty closely with Heather's mom at the Chamber of Commerce. I might be able to to help ease the news."

"I doubt it," J.J. said. "Finding out that your husband got whacked? That news can't be eased."

CHAPTER THREE

On a hilltop overlooking the town of Chester, nestled along the Ohio River, Chester Hill sported spacious contemporary houses.

Joshua met Cameron and Tracy at the Thornton home on Rock Springs Boulevard. Leaving her SUV in the driveway, Tracy climbed into the back seat of Cameron's cruiser, and they rode together to deliver the horrific news that would change their friends' lives forever.

"Poor Kathleen," Joshua said as Cameron turned out onto the road. "How long ago did Lindsay die in that car accident?" he asked Tracy.

"Three years ago. They've been in a nasty custody battle for Luke ever since."

"Luke?" Cameron made a left turn to drive her cruiser up the hill to where the Davis's white ranch-style home with black shutters rested at the end of a long twisting drive.

"Lindsay's son," Joshua said. "Lindsay and her husband Derek were very heavily into drugs."

"Lindsay wrapped her car around a tree," Tracy said. "Thank God she didn't hit another car and take others with her."

"Derek's addiction is so bad that he can't function," Joshua said. "After Lindsay was killed, the Davises easily won temporary custody. For the last three years, they've been fighting for full permanent custody."

Cameron pulled into the driveway to park next to another unmarked Pennsylvania cruiser. Tony climbed out. "How did Luke's father feel about them taking his son away?"

"According to what I heard from the family court lawyer," Joshua said, "he wasn't one bit happy."

"Unhappy enough to kill?" Cameron asked.

In the rear seat, Tracy leaned toward the back of Cameron's seat. "Didn't you say John Davis was stabbed?"

"Thirty-two times," Cameron answered Tracy's reflection in the rearview mirror.

"Derek stabbed a guy in high school."

Tracy's old friend, Heather, happened to be visiting her mother and nephew when she answered the call of the door chimes. Any question about why a group of friends would drop in unannounced was overtaken by Joshua's disheveled appearance. While exchanging greetings, Heather looked him up and down.

"I was helping J.J. do some work out at the farm," Joshua apologized while scraping the straw and mud that had collected on the bottom of his boots off on the doormat. Before he could step inside, a white furball shot from the bedroom wing of the house.

Twenty pounds of fur and teeth clamped itself around Joshua's leg and held on while the dog's seven-year-old master giggled.

"Luke, I told you to keep Munster in the bedroom," Heather told the little boy, who delighted in the sight of Joshua trying to shake the little dog off his leg.

39

Having concluded that he liked Joshua, Munster opted to stop biting and proceeded to hump his leg instead. Heather joined Cameron and Tracy in trying to peel the dog off Joshua. Unhappy about his offer of love being rejected, the little dog snarled and growled while Heather held him tucked under her arm.

Amused, Tony offered no aid. Instead, he stood laughing at the scene.

"A man is being attacked and all you can do is stand there and laugh?" Cameron asked him.

"You have to admit it was funny."

"Well, if it's so funny—" Cameron snatched the dog out of Heather's arms and tossed him in Tony's direction.

Seemingly in midair, Munster latched onto the detective's leg. While Tony fought to disengage the dog, Luke rolled on the floor with laughter. After his aunt detached the dog, she thrust him into Luke's arms and ordered him to take the dog back to his room and close the door.

"Sorry," Heather said. "Luke was begging for a dog and Dad just brought him home one day. Didn't even talk to Mom about it. That little monster has been a terror since day one. That's why we call him Munster." With a grimace, she rubbed her forehead. "I'm sorry. I woke up this morning with an awful headache." She took a bottle of aspirin from her jacket pocket." Mom's on the phone."

They exchanged glances filled with sympathy.

"Is there anything we can do—" Tracy offered. "You do look a little pale."

"Oh, it's just a sinus headache." Heather picked up a bottle of water from the coffee table. "I was getting an aspirin when I saw your SUV outside." She called into the study, located off the living room. "Mom, Mr. Thornton is here to see you." She turned to Tracy. "What's this about?"

Cell phone in hand, Kathleen Davis emerged from the study. Even though it was her day off, she was neatly dressed in slacks and a crisp clean sweater. Not a strand of her dark hair was out of place. "I think your father left his phone some place. I'm not getting any answer." She stopped when she saw Joshua Thornton in her living room. "Josh?" Her eyes landed on Cameron. "Is this an official visit?"

"Kathleen, I'm so sorry …" Joshua said.

Kathleen's face contorted. Her phone dropped to the floor. She covered her face with her hands.

"What's wrong with Grandma?" With his wide-eyed childish curiosity about the visitors, Luke had reemerged into the room.

A quick glance from Cameron set Tracy into action. "Hey, Luke, how about if you show me your room?"

Seconds later, they were gone.

Heather took her mother into her arms.

After introducing Tony, they sat in the living room, in which photos of the Davis family adorned the fireplace mantel and end tables. Cameron picked up a portrait of Kathleen with a slightly pudgy man with a round face. He had dark hair with gray patches at the temple. Based on the straight line between the silver and the dark hair, Cameron surmised the coloring was not natural.

"How did it happen?" Kathleen asked.

"Are you sure it was my father?" Heather stared down at her hands, in which she clutched her cell phone. "This has to be a mistake."

"They confirmed his identity by his fingerprints," Cameron said. "I'm afraid they're certain."

"How?" Heather's voice shook. "Where did they find him? How did he die?"

"I'm so sorry for your loss." Cameron placed the picture back in its place. "We're investigating his death as a homicide."

"When was he killed?" Heather asked. "Did he suffer?"

"It happened sometime last evening," Cameron said. "When was the last time you spoke to him?"

"Yesterday morning," Kathleen said. "He's been in Seattle on business. He was flying out yesterday. I expected him home last night."

"But he didn't come home," Tony said. "And you—"

"John travels a lot," Kathleen said. "Two or three times a month. Half the time his flights get cancelled and he has to reschedule. It's nothing for him to not come home when he says he'll be home."

"But you were trying to call him just now when we got here," Joshua said.

"Because he usually calls to let me know." Kathleen glanced at the phone on the floor. Joshua picked it up and handed it to her. "He's had trouble keeping track of his phone. So many times, he forgets his phone in a hotel or cab. Why, just a couple of weeks ago he lost his phone for a couple of days. He was on the verge of buying a new one when Heather found it."

"It'd fallen under the seat in his car," Heather said.

Cameron noticed Heather's fingertips flying across the screen of her phone while they spoke. She concluded she was texting the news to her brothers. One would think this type of news was best delivered with a call rather than a text message. "When did you last speak to your father, Heather?"

At the sound of her name, Heather jumped in her seat. "Excuse me?" She slipped the phone under her thigh.

"When was the last time you spoke to your father?" Cameron asked.

"I don't quite remember." Heather rubbed her forehead. "Sometime this week? Definitely, last weekend sometime. We always have dinner together on Sunday after Mass."

"Do you know who may have wanted—"

"Derek Ellison," Kathleen said forcibly. "He did it. He said he was going to kill us."

"In the courtroom after the judge awarded custody of Luke to Mom and Dad," Heather said. "He went bonkers. Screaming that we weren't going to live long enough to raise his son."

"It was our fault that Lindsay became an addict and killed herself," Kathleen said. "It was our fault that Derek is so stoned that he can't hold a job and take care of his son. Everything was our fault. So he was going to pay us back for taking his son away from him by—" She broke down.

Heather took her mother into her arms.

"Derek Ellison," Cameron said. "Does anyone know where we can find him?"

"I know." Joshua took his cell phone out of his pocket. "But you're not going without backup."

Tracy stayed at the Davis home to offer comfort to the grief-stricken family and to take care of Luke until Kathleen's two sons and their wives arrived.

Meanwhile, Joshua contacted Sheriff Curt Sawyer to meet them near Derek Ellison's dilapidated trailer tucked far back into the deep woods in Lawrenceville. They pulled onto a dirt road near Little Blue Run Lake and climbed out to wait for the sheriff and one of his deputies.

Little Blue Run Lake had once been a brilliantly blue man-made lake into which the power company had disposed of billions of gallons of coal waste. As a result, several residents in the areas had lost their homes after it had become a high-risk health hazard.

"This guy must be messed up in the head to willingly live here." Tony gestured at the dried up lakebed on the other side of the dead trees along the roadside.

"Must be suicidal," Cameron said. "Maybe he doesn't have to guts to do the deed himself, so he's hoping to get cancer—have the power company do it for him."

"What do you know about this guy?" Tony asked. "I mean, calling out the sheriff to go with you—"

"We're not in Pennsylvania anymore," Cameron said. "When we crossed that state line over there,"—she pointed in the general direction of the state line two miles away—"we left our jurisdiction. As a courtesy, we need to contact the Hancock County sheriff before going around questioning his citizens. He does the same when he comes over to our neck of the woods."

"I'm sure sleeping with their prosecutor helps keep things cordial, too."

Cameron laughed. "Doesn't hurt."

Two Hancock County sheriff's cruisers turned onto the side road and parked behind Tony's cruiser. Sheriff Curt Sawyer lowered the driver's side window of the first cruiser. Cameron recognized the deputy in the second cruiser as Hunter Gardner, her stepson-in-law. Joshua climbed out of her vehicle to join them.

"What'd Derek do now?" Curt asked Cameron after she had introduced Tony.

"John Davis was found in a hayfield in Hookstown last night," Cameron said. "Someone dumped his body and set fire to it."

"Cause of death was stabbing," Tony said. "Thirty-two times. Crime of passion."

"John Davis and his wife took Derek's son away from him," Joshua said.

"And he's been pretty passionate about wanting revenge on them," Sheriff Sawyer said. "When was Davis killed?"

"Sometime last evening," Cameron said. "Kathleen says he flew out from Seattle yesterday morning. So he would have gotten in last night. His body was found shortly after midnight."

"Less than a half hour from the airport," Tony said.

"All we want to do is talk to Derek," Cameron said. "Find out where he was. If he has an alibi."

"Good luck with that," the sheriff said. "His brain is so pickled that he can't remember where he was an hour ago, let alone yesterday." He hung out the window and gestured at Hunter. "I'll go in first. Gardner, you bring up the rear."

Hunter shot them a thumbs up sign and backed up to make room for them to pull out onto the road.

In Cameron's cruiser, Joshua reached under her seat and extracted one of her back up weapons. "Mind if I borrow this?"

"What's mine is yours, my love."

"Keep your weapon ready. Derek has some serious anger issues."

"Tell me about the kid Derek had stabbed in school," Cameron said.

"A friend of theirs," Joshua said while tucking the gun under his coat, into the back waistband of his pants. "Nice kid. Supposedly, he had disrespected a female friend of Derek's. He wasn't even supposed to be at the school. He had dropped out the year before. He snuck onto campus and hid in the boys' locker room. They went in after baseball practice and he knifed the boy. If Murphy hadn't been there, he would have killed him."

Following the sheriff, Cameron turned left onto a dirt road that took them deep into the woods. Beer bottles, boxes, and plastic bags littered the roadside. The road ended at what appeared to be a junk yard. Rusted cars rested on cement blocks. There were numerous piles of garbage bags scattered around the lot. Off to one side was an old trailer. A cement block stairway led up to the door.

Sheriff Curt Sawyer climbed out of his cruiser and pointed at a white truck marked with brown rust along the edges. "He's home. That's his truck."

"Wasn't his license revoked after his fourth DUI?" Joshua asked.

Sheriff Sawyer nodded his head. "My people have been watching and waiting to catch him driving to nail his butt."

Hunter pulled his cruiser up next to Cameron's and climbed out. He took a position next to his open door, so that he could easily grab his rifle if need be.

Cameron and Tony fell in step on either side of Sheriff Sawyer, a barrel-chested ex-marine, who still held onto his military bearing.

Fearing that the prosecutor's appearance would be too intimidating, Joshua opted to stand back with Cameron's weapon in his hand. He stayed close enough to be able to render assistance.

"You never should have accepted a plea deal when he stabbed Bryan," Hunter said in a low voice. "He'd still be in jail and Heather's father would still be alive."

Reminded that Hunter was yet another friend who had witnessed Derek's attack on the teenager, Joshua bit his lip. It was not the time or place to defend his decisions from nine years earlier.

Sheriff Sawyer ordered Cameron and Tony to wait at the bottom of the steps while he stood off to the side and pounded on the door. "Derek! Derek Ellison! It's Sheriff Sawyer! Open up!"

Cameron rested her hand on her service weapon—ready to pull it if things went sideways. She could hear Tony breathing hard behind her.

Receiving no answer, Sheriff Sawyer pounded again on the door—hard. "I know you're in there, Derek. Open up. We need to talk."

Again, there was silence.

"He's probably passed out," Cameron said as they heard a thump. The wall next to her rocked from an impact inside the trailer.

Sheriff Sawyer put out his hand to knock once again when the latch moved, and the door opened slightly.

Cameron saw the bloody knife before she saw the arm holding it. "Knife!" She yanked her gun out of the holster and aimed it at the emaciated young man staggering out onto the steps. "Put down the knife *now*!"

Sheriff Sawyer reached around the door to grab Derek by the back of the neck and force him down into his knees. "Drop the knife!"

Still, Derek clung to the knife that was streaked in dried blood.

Both Joshua and Hunter drew their weapons and aimed it at the young man whose withered frame was not unlike that of an elderly man. His face was gaunt. Across the driveway, Joshua could see that his eyes were hollow. The young man was so stoned that he had no idea what was happening.

Joshua rushed forward. "Do what they say, Derek! Don't make them shoot you! They'll shoot you unless you drop the knife *now*!"

"Drop the knife, Derek! Drop it now!" Cameron ran up the steps and aimed her gun at the side of his head.

Derek held his hands up—the knife tight in his grasp. He lifted his eyes to see Joshua running up to him.

"Derek, please! If you can't do it for yourself, do it for your mother! Please don't do this to her!"

Derek opened his hand. Cameron grasped the knife as it slid out of his grip.

Sheriff Sawyer snapped the cuffs onto his wrists.

"Derek Ellison," Cameron said, "I'm taking you in for questioning in suspicion for the murder of John Davis."

CHAPTER FOUR

Susan Livingston kicked her grief-stricken sobs up a notch in both pitch and energy.

Cameron glanced over at Tony. Seeing no sign of him offering John Davis's assistant a clean tissue, she went into the kitchen of the woman's home, tore a paper towel off the roll on the counter, and returned to the living room to offer it to her.

"Thank you," Susan said before wiping her face and blowing her nose.

When she offered the tissue back, Cameron declined. "Keep it."

"I just can't believe anyone would want to murder John," the pretty blonde said. "He was the kindest, gentlest man I—any of us at the office—have ever met." She looked back and forth between the two detectives who had delivered the tragic news. "I'm not just saying that. It's true. We all loved him." She caught herself. "I don't mean that as in romantic. John wasn't like that. He was devoted to Kathleen and his kids and his grandson. He treated everyone with respect—especially women. Why—he is"—she hiccupped—"was—the only vice president who had a staff entirely made up of women. We got paid equally what the male assistants at the plant got paid. He made sure of that!" Once more, she broke down into inaudible crying.

Patting the executive assistant on the back, Cameron waited for her to compose herself. She looked over at Tony, whose face was filled with boredom. He checked the screen on his phone.

There were other places he'd rather be—as he made abundantly clear upon discovering that Cameron had made an appointment to meet with John Davis's assistant after processing Derek at the jail.

"We got the guy," Tony objected. "He had the murder weapon on him."

"We don't know that for certain," Cameron said. "We'll know after forensics examines the knife. They're also going to examine Derek, his clothes, and trailer for further evidence. Until we have the results of all that, we have to make sure there aren't any lose ends. There's a lot we don't know."

"Like what?" Tony almost rolled his eyes at her—until he remembered that she was his boss.

She ticked off on her fingers. "Confirmation that the knife Derek had was the murder weapon. If so, where did it come from. Find the primary crime scene. We also need to find Davis's vehicle and examine it for physical evidence and clues to cement the prosecution's case. That's just a start." She jerked her chin toward the squad room door. "I'm driving."

Susan Livingston was an attractive middle-aged woman who lived in a single-family home in a neat subdivision. Upon hearing the news, she collapsed onto the sofa and wailed. It was a slow interview with several pauses to allow her to collect herself.

While Cameron offered comfort, Tony shifted in a chair across from them like a child with ants in his pants.

"Well, considering—" Cameron cleared her throat. "Someone obviously didn't love John since they killed him."

Susan's eyes lit up. "Maybe it was—" She covered her mouth with a gasp.

"Who did you just think of?"

Susan stared at her with wide tear-filled eyes. "But it couldn't be her."

"Her who?"

"Bea. But it couldn't possibly—"

Cameron was already writing down the name. "What's her last name?"

Instead of answering, Susan continued to stare at Cameron with her hand over her mouth.

"If she's innocent, then nothing bad will happen to her. If she did it, then we need to find that out, too. What's her last name, Susan?"

"Miller," she said grudgingly.

"Who is Bea Miller and why would you think of her?"

"She's a fruitcake," Susan said. "She was a clerk in accounting. She's like in her fifties and divorced three times. Almost two years ago, she put in for an opening for administrative assistant in our office. John hired someone else with more experience, and Bea slapped him with a sexual harassment claim. Of course, legal investigated and found that she had accused two other men in the last fifteen years of sexual harassment. Plus, on three separate occasions, she'd filed police reports accusing men of sexual assault. In every case the incidents were unfounded."

"The woman who cried rape." Cameron frowned.

"It was all he said, she said. Bea said the harassment happened during the interview. Of course, with John's long sterling reputation with the plant, and her checkered past, no one believed her. Word got around and she quit. She found a crackpot lawyer to represent her in a million-dollar lawsuit.

The men she had accused volunteered to testify for the defense, and the judge laughed her out of the courtroom before the case even got to trial. Four months ago, her house was foreclosed on. On that day, she showed up here at the plant and attacked John in the parking lot. Security was called in and John had her arrested for assault."

"When's her trial?"

"I don't know," Susan said with a shrug of her shoulders. "But it wasn't long after that that the threatening phone calls started. John got a restraining order against her, but the calls kept on coming. He blocked her calls, but then she'd change her phone number and kept on calling him."

"Sounds like I need to look this Bea Miller up," Cameron said. "Do you know where she is now?"

"I hear she's renting a trailer someplace."

"I'll find her," Cameron said. "Susan, when was the last time you spoke to Mr. Davis?"

"Yesterday afternoon before leaving work," Susan said while wiping her nose.

"How did he seem? Did he sound nervous or upset or worried about anything?"

Susan shook her head. "No, he was his old self. He was on the phone when I was leaving so"—she cleared her throat—"I never even got to say good-bye. If I had known, I would have waited for him to get off the phone, but I was meeting some friends for drinks and all I did was wave to him and told him to have a nice weekend and then I left." She wailed again.

"You poor thing," Cameron said. "It isn't like you knew that he was going—" Susan's statement hit her. She spun around to look at Tony, who was staring up at the ceiling. "Wait a minute! You didn't say good-bye?"

"I would have if—"

"John Davis was *on the phone* when you left?"

"His cell phone," she said with a nod of her head.

"You *saw* him?"

Susan's mouth hung open. Her eyes were wide. She nodded her head.

"Are you saying John Davis was in the office at the plant when you saw him last? In Shippingport?"

"That's where our office is located. Yes. Where did you think he was?"

Sensing that things were getting interesting, Tony sat up in his seat.

"We were told he was traveling," Cameron said.

"Was he killed on his way someplace?" Susan asked.

"More like coming back from someplace," Cameron said. "When was the last time Mr. Davis traveled for business with the nuclear power plant?"

Susan looked up at the ceiling. "I think … last spring … maybe …" Her voice trailed off.

"Did he come into work every day this week?"

"Oh, Mr. Davis never misses work. He was there morning to night every day. Why wouldn't he be?" Susan's eyes were wide. "Is something wrong? I mean, except for Mr. Davis being killed. What did I say?"

Joshua tapped the brass covered knight on two squares and across one on the chess board before setting it within striking distance of his opponent's silver-plated king. "Check." He shot a grin across the kitchen table in Izzy's direction.

Izzy dropped her spoon into her bowl of rocky road ice cream. Her mouth dropped open. She sat up onto her knees. Dressed in her pajamas and bathrobe, she had been sitting in the chair with her feet tucked under her. A drop of water dripped from her freshly washed hair to land on the wooden chess board while she studied the situation. "Where?"

With a chuckle, Joshua picked up his ice cream and sat back in his chair. "Look."

Seeing her predicament, she uttered a deep breath. "How did I miss that?" she seemed to ask Admiral, who was resting his head on top of the kitchen table. He was more interested in the ice cream than he was the chess match.

"You were so focused on protecting your queen that you left your king vulnerable."

"Because you were going after her." She moved her king one space back to protect him from the knight.

"That's what I wanted you to think. It's called a distraction." He slid his bishop across the board to snag her king. "What I was really after was your king." He set the chess piece on the table next to the board. "Check mate. Game over."

"You're sneaky." She dropped back into her seat.

"You've only just figured that out?"

Izzy's face brightened upon seeing Cameron push through the back door. "You're home!" She raced Irving and Admiral across the room to greet her.

Admiral won the race, with Irving a close second. After petting the animals, Cameron took Izzy into a tight hug. Izzy's moist curls tickled her nose.

While everyone greeted Cameron, Joshua placed the brass chess pieces into the wooden box and closed it shut. "Did you get Derek processed?"

With a roll of her eyes, she took off her utility belt and handed it to him to hang on the coat rack on his way to the cabinet where they kept the games. "For now. I'm betting he'll end up in the hospital with withdrawals before morning." Their bowls of ice cream reminded her of a possible dessert. She headed for the freezer. "Izzy, did you and Tracy get Poppy's gown taken care of?"

Izzy shot a suspicious look in Joshua's direction. One would have thought he was a spy from an enemy camp. "Poppy and I talked to Jessica."

Joshua narrowed his eyes in response to the suspicion Izzy cast his way.

Oblivious to the looks being fired back and forth across the kitchen, Cameron dug spoonfuls of ice cream into a bowl. Irving and Admiral pressed against her on either side—willing the ice cream to drop to the floor for them to devour. "Do you think Jessica can help find it?"

"Sshhh!" Izzy raced across the kitchen and waved her arms for Cameron to remain quiet.

Startled by the sudden outburst, Cameron dropped the ice scream scoop to the floor.

Irving and Admiral pounced. After delivering a paw filled with claws at Admiral's snout, Irving won possession of the scoop—only to discover that it was too heavy for him to carry away. He relented to sharing it with the big goof.

"Don't say anything," Izzy commanded.

"About what?" Cameron asked.

"About Poppy's gown." With her back to him, Izzy rolled her eyes and tossed her head in Joshua's direction. "He can't know."

"He's not the groom."

"But he's the groom's *father*. If you say anything to him about the bride's gown, then he'll tell the groom, and Poppy and J.J.'s wedding will be cursed, and we don't want them to be cursed before they even start." She pressed her index finger to her lips. "Say nothing."

"Well, if you can't trust Joshua, then you can't trust me. I am his wife and we don't keep secrets from each other."

"Do you want J.J. and Poppy to end up divorced? If they get divorced, then Poppy will leave, and she'll take Gulliver with her, and Comanche loves Gulliver and the two of them will be separated. Comanche may even die of a broken heart. I heard of that happening—animals dying of broken hearts. And if Comanche dies of a broken heart then I'll be heart broken and will probably die. You don't want me to die, do you?"

"I had no idea asking about a wedding gown could bring about such death and destruction," Joshua said. "I'm not even going to ask why you're calling Jessica in Washington about Poppy's gown for a wedding here in Chester. I can tell you this. If Jessica's getting that gown, it's going to be expensive. Jessica's contacts are high-end fashion designers and Poppy doesn't have much money."

"I'm not saying anything else." Izzy made a show of turning a key to lock her lips and dropping the key down the front of her bathrobe. She then kissed both Cameron and Joshua good night and trotted up the stairs.

Since Cameron had ice cream, Irving and Admiral chose to stay with her.

Once Izzy was in her room upstairs, Joshua's eyes met Cameron's. "Please tell me that Tracy and Jessica didn't talk Poppy into some horribly expensive, custom-designed gown. J.J. is paying for the wedding and they agreed on a budget. He's still got law school student loans to pay for. The last thing he needs is for this wedding to blow up out of control."

"You better not be talking about Poppy's gown!" Izzy yelled from upstairs.

"Go to bed!" Joshua replied in a loud voice.

After hearing the bedroom door shut, Cameron said in a low voice, "Poppy has a sensible head on her shoulders. No one is going to talk her into anything."

"Tracy and Jessica can be very persuasive." He followed her to the kitchen table where they sat next to each other. He asked about why she was so late getting home.

"Davis's executive assistant lived not too far from the police station, so Tony and I stopped in to break the news—just to see if there were any other suspects—possibly from his work at the power plant—who would want to see Davis dead."

Joshua dared to stick a finger into her bowl to steal a fingertip full of the dessert. "He is a vice president—an executive. It's not hard to imagine he'd make an enemy or two on the way to the top."

"According to Susan, John Davis did have an enemy. Bea Miller. A clerk who had applied for a job in his department. When she didn't get it, she accused him of sexual harassment. She appears to have a long history of accusing men of sexual assault and harassment."

"Sounds like a possible suspect."

"Davis did get a restraining order against her. Definitely on my list." She arched an eyebrow in his direction. Slowly, she twirled her spoon in the bowl of softening ice cream. "Susan's big regret was leaving work yesterday without saying good-bye to Davis."

"Leaving work without saying good-bye?" He blinked. "That suggests that he was at work yesterday."

"According to her, he was—all day," she said. "Kathleen told us that the last time she'd talked to John was yesterday morning when he'd called her from Seattle. She said he was flying home."

"Maybe he stopped in at the plant after flying into Pittsburgh. Shippingport is between the airport and Chester."

"John Davis was not booked on any flights coming in from Seattle. As a matter of fact, he was not booked on any flights arriving in Pittsburgh on Friday. He never left the area." Her dessert finished, she rose from the table and took the bowl to the sink. She turned around to face him. "He was in Shippingport yesterday morning. John Davis was at work every day this week. He just didn't go home after leaving work."

"Where did he go?"

"Good question. Where was Davis going after he left work every day? Where was he coming from when he went to work in the morning?"

"Mistress?" He frowned. "But I've known John Davis since we were teenagers. He dated Kathleen in high school. They got married right out of college. He's always been faithful to her. He was never a cheat. He adored Kathleen and the kids—bragged about them—"

"Josh, you're not naïve. You and I have both run into enough cases where everything seems honky dory to the outside world, but behind closed doors ..."

Joshua nodded his head in agreement. "I never would have thought that of John."

"My next question is this. Did Kathleen know about it? If she found out her husband was a cheat, it'd give her motive to kill him."

"Kathleen didn't act like she knew about it this afternoon."

"Operative word is acting. She's a smart woman. Certainly smart enough to have planned and executed the murder and plant that knife to frame their loser son-in-law who threatened to kill them."

"I've known Kathleen for years. I can't see her losing it and killing John like that." Joshua slowly shook his head.

"You also couldn't see John Davis as a cheat."

"You're just assuming he was a cheat," he said. "You don't know that for certain. He could have been doing something else when he told Kathleen he was traveling."

Cameron folded her arms across her chest. "Like what?"

At a lost for a suggestion, Joshua shrugged his shoulders.

"The medical examiner estimates the time of death to be between eight and ten last night. Susan left the office shortly after five o'clock, and Davis was alive and well then. We'll get a more precise time of when Davis left after security checks their cameras to see if something happened at the plant that we need to know about. Maybe this Bea Miller decided to violate the restraining order."

"Right now, we need to find out what John Davis was doing between five and eight o'clock. That's three hours." Joshua got up from the table and joined her at the counter. "He obviously didn't go home."

"We only have Kathleen's word for that. Maybe he did go home. She confronted him and killed him there."

"If Kathleen was going to kill her husband, she'd choose a neater method besides stabbing him multiple times and setting him on fire. You saw her house. Not a speck of dust. She never has a hair out of place. Her kids are the same way. Kathleen is very precise, very neat. If she was going to kill her husband, she would have used something clean and neat— like poison."

"Unless she was so enraged, she lost it." She placed her hand on her hip. "Forensics took Derek's clothes into evidence during check in. He was filthy. Clearly, he hadn't showered or changed his clothes in days. A cursory examination of him and his clothes show no blood."

"Davis was stabbed thirty-two times," Joshua said. "Whoever did it would be covered in blood."

"Maybe he changed out of the bloody clothes into dirty clothes without blood. But then, you'd think he'd have blood on his hands or in his hair…" With a sigh of exhaustion, Cameron wrapped her arms around him and laid her head on his shoulder. "My brain is tired. I can't think about it anymore."

He held her tight. "It sounds to me like you have some huge holes in your case."

"Where had John Davis been all week while Kathleen thought he was in Seattle? He couldn't have been up to anything good if he lied to her about it." She took in a deep breath. "I need to think about something else. What were we doing when I got the call about them finding Davis's body?"

"We had just acted out your dirty dream." He kissed her on the forehead.

She kissed him softly on the lips. "But we didn't get a chance to discuss your dirty dream."

He grinned at her.

"I believe it's your turn," she said.

He pulled away from her and went to the refrigerator. With a wicked smile, he opened the fridge, reached inside, and took a container of whipped cream out.

"Really?" She giggled.

He took her by the hand and led her up the stairs to their bedroom.

CHAPTER FIVE

By Monday morning, the news about Derek Ellison being charged with the murder of John Davis, husband and father of four, was all over the Ohio Valley. The bloody knife he had wielded in his hand when the police had arrived at his trailer proved to be the murder weapon used to stab John Davis thirty-two times.

Joshua would have considered it to be a dream case, if he were prosecuting it. Derek had motive, means, and no alibi—proving that he had opportunity. So why did he feel so guilty? It was the guilt that made him open the door to welcome Sadie Ellison into his home when she tearfully rang the doorbell.

Izzy was at school and Cameron was at the police station preparing for Derek Ellison's arraignment.

The lines on her face and bags under her eyes said it all. Derek's father had abandoned his family and left the area when his son was in middle school. Sadie cleaned houses and did odd jobs to put food on the table because the courts couldn't track down her ex-husband for child support. Eventually, their home had been foreclosed on, and they were forced to rent a small trailer in a park near the casino.

It was no wonder that Derek chose to act out on his feelings of abandonment.

Joshua took Sadie into a hug. "I am so sorry."

That was enough to turn on the faucet. Sadie collapsed into his arms and cried gut-wrenching tears into his shoulder. She let out a wail of grief that prompted Irving to arch his back, hop off the stairs in the foyer, and scurry down the hallway to the kitchen where he escaped through the pet door.

Joshua closed the door and ushered Sadie into his study, where he sat her on the sofa and retrieved a box of tissues for her. "Have you seen him?"

Sadie shook her head. "They won't let me. Only his lawyer can see him. Since we don't have any money, the court will appoint him one at the arraignment. I talked to the public defender in Beaver. He said Derek's best bet would be to ask for a plea bargain, which means he'll go back to jail. Since he's already been convicted of assault with a deadly weapon—" She lifted her eyes to his. "They know about that."

"It's on his permanent record."

"Derek would never have killed John," she said. "I know—"

"Derek threatened him. He has a history of violence."

Sadie collapsed against him into a sobbing mess. "What am I going to do? It isn't Derek's fault. He never did have a good male role model. Everyone who he has ever loved has been taken from him. His father. Lindsay. Luke. He's been so lost—"

"Being lost is no excuse to kill someone," Joshua said.

She sat up. "I just can't believe he did it. I know my son. Yes, he threatened John and I talked to him. I made him see that Luke needs him. That he had to pull himself together and needed to straighten himself out and maybe then he could get the Davises to let him be a part of Luke's life. I made him see that he had to give Luke up for now for him—make that sacrifice. I thought I had made him see that. He was determined to clean himself up. If he killed John Davis, then he wouldn't ever get to see Luke again."

"Was Derek clear thinking enough to see it that way?" Joshua asked.

"I'm sure he was." Sadie grasped his hand. "The public defender is going to make Derek cop a plea. He'll go to jail. If he goes to prison, then I know I'll lose my son forever. Josh, can you—"

"I can't defend him," Joshua said. "I've got a contract with the county. I can't take any other cases."

"But don't you know someone who can help Derek?"

Joshua sighed. "With everything that they have against him, if Derek doesn't want to take a deal, he's going to need a pit bull for a defense attorney."

"Do you know a pit bull?"

"Teaches me to drop in without calling first," Joshua told himself when he turned the corner of J.J.'s barnyard to find that the spot where he usually parked his truck was vacant.

Joshua had driven to J.J.'s farm because he had concluded that he would be more persuasive in person.

Discovering that his son was not home, Joshua brought his SUV to a halt and backed up to turn it around to leave. While turning the steering wheel, he saw two pairs of eyes watching him.

One pair belonged to Charley, J.J.'s "watch" rooster. Equal in size to a tom turkey, the territorial bird was nastier than the farm's half a dozen mixed-breed dogs, who were napping in a patch of sun along a fence by the hen house.

The pack noted Joshua's arrival with lifted heads and perked ears. Once they determined that he wasn't going to run over them with his SUV, they resumed snoozing.

The rooster was a different story. Charley surveilled Joshua with unblinking eyes from his perch on top of the porch railing.

The other pair of eyes belonged to Ollie, an orphaned lamb who Poppy had adopted the previous spring. The farm didn't raise sheep, and no one had the heart to tell the hundred-pound farm animal that he wasn't a lap dog. His head cocked, lamb watched Joshua from the front porch.

Charley rose up onto his feet and let out a crow that sounded like a warning against trespassing.

"I'm leaving already," Joshua told him.

As he pulled the SUV forward, he noticed that Poppy's truck was parked in its usual spot in front of the barn. He wondered why she hadn't checked to see who was visiting. That was when he noticed the two-horse trailer missing from its spot between the paddock and the hen house.

Before Joshua could put two and two together, he saw J.J.'s truck traveling along the road leading to the farm's main entrance. The full-sized dually-wheeled truck pulled the horse trailer behind it.

"Don't tell me," Joshua muttered. "Poppy talked him into another horse."

As if to answer his question, Gulliver, Comanche, and three of J.J.'s mares galloped across the pasture. They stuck their noses up in the air to sniff out the newcomer.

An Appaloosa, Gulliver was Poppy's horse, a gelding. Like his freckled owner, he had spots all over his body. A mare, Comanche was a palomino who J.J.'s late partner had gifted to Izzy. Comanche had been rescued from a situation in which she had been badly neglected. The two outsiders living at a quarter horse farm were best buddies.

In the adjacent pasture, Captain Blackbeard, the farm's champion quarter horse stallion, followed the trailer with his nose up in the air. He snorted and shook his head is if to veto the newcomer's application to the herd.

Joshua parked his SUV next to the house and climbed out. As he had concluded, there was a horse in the trailer.

J.J. parked the truck in front of the barn. Poppy jumped out of the passenger seat and hurried to the rear of the trailer.

"What bloodline is this one from?" Joshua called to them while making his way across the barnyard.

Ollie galloped ahead of him to greet J.J. when he slid out of the driver's seat. His hair was disheveled, and he was un-shaven. Dressed in his stained work coat and muddy boots, one would never have guessed that he had graduated top of his class from one of the best law schools in the country. "We have no idea."

As he drew nearer to the trailer, Joshua saw that the horse was a black and white paint. Nervous, she moved back and forth in the trailer. Uncertain of the horse's temperament, he stood back to allow Poppy to direct them. "You bought a horse without knowing its bloodline?"

"Red-blooded horses have a right to live, too." Poppy un-latched the rear door of the trailer.

"Ah, she's a rescue," Joshua said with a nod of his head.

J.J. pulled the ramp from the trailer to the ground and secured it. "Someone called Poppy last night to tell her that this pregnant mare was at a slaughterhouse auction. She and her baby were going to be slaughtered. So she woke me up first thing this morning and we drove out there to buy her and bring her home."

"Slaughterhouse auction? Where—"

"An hour and forty-five minutes away," J.J. said. "We left before six this morning. Got there when they opened. Paid cash to save her."

"Cash?"

From inside the trailer, Poppy smiled through the slats. "J.J. took all the money he had in the house and we prayed it'd be enough to rescue her."

J.J. rolled his eyes. "Poppy cried when she saw the place. If we had enough money, we would have crammed three more horses into the trailer, strapped one on the roof, and ridden with one in our lap to bring them home."

"Where there is love, there's always room for one more," Poppy called out.

"Your mother used to say the same thing to me." In a low voice, Joshua added, "Usually after telling me that she was pregnant."

J.J. uttered a low laugh, before turning serious. "It was sad. But we did save this one and her baby."

Poppy spoke softly to the horse while backing her out of the trailer.

The black and white horse was filthy with mud and manure caked in her fur. While her pregnant tummy bulged, her ribs stuck out to show that she was malnourished. She hung her head and coughed. Joshua didn't know much about horses, but he could see that she was not healthy. "What if she's sick with something contagious?" He felt like a heel being more worried about the sick and pregnant horse making Izzy's Comanche sick than her own well being.

"We'll keep her away from the other horses until she gets a clean bill of health." Poppy handed the rope to J.J. "Rod is coming by this afternoon to give her a thorough checkup."

"We already know she's going to need to be wormed," J.J. said.

"What's her name?" Joshua asked J.J., who turned to Poppy.

She stroked the mare's face while murmuring softly to her. "Pilgrim."

"The horse in *The Horse Whisperer*," Joshua said.

"She's a survivor, just like that horse." She delivered a long lingering kiss to J.J. while taking the rope from him. She led the horse into the barn with Ollie galloping ahead of them as if to lead the way.

"She has you wrapped around her pretty little finger," Joshua whispered to him as they watched her walk away.

"I know." He shot Joshua a grin. "And I wouldn't have it any other way." He patted him on the back before trotting toward the house. "Want some coffee? I've only had two cups this morning and I haven't eaten yet today."

Once they were inside the French country home, J.J. dumped the old coffee into the sink and refilled the pot with clean water. He waited until the coffee was brewing to shrug out of his coat and drape it across the back of a chair.

Joshua took a seat at the table. "I just stopped by to ask about how your law practice is going."

"It's not. I've defended a couple of DUIs. One B and E. An assault." J.J. paused in taking two mugs out of the cupboard. "You drove all the way over here to ask me that?"

"I wanted to check on Comanche," Joshua lied. "You're licensed in Pennsylvania. Have you taken any public defender cases over there?"

Looking doubtful, J.J. set the mugs on the counter next to the coffeemaker. "I had one last year. That was the breaking and entering. I plea bargained that one. They caught him with all of the stuff in his house."

"You haven't defended anyone charged with murder yet?"

"You know I haven't." J.J. opened the refrigerator to peer inside in hopes of finding something quick and easy to eat.

"Do you think you're ready to take one on?"

Holding the door open, J.J. slowly turned from the fridge to face him. "What murder—" Seeing his expression, he threw the door shut. "No! No way! Derek Ellison deserves to rot in jail!"

"He has a *right* to the best defense possible," Joshua said.

"He stabbed one of my friends."

"He's paid for that," Joshua said. "The John Davis murder is a whole different case."

"He would have killed Bryan if Murphy hadn't stopped him. Bryan has an ugly scar in his side because of that animal."

"That animal is a human being who's been dealt a bad hand." Joshua gestured toward the barn. "Not unlike that horse that you just spent all morning driving across the state to save."

"That horse never stabbed anyone!"

"You don't know that. You know nothing about that horse. She could be carrying the Son of Sam as far as you know."

"You've lost your mind!" J.J. slammed his hand down on the counter between them. "Why do you keep defending Ellison?"

"I can't defend him. That's why I'm asking you to."

"He'll get a court-appointed attorney in Pennsylvania."

"Who will talk him into taking a plea, and then he'll spend the rest of his life in jail."

"Where he belongs." J.J. threw up his arms. "My whole life, you've preached about being man enough to take responsibility for our bad decisions. When you make a mistake, you don't blame society. You don't blame your mother or father. You admit you're wrong, and you pay the price for your mistakes. But when it comes to Derek Ellison—it's a whole different story. He trespassed onto school property and hid in the locker room to stab Bryan, and you accepted a plea bargain for four years. He was out in three and went on to kill John Davis, the father of another friend of mine! Now, you stand there and ask me to defend him? What is it with you?"

"Everyone is innocent until proven guilty," Joshua said in a steady tone. "That's the foundation of a civilized society. It is up to the prosecution to prove Derek Ellison killed John Davis. Unless they can prove beyond a reasonable doubt that he did kill John Davis, then he's innocent. Except for his mother, this man has never had anyone willing to stand in his corner to defend him against anything. It's been him against the world his whole life." He shook his head. "You've never been alone, J.J. Not you, your brothers, or your sisters. You get up in the morning knowing that you have your entire family in your corner. If anything happens, we'll all be there for you. Imagine what your life would have been like if you had to deal with what you've gone up against alone. Losing Suellen. Getting shot."

J.J. dropped his eyes to the floor, where Ollie was chewing on his shoe laces. The orphaned lamb had climbed through the doggie door to join them without either of them noticing.

"Derek and you do have something in common," Joshua said. "He loved Lindsay—just like you loved Suellen. When you lost Suellen, we were all here to help you go through it. When Derek lost Lindsay, the only one who was there for him was his mother. No other family. No friends. A lot of folks, myself included, kind of thought they had it coming because both of them were a couple of addicts." He sighed. "And then society took his son away from him on top of all that."

"If you're trying to make me feel sorry for the guy, I do," J.J. said. "But the thing is, all of these things that have happened to him have been the result of his and Lindsay's own bad choices."

"Derek didn't start out as the man he is now," Joshua said. "Abandoned by his father—rejected as a bad boy—I admit it—even by me. With everyone against him—no one to defend him. After a while, that type of adversity breaks a man."

"Would you have approved if Tracy had brought Derek home and wanted to marry him?"

Joshua grit his teeth and slumped against the breakfast bar.

J.J. laughed. "Where's your compassion now?"

Joshua's eyes met his. "Derek doesn't remember where he was at the time of the murder."

"Which means he has no alibi. He had the murder weapon."

"And you had Hawkeye in your locker."

J.J. stood up straight. Joshua's statement cut him like a knife.

"You remember Hawkeye, don't you? Middle school. Oakland, California. The school mascot went missing from the display case. The principal was looking for it. When you opened your locker, it fell out and landed at his feet."

"I didn't steal it," J.J. said.

"But you were in possession of it." Joshua jabbed him in the chest. "As far as your principal was concerned, that was evidence enough to convict you—suspend you from school."

"The real thief saw someone coming and stuffed it in my locker," J.J. said.

"Who?"

J.J. closed his mouth.

Joshua shook a finger at him. "I've always suspected that you knew. But you refused to give him up and took the three-day suspension, because you didn't have as much to lose as he did."

"Actually, I'd hoped the real thief would be man enough to come forward on his own and confess. He didn't, and our friendship ended."

"Point is, you were wrongfully convicted because you looked guilty. You have a unique perspective that most of us don't. You've been there."

J.J. lifted his eyes to meet Joshua's. "What do you know that you aren't telling me?"

"It's not what I know. It's what the lead investigator on the case doesn't know."

"I don't have any cash." J.J. let out a deep sigh. "Can you give me money for lunch?"

CHAPTER SIX

"Why do you look so worried?" Tony asked Cameron when he arrived at the courthouse in Beaver, Pennsylvania, to find that she didn't have the same confident expression as he had. "We got him. We caught him with the murder weapon in his hand. His fingerprints on it. No alibi." With a chuckle, he watched the spectators flowing into the courtroom for the arraignment. "Not bad for my first murder case in homicide, huh?"

Cameron extracted a folder from her briefcase. "Have you looked at the victim's financials?"

Tony shrugged his shoulders. "Just the usual stuff you'd expect to see in a vice president's financials."

She took a printout from the folder and pointed to a line on it. "What do you see there?"

Tony took the printout from her and read the line. "Davis withdrew ten thousand dollars from his personal savings account."

"On what day?"

Tony looked at the statement again. "Friday."

"The day he was killed."

"So?" Tony said. "The guy made a hell of a lot of money. Ten thousand was like—"

"He took it out in cash. That means he was walking around with ten thousand dollars in cash. Where is that money now?" Cameron stared at him while waiting for an answer. After receiving none, she said, "His wife made no mention about ten thousand dollars."

"Probably because it's not missing. He must have given it to whoever he took it out for."

"When did he give it to them and for what?" Cameron shoved the folder back into her briefcase. "Did he give the money to them or did they take it—after killing him? Have you located Davis's car yet?"

"Ellison sold it and used the money to buy booze and drugs."

"We don't have any proof of that. We haven't found the primary crime scene, and we don't know where Davis was living during the week while his wife thought he was in Seattle."

"Have you told the widow about her husband lying about his business trips?"

"No." She wagged a finger at him. "And I don't want you telling her. I want to keep this under our hats. If she did know, then she may slip up and that's when we'll get her."

"Wait a minute," Tony objected. "You can't be thinking Ellison didn't do this. He had the murder weapon."

"He's a stoner," Cameron said. "If Davis's wife found out he was stepping out on her, then she had the motive, means, and opportunity to kill him and frame Ellison. Kill two birds with one stone. Gets rid of a cheating husband and gets rid of her grandson's loser father."

"But—"

"The only reason Sanders took the case is because she's coming up for re-election and she wants to get a high-profile conviction under her belt. What's more high-profile than a successful family man getting brutally murdered by his druggie son-in-law. Ellison is a loser and Sanders expects the public defender to roll over and play dead."

"All the better for us. We get another animal off the streets."

"What if that animal didn't do it? Then the real animal who killed Davis is still out there," Cameron said in a low voice when she noticed a familiar face emerge from the top of the stairs. "I'll see you inside."

With a roll of his eyes, Tony went into the courtroom to await the arraignment.

J.J. looked embarrassed to be there when she stepped up to him.

"What are you doing here?" She noticed his slacks and suitcoat worn over a sweater. His clean-shaven face said it all. "No."

"Dad asked. I called the public defender. He jumped at my offer to—"

"You've never defended someone on a murder charge," Cameron said in a low voice.

"But I am a Thornton." J.J. held the door open for her to go into the courtroom ahead of him.

The arraignment was just a hearing for the court to read the charges, Derek to enter a plea, and for the prosecutor and defense attorney to argue about bail.

Considering Derek Ellison's living conditions, J.J. assumed and hoped the prosecutor would request bail be denied. His assumption was confirmed when he saw Derek stagger into the courtroom in shackles and drop into the chair next to him. His stench was enough to make J.J. gag.

"Derek, I'm Joshua Thornton Junior, your court appointed counsel."

Derek lifted his head and looked up at him through eyes narrowed to slits. He uttered a loud groan.

J.J. turned to look back at Cameron and Tony. The young detective was chuckling. A recovering alcoholic, Cameron was not.

She moved over to take a seat in the gallery behind J.J. "He's going through withdrawal," she told him in a low voice.

Derek threw his head back and wailed.

"I thought he was in a holding cell for the last two days," J.J. said.

"Depending on what drugs he's been taking, it's probably still in his system," she said. "He needs to go to the hospital. He needs detox."

"Pennsylvania versus Derek Ellison. Charges are murder in the first degree and second degree," the bailiff announced.

J.J. and the assistant prosecuting attorney rose to their feet. When Derek didn't stand, J.J. reached down to grab him by the arm and lift him physically to his feet.

"Does the defendant have an attorney present?" the judge asked.

"Joshua Thornton, Junior, for the defense, your honor," J.J. said.

For the first time, the judge lifted his eyes from the paperwork before him to look down at the defense attorney. "Joshua Thornton, *Junior*?"

J.J. suppressed a grin. "Yes, sir."

"Any relation—"

"He's my father."

The judge smirked. "Well, this case promises to be fun. How does your client plead, Mr. Thornton?"

"Not guilty, your honor," J.J. replied while pulling Derek up when he tried to slip down into his chair.

Derek let loose with a moan that resembled the call of a walrus.

"Bail?" the judge asked.

"The defendant brutally murdered a respected husband and father and then set his body on fire, your honor," the prosecutor said. "He has a history of violent crime. For the safety of the community, we ask that the defendant remain in jail without bail until his trial."

"Mr. Thornton?" the judge asked.

Unable to hold Derek up any longer, J.J. released his arm to allow him to drop into the chair. Upon hitting the chair, Derek slid to the floor—unconscious. "The defense has no objection, your honor. However, we do request that my client be held in a drug rehab facility so that he can get the medical help that he so obviously needs. As you can see, currently, he is in no condition to defend himself against these charges."

The judge peered over the top of his eye glasses to observe the young man in shackles who had oozed to the floor from his chair. "Does the prosecution have any objection?"

The prosecutor let out a breath. "No, your honor."

"The court will have the defendant transported to the hospital for detox until he can be admitted into a state-run drug rehabilitation facility."

What have I gotten myself into? J.J. shot a glance over his shoulder to Cameron who was rushing out of the courtroom with her cell phone to her ear. Tony was directly behind her.

The arraignment concluded. Two guards rushed in to pick Derek up and drag him out to await an ambulance to take him away to the hospital.

Before J.J. had time to turn around, the prosecutor, a young man who J.J. had seen around the courthouse but never met, stuck his hand out. A wide grin crossed his face as he introduced himself as Seth Booker. "Thornton, huh? Your old man's a legend in these parts."

"So I hear."

"Give you time, and maybe you'll work up to fill his shoes." Seth jabbed him in the ribs with his elbow. "Too bad you got such a dog with this case, though. What kind of deal are you looking for?"

J.J. was about to ask him what kind he wanted to offer when he saw Heather Davis at the back of the courtroom. Her eyes met his. "I'll give you a call."

"Don't wait too long," Seth said before slipping past Heather and going out the door.

"Hello, Heather." J.J. took note of her dark red sweater over a long skirt. She looked as attractive as she did back when they were teenagers and all the boys wanted a date with her. "I'm sorry about your dad."

She responded with a slap across his face.

The sting from her slap traveled up and along his eyebrow. He was still recoiling from the assault when he heard her whisper, "I can't believe you said that with a straight face. I thought we were friends. How could you, J.J.? How can you stand there and tell me how sorry you are about me losing my dad when you're defending the bastard who took him from me?"

J.J. rubbed his hand across the welt he felt growing on his cheek. When he opened his eyes against the pain, he was aware of the clerks, journalists, and various court house employees watching him with their mouths hanging open.

Heather Davis had left.

Shame washed over him. He stepped out into the corridor, where he found Cameron sitting with two women on a bench near the stairwell.

There was yet another familiar face from his past.

Madison Whitaker. Ah, man!

He glanced up and down the corridor. There was another stairwell at the other end of the hall. He spun on his heels.

"J.J., is that you?"

He stopped. Slowly, he turned around. Pasting a smile on his face, he stepped toward the slender blonde clad in a royal blue winter cape and stylish hat. "Madison! I thought you'd moved to New York." He accepted her hug and kissed her on the cheek.

"I'm back. Didn't Tracy tell you?"

He shook his head. "I guess it slipped her mind."

"Probably between opening her restaurant and wedding stuff." She licked her lips. "I hear some lucky girl has managed to take you off the market for good."

"Poppy. She's … awesome. That's the only way to describe her."

"Is she from around here?" Madison asked.

"No. She's from Montana. She's a horse trainer. One of the best." He noticed that Cameron and the woman he recognized as Madison's mother wore expressions of concern. "Is everything okay?"

"We haven't heard from my dad since Friday," Madison said. "Mom was afraid that maybe something awful happened to him."

"Why would someone want to hurt your father?"

"My dad drives truck cross-country," Madison said, "and he meets a lot of people—all types. A few months ago, he had stopped to help a woman whose car was broken down at a rest stop. She's been calling him non-stop ever since."

"How did she get his number?"

"He gave it to her in case she broke down again before she could get home."

"What was her name?"

Madison sighed. "He never told me. Maybe he told Mom."

J.J. stepped over to Cameron.

"Shawn only gave me her first name," Sherry said. "Bea."

"Bea?" Recalling the name of John Davis's former employee, Cameron was startled. "Are you sure?"

"Definitely." Sherry's voice trembled. "Since John Davis was killed on the same day Shawn disappeared, I'm afraid that maybe his murderer did something to my Shawn. Maybe he was a witness and they killed him to keep him from saying anything."

"How could they?" Madison asked. "Dad and Mr. Davis traveled in two different circles."

"Since Shawn's a trucker, maybe the murderer forced him to help him escape the area." Sherry's face brightened. "Maybe he's still alive."

"If he is, we'll find him." Cameron stood up. "Detective Seavers will take you down to the station to fill out a missing person's report and we'll start looking to see if there's more of a connection to this than meets the eye."

Taking Tony by the elbow, she led him away. "Any word yet in our BOLO for Bea Miller?" she asked him in a low voice.

"The former clerk at the plant who John Davis had a restraining order against?" Tony asked. "I've heard nothing."

"Four months ago, Bea Miller assaulted Davis and he got a restraining order against her. A few months ago, Shawn Whitaker started getting unwanted phone calls from a woman by the name of Bea." She winked at Tony. "I don't believe in coincidences. We need to find Miller."

"Are you going to investigate my dad's case, J.J.?" Madison gazed up at him with wide blue eyes.

"I'll certainly be interested in what happens with it," J.J. said.

"Maddie." Sherry took her daughter by the arm. "We need to go with the detective to fill out the missing person's report."

Madison couldn't resist one last look over her shoulder before her mother led her away to follow Tony.

"Boy, she's got it bad," Cameron told him in a low voice.

"She was a very nice girl."

"And she knows you're engaged. Based on the way she's eyeing you, she doesn't care." She swiped her fingers across the screen on her tablet.

"I may not have a ring on my finger yet, but I consider myself taken," he said.

"Good boy. You're going to make Poppy a fine husband." She stepped over to stand next to him and held her tablet out for him to see. "Did you ever meet Heather's dad?"

"Sure. Dad and him go way back."

Cameron pressed a button on her tablet and a portrait picture of John Davis filled the screen. The executive was dressed in a suit, white shirt, and tie. The middle-aged man was attractive with a clean-shaven round face and a receding hairline. "That's John Davis," she said.

J.J. nodded his head. "The victim in the murder case I'm defending."

Cameron reached into her valise and extracted a photograph. "This is the picture that Sherry Whitaker just gave me of her husband, Shawn Whitaker, who was last seen Friday morning." She rested the picture on top of the tablet, to the side of the screen for J.J. to see the two images together.

Shawn Whitaker was a middle-aged man, with a round face, and receding hairline. Grinning with pride, he posed in front of a big white pick-up truck. He appeared comfortable dressed down in jeans and a plaid shirt.

There was no mistake. It was the same man in both pictures.

"Maybe they're twins," J.J. said.

"Two different last names?" Cameron said.

"Separated at birth?" Even as he said it, J.J. shook his head. "What did you tell—"

"I said nothing," she said. "I sent her to fill out a missing person's report so that I can be sure. In the meantime, the Columbiana County Sheriff's department has located John Davis's car in Calcutta. Do you want to come with me to check it out?"

"You asked me that like you think you can stop me."

Chapter Seven

The Columbiana County police had spotted John Davis's burgundy Audi in a small apartment complex tucked between two shopping centers in Calcutta, a rural town north of the Ohio River that consisted mostly of shopping centers, convenience stores, automotive dealerships, and business parks. The complex consisted of five four-story apartment buildings forming a pentagon around a grassy courtyard and playground.

When she pulled into the complex, Cameron let out a deep breath upon recognizing the dark SUV parked in the visitor's lot. Its owner was too busy examining the Audi while chatting with the two uniformed police officers and a barrel-chested man clad in a flannel vest to notice her.

"Who called you?" she asked after parking and throwing her door open.

Joshua pointed at J.J. who was climbing out of his truck.

"He's my investigator," J.J. said. "As defense counsel, I'm entitled to an investigator."

"I thought you can't—" she started to say.

"I'm not allowed to work as legal counsel. My contract says nothing about investigating." Joshua pointed through the Audi's driver side window. "This is definitely John's car. I see a folder on the driver's seat with the nuclear power plant's logo."

"The parking in this area is reserved," the man in the flannel vest said. "The number painted on the curb says which apartment the vehicles belong to."

Joshua introduced J.J. and Cameron to Ross Bayles, the apartment manager.

"We were answering a call for a domestic dispute," one of the uniformed officers said, "when we noticed the Audi and remembered seeing the BOLO for one with West Virginia plates. We don't see many Audis around here."

"Which apartment is this parking space assigned to?" J.J. asked Ross.

The manager pointed up the walkway to a building behind them. "Ground floor corner unit. Number A-one-sixteen. Name's Bishop Moore."

"Have you ever seen this car parked here before?" Joshua asked.

"He told me it belonged to a friend of his," Ross said while watching Cameron examining the white truck parked next to the Audi. "His bud traveled a lot and wanted to keep his car someplace safe while he was out of town."

Cameron was more interested in the Ford pick-up with Pennsylvania plates parked next to the Audi. She extracted the photo that Sherry Whitaker had given to her of her missing husband. The license plate was plainly displayed on the truck in the picture. When she compared the license numbers, they matched.

"And the truck?" she asked the manager.

"Another friend," Ross said.

"And this Moore guy?" Cameron asked. "What does he drive?"

The apartment manager's face was blank. "Nothing."

"Nothing?" J.J. said. "Are you saying he doesn't have a vehicle?"

"I've only seen him driving his friends' cars," Ross said. "He works for a travel agency. He's gone more than he's here. He says it's not worth the expense of a owning a vehicle to sit in an airport parking lot most of the time. The apartment is basically a place for him and his friends to crash between trips."

"Is Moore here now?" Cameron turned to him to ask. She saw Joshua cock his head with a questioning look in his blue eyes.

"Is Moore in trouble?" Ross asked.

"We just have some questions for him," she replied.

Ross took a full moment to respond. "Knock on the door and see if anyone answers." He pointed in the direction of the ground floor apartment.

Cameron stepped through them to stride up the walkway toward the ground-floor apartment. The two buildings at the end of the walkway were connected by an open stairwell.

"What was that about the truck?" Joshua fell into step with her to ask in a low voice.

She cast a glance over her shoulder at the uniformed officers and apartment manager. "Tell you later." She used the knocker to rap on the door.

The stairwell acted as a wind tunnel for the January breeze to whip through to chill them to the bone. Cameron, Joshua, and J.J. bounced on the balls of their feet to warm up.

Cameron rapped on the door once more before turning to the apartment manager watching them with wide eyes from a position several feet behind the uniformed officers. "Do you have a master key to let us in?"

"Don't you need a warrant?"

"We can get one," Joshua said. "That Audi is registered to a murder victim."

Ross spun on his heels and trotted down the walkway.

Catching Joshua's silent message sent via a toss of his head, J.J. hurried to catch up with the manager to extract what information he knew about the relationship between the renter of the apartment and John Davis.

Joshua stepped around to put his back to the wind to shelter Cameron, who was shivering. "What's the story with the truck?"

She moved in closer to him and peered up into his blue eyes. "That's Shawn Whitaker's truck."

"Shawn Whitaker?" Joshua's brow furrowed.

"A missing husband," Cameron said. "Truck driver. He disappeared the same night that John Davis was killed. Not only that, but Davis's body was dumped on Whitaker's in-laws' farm."

"And his name was Shawn Whitaker?" Joshua brought his face close to hers. "Are you certain?"

"Positive. What does that name mean to you?"

Joshua shook his head. "It could just be a coincidence."

"I don't believe in coincidences," she said. "Tell me about Shawn Whitaker."

"Kathleen Davis used to be Kathleen Whitaker and she had an older brother—Shawn Whitaker. He joined the army out of high school and was killed in a training exercise."

"How long has ..." J.J. paused to recall the name of the renter while walking across the complex with the manager

"Bishop Moore."

J.J. followed him to an apartment with a wooden sign reading "Apartment Manager" attached to the door. He could hear a television blasting from inside. "How long has Bishop Moore been renting here?"

"Have no idea." Ross pushed through the door. "My wife and I only moved here four months ago after I got hired to manage the place. I'm retired from General Motors. I worked in maintenance at their plant in Lordstown. Thought getting out of Youngstown would do her some good."

J.J. followed Ross into the office, which appeared to have been an apartment in a previous life. A cloud of cigarette smoke hit J.J. in the face. He let out a cough. Instantly his throat became sore.

The first room in the office was a converted kitchen. A printer rested on the counter. A desk had been pushed up against the wall. A cupboard door hung open to display rows upon rows of hooks with keys hanging from them.

A motorized wheelchair rested inside the living room where a heavy-set older woman was sprawled out in a recliner. A talk show was blasting on a wide screen television. Even though it was the middle of the afternoon, the woman was dressed in a worn bathrobe with slippers. A plume of cigarette smoke rose from the ashtray on the end table, which rested next to a can of beer.

The television's volume was so loud that J.J. could not hear what Ross was saying while thrashing through folders in a file cabinet.

"Excuse me." J.J. gestured that he couldn't hear him.

"Brenda! Turn that dang TV down!" Folder in his hand, Ross stomped into the living room. "We can't hear ourselves think."

Brenda jumped as if she had been awakened. Blinking her eyes, she looked beyond her husband to J.J. in the office. "Who's that?"

"The police," Ross said. "They're lookin' for Bishop Moore."

With a glare at J.J., she uttered a slurred curse.

"Excuse me. What did you say?" J.J. asked.

Turning his back to Brenda, Ross made a gesture with his hand to indicate that she had been drinking and ushered him back into the kitchen. "Moore signed a three-year lease on that apartment seven months ago." He handed the folder to J.J. who leafed through a thick stack of legal agreements. "Looks like he's been here a while."

J.J. read the date on the oldest lease. "Twelve years."

"Longtime resident."

J.J. handed the folder back to the manager, who set it on his desk. "If he's making good money, why rent?"

"He probably split the rent with his two friends."

"Maybe," J.J. said with a shrug. "Still, it's better to invest in a place that you own rather than rent."

"Obviously, there's a connection between Shawn Whitaker and John Davis," Joshua said.

"And I know what it is." Cameron extracted the picture from her bag and handed it to him.

Recognizing the image of his old friend, Joshua shrugged his shoulders and looked down into her face.

"Sherry Whitaker gave me that picture when she told me that he was missing. She hasn't heard from him since he left for a cross-country haul Friday morning. She says he calls her every night when he's on the road. John's body was dumped on her parents' farm the same day. She wondered if John's murder and her husband's disappearance could be connected."

"Like that Whitaker witnessed Davis's murder?"

Cameron tapped the man's image in the photograph. "This is Shawn Whitaker. He was with his wife, Sherry, all last week—during the time period that Kathleen's husband was in Seattle on a business trip."

"A business trip that Davis's assistant says never happened," Joshua said with a sigh.

"We wanted to know where John was going after he left work." She took the picture from Joshua's hands. "Now we know. He was going home to his other family."

"I don't believe it. John Davis was not a cheater."

"Which do you find easier to believe? That your friend John Davis was bouncing back and forth between two wives or that the man in this picture is his identical twin and the two of them were separated at birth?"

J.J. trotted up the walkway with the apartment manager. "Bishop Moore has been renting here for the last twelve years," he told them while Ross unlocked the door with his spare key.

"Is he from around here?" Joshua accepted a pair of evidence gloves from Cameron who extracted a pack from her valise. She also handed a pair to J.J.

"He's from Canfield." Ross threw open the door and held it for them to step inside.

They each glanced around the apartment while walking through the combined living room-kitchenette, bedroom, and bath. The furnishings were a few inexpensive pieces—a sofa, chair, coffee table and small television. The kitchenette had a table with one chair. A sliding glass door opened to a bare patio.

Cameron looked inside the fridge. It contained a carton of eggs, milk, and six-pack of beer. In the freezer, she found a half-dozen frozen dinners. "Obviously, Bishop Moore is not a gourmet." The cupboard contained a cheap dishes that looked almost new.

"This is definitely a crash pad," Joshua said while poking through a shelving unit resting against one wall. "No personal items like family pictures or books. Just the bare essentials."

When Cameron turned to respond, she noticed Ross standing at the door. His eyes were wide. His mouth hung open. "We may be a while. How about if you leave us the key and we'll bring it over to your office when we're through."

After a moment of hesitation, the apartment manager handed the key to her. "Be sure to lock up when you leave." He took one last glance over his shoulder before leaving.

"Nosy," she muttered while tucking the key into her jacket pocket.

Joshua stepped into the kitchenette, where he took note of the empty trash can. He picked it up to show her that there wasn't a liner in it. "Someone took out the trash."

"Moore took the trash out when he left. How responsible of him."

"I'm talking about the condition of this kitchen." He placed the bin back on the floor next to the counter. "This is sterilized clean."

She frowned when she noticed a splatter of red spots on the side of the trash bin. "Not exactly sterilized." She picked the bin up and held it sideways to show him a spray of red splatters across the bottom half of the bin. "Does that look like blood to you?"

Joshua glanced at the knife block on the counter. "The butcher knife is missing."

Cameron knelt to examine the linoleum floor. She could see red stains along the seams. "We found the crime scene."

J.J. stepped into the bedroom doorway. "You're going to want to see this." He crooked his finger for them to follow him.

In the bedroom, Cameron noticed that there was no comforter on the queen-size bed. "Now we know where the comforter Davis was wrapped up in came from."

The walk-in closet door was open. J.J. swept his arm for them to step inside. "Take a look at his clothes."

The closet had racks to hang clothes on both sides of the small room. One side contained flannel shirts, work pants hanging clumsily from hangers or loosely folded and stacked on shelves. Soiled work boots were scattered along the floor. There were jeans and thick belts with big decorative buckles.

The other side was a picture of contrast. Suits, sports coats, dress slacks, and ties were neatly hung up. Dress shoes were arranged in a straight row against the wall.

Joshua picked up a pair of shiny leather dress shoes. "I'm guessing this side of the closet is for the up-tight executive."

Cameron picked up a sweater from the floor. "And this side is the easy-going truck driver."

J.J. held up two cell phones from the dresser. "He had both families completely separated right down to the phones."

"Madison is—" Joshua looked at J.J. to confirm. "Isn't she the same age as Tracy?"

"They graduated the same year in high school."

"Could John have been a bigamist and gotten away with it for like twenty-five—"

"Sherry Whitaker says they were married for twenty-seven years," Cameron said. "And now I'm thinking someone found out about it. Davis or Whitaker or whatever his name is took ten thousand dollars out of Davis's savings account on Friday—the day he was killed. He got cash. I can't find anything to account for where that money went to."

"Seeing this," Joshua said, "the first thing to comes to my mind is blackmail."

"What role does Bishop Moore play in all this?" J.J. asked.

"Is there even a Bishop Moore?" Joshua asked. "Take a look at this place. I couldn't even find any mail addressed to occupant."

"Minimal furniture and food in the kitchen," Cameron said. "This is just a crash pad for Davis-slash-Whitaker to change from one personality to the other. I doubt if Bishop Moore even exists. I'll still run a background check on him."

"Then the question remains," J.J. asked, "which identity was the intended murder victim? John Davis or Shawn Whitaker?"

CHAPTER EIGHT

One would have found it difficult to believe that Cameron outranked Tony when he arrived at Bishop Moore's apartment. The forensics team had only just started examining it for evidence of John Davis's murder.

"Are you kidding me?" The young detective laid into Cameron after she finished showing the crime scene investigators where she had found traces of blood in the kitchen. "You brought your husband to uncover crucial evidence, but left me at the office filling out a missing person's report?" He gestured to where Joshua was leaning against the wall across from the ground floor apartment in the open stairwell.

"We needed the information from the missing person's report to follow up on my suspicion that Davis and Whitaker are the same man," Cameron said.

"A suspicion you kept from your partner," Tony said. "Yet you had no problem bringing in your husband, who isn't even a member of the police force."

"You're sounding like a jealous girlfriend."

"And you're acting like a first-class—"

"Hey, Cam, is that Kevin Bacon ever there?" Joshua blurted out to cut Tony off.

Both detectives stopped to glare in his direction. Joshua crooked at finger at Cameron. Her eyes blazing, she stepped across the breezeway.

"He's right," Joshua told her in a soft whisper.

"Are you—"

"You've always been the subordinate team member. Your partner has always outranked you. Think about it. If any of your partners had left you out in the cold, the way you did Tony—"

"Hey, you invited yourself here," she said with a hiss. "I didn't."

"But who invited J.J.—after sending Tony back to the office?" Joshua shrugged his shoulders.

"I never did played well with others." With a low growl, she crossed the breezeway. "Okay, Seavers. You were right."

Tony's eyes grew big. He shot a glance in Joshua's direction before asking, "What was I right about?"

"I should have read you in and invited you to follow up this lead with me instead of sending you back to the office."

"All right!" Tony pumped his fist up into the air.

"Don't get cocky," she said. "I'm still your supervisor, and I can get your ass demoted. So don't mess with me."

"Yes, ma'am." Tony nodded his head. "Apology accepted."

"I didn't apologize."

"But you just said you were wrong."

"I never said I was wrong. I said you were right."

"But if I was right, then that means you were wrong."

"Are you arguing with me, detective?"

"No, ma'am."

"Good," Cameron said. "Now that we have that sorted out, let's get back to the case. The murder weapon is the same type and brand of knife missing from the block in the kitchen. If we're right, the victim was leading a double life, which means we have at least two suspects with motive to kill him in a crime of—"

"Assuming they knew about his double life," he said.

"Did Sherry Whitaker give you the phone number for her husband's dentist? Let's have him compare Whitaker's latest x-rays with our murder victim."

"How about the guy renting this apartment?" Tony asked.

"Bishop Moore," she said. "No one knows where he is."

"I'm betting he's in the morgue listed under the name John Davis," Joshua said. "The phone number listed on his apartment lease is for a travel agency in Youngstown that went out of business ten years ago."

"Run a background check on Bishop Moore," Cameron told Tony. "I'm thinking someone knew about Davis's double life. He withdrew ten thousand dollars out of his savings on the same day he was killed. We need to find out what that withdrawal was for. Hunt down everything you can about Bishop Moore, starting with finding out if he's even a real person. Also, don't forget to get in touch with Shawn Whitaker's dentist so that we can find out if he's alive or dead."

"Yes, ma'am." Tony spun on his heels and took out his tablet to get to work. As he hurried away, Joshua noticed the apartment manager and a woman in an electronic wheelchair watching from the end of the walkway.

Turning away, Joshua noticed a security camera erected in the upper corner of the breezeway. It was aimed at the walkway leading to the parking lot. "Where are these security recordings kept?" he called to the apartment manager.

A sheepish expression filled Ross Bayles's face. He trotted up the walkway before answering in a low voice. "Nowhere."

"What do you mean 'nowhere?'" Joshua asked, though he suspected he knew the answer. The security cameras were for show, in hopes of scaring away potential criminals.

"People kept breaking them or they'd break on their own," Ross said. "They were more trouble than they were worth. So ..." His voice trailed off.

Clad in a heavy winter coat, a woman with short salt and pepper hair trotted around the crowd of curious onlookers. Digging into her handbag, she craned her neck to study the police activity. With a pleasant grin in Joshua's direction, she extracted a key chain.

"Don't tell anyone," Ross said before flashing a pleasant grin at the tenant heading toward them.

Realizing that he was blocking the door to her apartment, Joshua stepped aside.

"What's going on?" she asked while turning the key in the deadbolt to her door.

"Police are investigating a suspected crime scene." Not wanting to give away too much information on an open case, Joshua tried to be as vague as possible.

She pulled the key from the deadbolt. "Is Bishop okay?"

"We're still investigating."

"I assure you our apartments are completely safe and secure," Ross said before hurrying away.

"Did you know the man who lived in that apartment?" Joshua asked.

She hesitated before nodding her head. "He's very nice. Charming even. He travels a lot in his job with the travel agency. He'll bring me little gifts from places he's been."

"What kind of gifts?"

"Little things. Nothing really expensive, but sweet stuff." She opened the door and invited Joshua into her apartment. The layout was identical to the one across the stairwell.

After setting her purse on the kitchen table, she pointed at a blue painted vase with paper flowers acting as center piece. "He brought me that vase from France."

He picked up the vase to examine it. "I didn't catch your name, by the way?"

With a laugh, she said, "How stupid of me? I just assumed with all the police around that you were a detective."

"Lawyer." He shook her hand. "Joshua Thornton."

"Rosie Danza. Let me show you what else he brought me." She hurried to a curio cabinet in the living room.

Joshua read a tiny label on the bottom of the vase. "Duty Free."

"Bishop brought me this doll from China." Rosie went on to show him a wide variety of gifts she had received from her neighbor. Many were small decorative items or jewelry.

"He certainly has given you a lot of nice things," Joshua said while examining many of them. "What was exactly your relationship with Mr. Moore?"

"Now you sound like a detective investigating a murder." Her smile fell. "We were just friends. Maybe I hoped that we could have become more later on, but I've been gun shy since my divorce and he knew that. We'd just have dinner once in a while. That's all."

"When was the last time you saw your neighbor?"

"Did something bad happen to—" She gasped. "They killed him, didn't they?" She dropped onto the sofa. "I knew I should have called the police, but I didn't want to seem like one of those nosy busybody neighbors."

"Right now, no one knows where Bishop Moore is." Joshua sat next to her. "What happened? When did you think about calling the police?"

She took in a shuddering breath. "I think …" She paused. "Friday. It was Friday night. It was after dinner. Seven. Maybe it was closer to eight? I'm not sure. But I heard a lot of yelling and he's usually very quiet. Very. So it was unusual. It was a big loud fight."

"Physical?"

Rosie shook her head. "Yelling. Shrieking. Crying. Definitely two women and him. But they were doing all the talking."

"Two? You're sure."

Rosie pointed out her living room window to the parking lot. "I was nosy enough to look out the window after I heard the door slam shut over there. I saw two women leaving. They went down the walkway and over to the visitors' lot. I didn't see what they were driving when they left." She bit her bottom lip. "To tell you the truth, I only saw them go down the walkway." Her eyes grew wide. "Maybe they doubled back and did something awful to Bishop."

"Could you describe them?"

"Tall. Skinny. Pretty, I'm sure. I didn't see either of their faces, but I saw their backs. One was blond. The other was brunette." She covered her mouth with her hands. "Was he dismembered?"

"Why would you ask that?" Joshua asked.

"I heard what sounded like a saw later on that night. It not something that you usually hear around here. That's why I wondered if maybe they killed him and cut him into little pieces and carried him away. I mean, think about it. How would they have gotten rid of the body?" She noticed Joshua looking at her with curiosity. "I read a lot of murder mysteries."

There was a knock in the door. Rosie jumped to her feet to answer it.

Cameron was in the doorway. "Have you seen a good-looking man with silver hair?"

Rosie swept her arm in Joshua's direction. "He's all yours."

"He most certainly is." Cameron crooked her finger for Joshua to follow her. "The investigators have located our crime scene."

Joshua followed her into the kitchen where they had dimmed the lights in order to illuminate the floor and cabinets under an ultraviolet lamp. The floor and cabinets glowed with purple streaks and blood splatters.

"We sprayed the area with luminal and this is what we turned up," the head of the crime scene unit explained. "Based on all this blood, this is definitely a crime scene. They did a good job of covering it up. Some of the blood had drained into the seams for the linoleum."

"I bet the killer used bleach to clean it up," Cameron said.

"We found traces of bleach all right," the investigator said. "But he did miss a few drops of blood that splattered onto the underside of the cupboard above the sink." He pointed to the upper cabinet. "We'll be able to get DNA. If it's a match to your victim, then I believe you found a crime scene."

"Good job." Cameron bumped fists with the investigator before turning to Joshua. "Now all we have to do is figure out which of our victim's women took him out."

"According to Moore's neighbor, it could be both."

CHAPTER NINE

With a heavy sigh, Poppy dropped her head into her arms. "At the rate I'm going, I'll finish school when Izzy is getting her degree in veterinary medicine."

Seated next to her at the Thornton kitchen table, Izzy wrapped her arms around Poppy's shoulders. "It only feels like that now. Once you get algebra down, then it'll be downhill from there" —she winked at J.J. from behind Poppy's back— "until you hit calculus."

Poppy sat up. "I don't need calculus to get my high school diploma." She turned to where J.J. was going over her homework for that night's GED class. "Do I?"

"No, you don't need calculus." J.J. reached around her to tap a giggly Izzy on the arm.

"I'm never going to get algebra." Poppy slapped her laptop shut. "I've got a career that I love. I'm marrying the love of my life. I have friends and a family. Why do I need to make myself feel like an idiot by going back to school—especially in the middle of planning a wedding?"

"Because you're not an idiot." J.J. kissed her. "One day, you're going to need that slip of paper. Maybe not now, but

THE ROOT OF MURDER

one day. Like maybe you'll decide later to go to veterinary school."

"We can go to veterinary school together," Izzy said with a broad grin.

"Not if I have to learn calculus," Poppy said.

Admiral galloped into the kitchen from where he had been sleeping on the living room sofa. The giant dog hit the rug, slid across the room, and collided with the back door at the same time Cameron was opening it from the other side. Smelling oriental food, Irving launched himself from the window sill to join the dog in greeting Cameron and Joshua.

"Honey, I'm home," Joshua sang out while holding up the brown paper bags.

"Did you get veggie egg foo young?" Izzy ran to the cupboard to take out plates.

"And egg drop soup and spring rolls. We got enough to feed an army." Cameron helped Joshua unload the bags.

Admiral ran his nose along the counter's edge to sniff out the possibilities for food theft.

"Did the forensics investigators locate the crime scene?" J.J. asked while holding out a bowl for Cameron to ladle soup into.

"If you'd stuck around, you'd know the answer to that." The corners of her lips curled.

"I had to pick *your* kid up from school." J.J. handed the bowl to Poppy who switched it for an empty bowl.

"That kid is your sister." Joshua set the opened boxes in the middle of the table. He placed serving spoons into each one.

"I like it when J.J. picks me up from school." Izzy ripped open a package containing a pair of chopsticks. "Then I get to go to the farm before doing my homework."

"Delaying the inevitable," Joshua said.

"Did you see Pilgrim?" Izzy plunged on without waiting for Joshua's answer. "Poppy and I gave her a bath and combed out her mane and tail. We trimmed them, too. She's going to have her baby at the end of March—right about when J.J. and Poppy get married." Her mouth dropped open. "Wouldn't it be *awesome* if Pilgrim had her colt on your wedding day?"

"What else did Rod say about Pilgrim? How sick is she?" Joshua held back the urge to ask if the new horse had a contagious ailment that would infect J.J.'s champion quarter horses.

"She's full of parasites and malnourished, but with a lot of TLC, she'll be fine." Poppy flashed Joshua a grin of reassurance. "We'll keep her in quarantine until the vet gives her a clean bill of health."

Everyone dove into their dinner. Once their plates were filled, J.J. repeated his question. "Did the forensics investigators find any evidence in the Moore apartment to prove Derek innocent?"

"You don't have to prove his innocence," Joshua said. "All you have to prove is reasonable doubt. The burden is on the prosecution to prove guilt."

"Which is my job," Cameron said, while grabbing her buzzing phone. She got up from the table as she put it to her ear. "Yes, Seavers, what have you got?" She left the kitchen to talk to him in a quieter location.

While shooing Admiral and Irving away from Cameron's plate, Joshua told J.J., "Unless the prosecution can find evidence putting Derek in that apartment, you've got grounds to move for a dismissal."

"Bishop Moore is dead," Cameron heard Tony say while she rushed into the study.

"Why am I not surprised?" She flopped into the leather executive chair behind Joshua's desk.

"Now here is the surprise," Tony said. "His last known legitimate address was North Jackson. He tended bar in Austintown and was killed in a hit and run thirteen years ago."

"Are you sure it's the same Bishop Moore? This Bishop Moore is a travel agent."

"I used the information on his lease application for the background check," Tony said. "All the management did back then was run a credit check. They didn't check to see if the guy was alive. I guess they assumed he'd be alive if he was well enough to rent an apartment."

"So the real Bishop Moore was hit by a car—probably one of the drunks—"

"Based on the crime scene report, he was murdered," Tony said. "He was hit, then the vehicle backed over him, and ran over him again. The detectives do have a suspect—his girlfriend's ex—but they were never able to pin it on him. The guy had an alibi and they've never been able to break it."

"The point is Bishop Moore was killed thirteen years ago, and he's been renting an apartment in Calcutta for the last twelve," Cameron said.

"I think John Davis stole his ID," he said. "You were right. The ME said Shawn Whitaker's dental X-rays are an exact match for John Davis's body."

"And the fingerprints are a match for John Davis's," she said. "Shawn Whitaker and John Davis are one and the same. That gives us two pools of suspects to choose from."

"But Derek had the murder weapon—"

"Which matches the knives in Moore's apartment," Cameron said. "Plus, forensics found blood splatters and blood on the scene to indicate the murder happened there."

"Derek publicly threatened the victim."

"But we can't put him in the apartment," she said. "No fingerprints—"

"The place was wiped down," he said. "He cleaned up afterwards."

"Were you in that courtroom today?"

"Yeah," he said with a scoff. "Why?"

"Do you really think Derek Ellison has the mental capacity to think through moving a body and cleaning up a crime scene to conceal his crime?"

"His fingerprints are on the knife which came from the victim's apartment."

"Oh, and then, after cleaning up the crime scene and moving the body, he was stupid enough to take the bloody murder weapon home with him," she said. "If he was swift enough to clean up and dump the body, then he'd be smart enough to ditch the murder weapon where it wouldn't implicate him. You're right. He did threaten the victim, which made him an excellent patsy to frame for the murder. Based on this new information, I'm going to tell Sanders that we need to get a continuance or drop the charges until we can fully investigate this new evidence."

"You're the boss," Tony said with an edge in his voice.

"That's right," she said. "Here's what we're going to do. Have you told anyone about Whitaker's dental records being a match for Davis's body? Did you contact the family?"

"No, I thought I'd leave that news up to you."

"Good. Tell no one."

"No one? How about the victim's wife? I mean, second wife."

"Especially not the victim's family—either of them. Contact the medical examiner and tell her not to let this news go anywhere. That includes her staff. As far as everyone's concerned, Shawn Whitaker is a missing person."

"Will do. Anything else?"

"Bea Miller. Does anyone know where she is?"

"I checked on the restraining order. It's still in place," Tony said. "Her last known address is a rental at a trailer park in Calcutta."

"Weren't we just in Calcutta?" Cameron asked.

"Yeah," Tony said. "Bea Miller lives practically across the street from our victim."

"Very interesting."

"Whoever cleaned up the murder scene missed blood splatter on the underside of the upper cabinets," Joshua was telling J.J. when Cameron returned to the kitchen. "The pattern indicates high velocity blood splatter—a violent death. There's enough blood for them to run a DNA comparison."

"And if it is John Davis's blood, that means he was killed there and his body was dumped at the Newhart farm, which belonged to Shawn Whitaker's in-laws," J.J. said.

"Who were also Davis's in-laws because Whitaker was Davis," Cameron said as she took her seat.

"What about Bishop Moore?" J.J. asked. "Is he a third identity of the same man or an accomplice who helped Davis and Whitaker—what should we call him?"

"Right now, I'm leaning toward Moore being a third identity," Cameron said. "Our background check indicates that Moore died thirteen years ago—one year before his identity was used to rent that apartment."

"Somehow, Davis got his hands on Bishop Moore's information and used it to rent a place to rest between wives," J.J. said.

"John Davis has to be the primary identity. I'd known the man since high school." Joshua set down his fork. "Which is why I find this so unbelievable. John was never a big womanizer. He always treated women with respect—never leering or making rude jokes. He liked—I mean really liked women and obviously, they liked him—"

"Obviously," Poppy said with a sly grin.

"He wasn't that attractive," Joshua said. "He wasn't the type of man that women chased after and he didn't chase after them. So how did he end up with two wives?"

"Well," Cameron mused, "when you look at it from an investigative point of view—everything you've described makes John Davis above suspicion for being a bigamist."

"Cam's got a point," J.J. said.

"John dated Kathleen all through school," Joshua said. "He married her well over thirty years ago."

"He was married to Sherry Whitaker for twenty-seven years," Cameron said.

"Shawn Whitaker died like thirty years ago," Joshua said. "Kathleen was the executor of her brother's estate. That would have given her access to everything John needed to file for a birth certificate and get a social security card to create a second identity."

"Madison Whitaker is the same age as Tracy. And so is Heather." J.J.'s mouth dropped open in a gasp. "If John Davis and Shawn Whitaker are the same man, that means Heather and Madison are sisters."

"Half-sisters," Joshua said. "I can't believe with all the stuff that went down between those two in high school that no one ever found out that they had the same father." He chuckled. "You gotta hand it to John. Two families—living how far apart?"

Cameron was already checking on her tablet. "The two women's addresses are twenty miles apart—with the state line dividing them."

"My big question is why," Joshua said. "What man in his right mind starts a family with two different women?"

THE ROOT OF MURDER

"Do they know each other?" Cameron asked.

"I'm sure they'd met when Heather and Madison were in dance together at Miss Charlotte's Dance Studio," J.J. said. "They were never friends from what I saw. Not enemies. Just from different worlds."

"If they had been, I'm sure their friendship ended after you entered their daughters' lives," Joshua said with a chuckle.

"What did you do to them?" Poppy asked J.J.

"I did *nothing* to them."

The women around the table turned to Joshua for the answer.

"J.J. dated both of them at the same time."

"Not at the same time," J.J. said.

When the women turned to Joshua to confirm J.J.'s statement, he nodded his head to indicate that he did.

"I bounced back and forth between them like a ping pong ball, but I was upfront about it," J.J. said. "I couldn't decide between them. I started out dating Heather. She was co-captain of the cheerleading squad with Tracy. She was so sharp and organized and really had her head on straight. She always knew what she wanted to do."

"She graduated from WVU with her MBA in five years," Joshua said. "She works for a big marketing company out in Robinson."

"She was taking dance lessons at the same studio as Tracy," J.J. said. "I went there to pick them up a few times. That was where I met Madison. She was a fantastic dancer."

"Wasn't Heather's sister taking lessons there, too?" Joshua asked.

"Heather's sister?" Cameron asked. "Are you talking about Derek's wife?"

"Lindsay." J.J. shook his fork in Joshua's direction while slowly saying, "I forgot all about her. I think Lindsay enjoyed dancing more than Heather. But then she loved partying more than dance."

"She had to drop out when she got pregnant in her junior year of high school," Joshua said. "She was eight months pregnant at Heather's graduation. Kathleen was horrified with embarrassment."

"Didn't she die in a drunk driving accident three years ago?" Cameron asked. "Supposedly, that's what sent Derek off the deep end."

Joshua and Cameron noticed a shadow cross J.J.'s face before he turned his full attention to the food on his plate.

"Are we missing something?" Cameron asked.

"I wasn't here when Lindsay died." J.J. glanced from one of them to the other. "I've only heard rumors."

"What kind of rumors?" Joshua asked.

"About Lindsay's accident." J.J. cast a nervous glance in Izzy's direction.

Aware of all eyes aimed at her, Izzy lifted her shoulders. "I know how babies are made and where they come from."

"She even assisted in birthing a foal last spring," Poppy said.

"This isn't about sex," J.J. said.

"I know about death, too," Izzy said. "Have you forgotten that my mom was murdered? That's how I ended up here."

"She does have a point," Joshua said.

Relenting, Cameron said, "Just don't go repeating what we're talking about, Izzy. It may be helpful in catching a killer."

With a shrug of her shoulders, Izzy returned to eating her spring roll.

"Out with it," Joshua ordered J.J.

"There's nothing concrete to come out with," J.J. said. "Rumor has it that Lindsay committed suicide."

"Sheriff Sawyer investigated that crash out on Washington School Road," Joshua said. "She had gone out drinking—"

"After having a huge fight with Heather," J.J. said.

"What were they fighting about?" Cameron asked.

"Heather blew off coming back home for Luke's birthday party," J.J. said. "She chose to go to a conference instead. Lindsay took it personally."

"Even if she took it personally, that doesn't mean she purposely wrapped her car around a tree," Joshua said. "She was on methamphetamine and had a blood alcohol level of point four. She never should have gotten behind that wheel. We can only thank God she didn't take someone else out with her."

"I'm only telling you what I heard," J.J. said. "Lindsay had a lot of regrets about decisions she had made. She knew she had a problem with drugs and booze. She was afraid of how Luke was going to turn out with her as his mother."

"Did she leave a note saying that?" Cameron asked.

J.J. shook his head. "I can't even tell you where I heard it. It's just been going around."

"What does Derek say?" Cameron asked Joshua.

"He says Lindsay wrapped her car around that tree by accident," Joshua said. "According to what Sawyer uncovered during his investigation, Lindsay did have a big fight with Heather about not coming home for Luke's birthday. She told Derek that she needed to go out. That was about seven o'clock in the evening—right after dinner. He gave her a twenty-dollar bill and she left him home with Luke, who was already in bed. Witnesses saw her eating pizza and drinking in Chester Park. It was close to three o'clock in the morning when one of Sawyer's deputies discovered the wreck on Washington School Road. Her body was in the middle of the road. There were skid marks all over. Sawyer concluded she had lost control of the car going around the hairpin curve. She got thrown from the car and it rolled over her before going over the hill. The broken clock on the dash registered the wreck as being close to one-thirty in the morning. They lived right down the road. She must have been going home when it happened."

"What a waste," Cameron said.

"Lindsay loved to dance," J.J. said. "She wanted to be a professional dancer until she got caught up in drugs."

"It was Heather who went to competition," Joshua said. "Madison was her arch rival. She'd win every time with Heather coming in right behind her—just missing that big trophy. That drove Heather, who has always been very competitive, crazy. When J.J. decided to step out with Madison—"

"Dad, you make it sound like I was cheating on Heather." Aware of Poppy looking at him out of the corner of his eye, J.J. turned to her. "Heather and I did not have an exclusive relationship. Madison invited me to go dancing with her one night, and I like to dance. We had a good time. Then, she asked me to be her date for homecoming at her school and—"

"Boom!" Joshua threw up in hands in a gesture of an explosion.

"Boom?" Poppy asked.

"I didn't do anything wrong," J.J. said.

Breathless with excitement, Izzy asked Joshua, "What happened?"

"J.J. took Madison," Joshua said. "According to Tracy, Heather went a little crazy. She called up a boy from that school who had a thing for her and charmed him into taking her so that she could keep an eye on them."

"I smell trouble," Cameron said.

Frowning, Joshua shook his head. "Oh, it was bad."

J.J. hung his head. "Do we really have to talk about this?"

"You can't stop in the middle of a story." With a grin, Poppy turned to Joshua. "How bad was it?"

"How bad was it?" Laughing, Joshua threw down his fork. "Let's see. It was so bad that the police were called in."

"Dad, I want this woman to marry me." J.J. pointed to Poppy. "I was outside when the first punch was thrown."

"Cat fight, huh?" Cameron asked. "Over J.J.?"

"Tracy knew it would be all-out war when both girls showed up in the same dress," Joshua said.

The women cringed.

"Heather bought her dress from an exclusive dress shop in Beaver," J.J. said. "She paid four hundred dollars for it. Witnesses in the bathroom said Heather threw the first punch after Madison told her that she bought her dress at J.C. Penney's for eighty dollars."

"Both dresses got shredded in the fight," Joshua said, "and J.J. got four stitches."

J.J. shook his head. "No, that was the fight where I got the black eye. I got the four stitches during the Christmas formal when I got hit in the face with a punch bowl."

"I thought you got the broken wrist at the Christmas dance."

"No, the broken wrist happened at the dance recital in the spring," J.J. said.

"And the broken ribs?"

"That was prom." In response to Poppy's questioning expression, J.J. said, "At which point, I dumped them both."

"Whatever for?" Cameron asked with a laugh. "The three of you seemed to be having so much fun."

"Doctor's orders," Joshua said.

"Funny," Poppy said. "You never told me you were a cheat."

"They never do," Cameron said.

"I'm not a cheat," J.J. said. "I honestly could not decide between them. Madison was a lot of fun. Heather was so serious, so focused. The cheerleading and dance lessons—she did them strictly for her resume. She honestly did not know how to just have fun. With Madison, I could just cut loose."

"So you liked Madison," Cameron said.

"But I couldn't have a serious conversation with Madison," J.J. said. "She didn't like books or studying. She couldn't see past tomorrow—except that she was going to New York as soon as she graduated. When I'd ask about specifics—like where are you going to live and what are you going to do for food—" He lifted a shoulder. "She'd cross that bridge when she came to it."

"When you felt like being with a woman who you could talk to," Poppy said, "you'd ditch Madison and take up with Heather."

"More or less."

"That doesn't sound quite fair to Heather and Madison," Cameron said. "How long did you bounce back and forth between them? It sounds like your entire junior year."

"I'm not a cheat," J.J. said. "I was up front with both of them."

"And he didn't get one bit of enjoyment out of two women fighting over him," Joshua said with a sly grin.

"You were a heel," Izzy said.

"I know," J.J. said with a sigh.

"Going back to the murder case," Joshua said, "when you think about it, John Davis was really good."

"He was rotten," Cameron said. "He went beyond J.J. here. He didn't just date two women, he married them and started whole families without either of them knowing it."

"I know but think about it. Both girls took dance lessons at the same dance school for years. They dated the same boy for almost a full school year. Yet, no one realized that they had the same father."

"Didn't these girls' father ever have that talk with you when you went to pick them up?" Cameron asked J.J. "You know the talk. 'Mess with my daughter and I'll break your kneecaps.'"

"I'd met Heather's dad. I mean, Davis was a friend of Dad's. But I'd never met Madison's father. He was a truck driver and always on the road."

"Wouldn't you think the Whitakers would have had pictures of Shawn up at the house?" Recalling the Newhart home, Cameron shook her head. "Their grandparents had pictures of Madison and Sherry, but not Shawn."

"Some people are camera shy," Joshua said. "When you think about it, it wasn't really that hard. Whitaker was always on the road, which gave him an excuse to never be at any events where both families were likely to show up."

"Never allow his picture to be displayed where the other family was likely to see it," J.J. said.

"Two completely different cell phones. Thus, separating all contact between the two families." Cameron cocked her head. "Do you really think his wives didn't know? We're talking about a deception that went on for close to three decades."

In silence, they exchanged glances.

"I was just a little kid when my mom was cheating on my dad—right before he went missing," Poppy said in a soft voice. "I remember once, Dad and I were doing chores in the barn. Mom came out. She was all dressed up. She said she was going to some sort of meeting or something. I don't even remember where she said she was going. When she left, I saw this really sad expression on my dad's face. It was just a glimpse. Years later, when I realized what had been going on, and folks told me that Dad had no idea about her cheating on him—I remembered that expression. His heart was breaking." She nodded her head. "He knew. He may have never told anyone. He may never have even admitted it to himself, but he knew." She raised her eyes to look at Cameron and Joshua. "It's called blissful ignorance for a reason."

CHAPTER TEN

Poppy gathered her school supplies and left for her GED class as soon as she had finished dinner. Izzy went to her room to work on a school project. As usual, Irving and Admiral followed her, their favorite human.

After seeing Poppy off, J.J. went back into the house to tell Joshua and Cameron good-night. He found them in the study. Joshua sat behind his desk. His cell phone rested in the center of the desktop.

Cameron held a brandy snifter to J.J. "Your father is calling Tracy."

J.J. took the glass. "What for?" He took a sip of the brandy.

"Confirmation," she said with a wink.

Tracy's voice floated from the speakers. "Hey, Dad! What's up?"

"I'm here with your brother and Cam. We're calling for some information."

"What about?"

Cameron interjected, "Is Hunter there with you?"

"He's sleeping. He's got the early shift tomorrow. I'm decorating a cake for a birthday party. Oh, J.J., he'll meet you at the house after work to help you with whatever you need

113

done. Text him if you need him to bring some of his tools." She shifted back to the reason for the call. "Why are you asking about Hunter? Do you need me to wake him up?"

"No," Cameron said. "This is about my investigation and we need our conversation to be on the DL."

Tracy let out a girlish squeal. "Tell me more."

They exchanged glances. Wordlessly, they asked who should lead, how much to divulge, and how to extract information from Tracy without accidentally leading her in what could possibly be the wrong direction.

Cameron plunged in. "Tracy, did you know that Sherry Whitaker reported her husband, Madison's father, missing?"

"No." She gasped. "When did he go missing?"

"Sherry told us that the last time she saw him was Friday morning," Cameron said. "He was driving a rig cross-country to Montana. He calls her every night when he's on the road and she hasn't heard from him."

"Maybe he had an accident," Tracy said. "But then, if you believed that, you wouldn't be talking to me on the down-low, would you?"

"Smart girl," J.J. said.

"Our question for you is simple," Joshua said. "Have you ever met Shawn Whitaker?"

"No. Why?" Tracy replied.

"You were friends with Maddie," J.J. said.

"You *dated* Maddie," his sister countered.

"And I never met her father," J.J. said.

"Are you saying he doesn't exist?" Tracy laughed. "Like that movie *Psycho*. Sherry Whitaker dresses up as a truck driver and goes around knifing unsuspecting dog owners who come to her for training."

"That actually seems more believable," Cameron muttered.

"Tracy," J.J. asked, "you've been to their house—"

"So have you."

"Do you remember ever seeing pictures of Maddie's dad?"

"Yes," Tracy replied. "They have a picture of him standing in front of his big rig."

J.J., Cameron, and Joshua exchanged questioning glances while she rattled on.

"It's in the book case in the corner of their living room. Maddie's mom said he was very proud of his truck."

"I remember that picture now that you mention it," J.J. said. "It was a full picture of the truck—trailer and all." A sly grin crossed his face. "He looked small and blurry because the truck was so big."

"Not a clear picture of him, huh?" Joshua asked.

"He was wearing a cowboy hat, too," J.J. said.

"Sherry and Madison probably insisted on having a picture of him," Cameron said. "He chose to have it taken with his big rig knowing that his image would be too small to be recognizable."

"What's this about?" Tracy asked.

"Have you ever met Shawn Whitaker personally?" Cameron asked.

"No. But then, I've never met a lot of my friends' parents when I was in school, especially at the dance school. Most of the fathers didn't go to the recital because it was a mother-daughter type thing. Dad, you went to the dance recitals. How many fathers did you see there?"

"Not many," Joshua said. "Maybe one or two. I remember now that John Davis never went near that dance studio."

"Heather's dad? What does he have to do with this? Are you thinking Derek killed Maddie's dad, too?"

"Did you ever see Maddie's and Heather's mothers together?" Cameron asked.

Tracy scoffed. "They were from two totally different worlds. Kathleen is extremely organized. You think I'm organized? She's beyond that. Total workaholic. Driven and all about appearances."

"Like Heather," J.J. said.

"Sherry is like Maddie," Tracy said. "One day at a time. Carpe diem. Seize the day. Sherry Whitaker thinks nothing of going out of the house without makeup and her hair combed. Though, I have to admit, she still looks good. She's one of those natural beauties. She says, 'This is who I am. Deal with it.' She lets the dogs she's training run loose in the house, jump on the furniture, kiss her on the lips. She's loads of fun."

"I remember that," J.J. said.

"Kathleen would have a stroke if one of her puppies peed on her expensive oriental rug."

Cameron shot a questioning glance at Joshua. "Puppies?"

"Sherry is a dog trainer," Tracy said. "She's also a breeder. A good one, too. She breeds champion Bichon Frises."

"Like the one who took a liking to your father's leg the other day," Cameron said.

"That's the breed," Tracy said. "Yes."

"And Heather said her father just showed up with Munster one day," Cameron said. "I wonder where he got him."

"Heather told me after you guys left that Munster had been a show dog, though she had her doubts because he's so unruly," Tracy said. "He chipped his tooth and the owner couldn't show him anymore. The trainer told John. Luke had been begging for a dog, so he bought him. Paid over twelve hundred dollars for that little terror."

"And Sherry Whitaker is a dog trainer," J.J. told Cameron in a low voice.

"Speaking of Maddie's dad," Tracy said. "She once told me that she'd be too embarrassed to have her father show up at one of her recitals because her parents couldn't keep their hands off each other. He traveled so much and anytime her parents were in the room, they'd be touching and kissing and calling each other pet names. Worse than you and Cam, Dad. Now tell me what this is about."

"We're thinking John Davis was Shawn Whitaker," J.J. said.

There was a long silence on the other end of the call before Tracy responded. "Excuse me?"

"Tracy, you can't tell anyone about this," Cameron said in a firm tone. "It's important to our investigation. Dental records confirm that the body found at the Newhart farm was Shawn Whitaker. Fingerprints are a match for John Davis."

"Which means Shawn Whitaker was John Davis," J.J. said. "That means Maddie and Heather are half-sisters."

"Here's the million-dollar question," Joshua said. "Did his wives know?"

"We have not told either family and we're not going to yet," Cameron said. "If the motive was because of Davis's double life, then we're hoping the killer will give themselves away by revealing that they knew about it."

"Sherry Whitaker and Kathleen Davis only came together at the dance school," Tracy said. "That was six years ago. Their daughters hated each other. They had never been to each other's houses. If Maddie had been to Heather's house, she would have known instantly because they have family pictures all over and John is in a lot of them."

"I'm willing to bet John Davis got Munster from Sherry Whitaker," Joshua said.

"Sherry would never have let that dog go without knowing if he was going to a good home," J.J. said. "That tells me that she did know."

"Sherry wouldn't hurt a flea," Tracy said. "Kathleen? Maybe."

"Obviously, John Davis is very good at lying," Joshua said. "He had to be in order to have pulled this off for so long. He must have come up with a good story to get Sherry to arrange letting him have that little white monster."

"I don't think Munster came from Sherry," Tracy said. "He wouldn't act the way he does if she had trained him."

"Not necessarily," J.J. said as he refilled his drink. "The Davises never had a dog. Dogs are the same as horses when it comes to training. You put someone who knows nothing about horses on a horse, and that horse will walk all over them because they know they can get away with it. Put someone who knows horses on, and that rider will be in control."

"I talked to a witness who heard Davis arguing with two women on the night of the murder," Joshua held out his snifter to J.J. to refill. "One blonde. The other was a brunette."

"And he had two wives," J.J. said. "If Kathleen the brunette found out about Sherry the blonde—"

"Kathleen knew all about Derek threatening him," Joshua said, "and she knew where he lived to plant the knife."

"Oh, I don't like where this conversation is going," Tracy said. "Heather is my friend. So is Maddie."

"Why dump the body at the Newhart farm?" J.J. asked.

"To point the finger at her rival, just in case we didn't buy Derek as a prime suspect," Cameron said.

"The killer must have known about John Davis's triple life," Joshua said.

"Triple life!" Tracy gasped. "What other friends was Davis deceiving?"

"Was it really a triple life?" Cameron asked. "We saw that apartment. It was more like a halfway house. Davis would go there to change from one identity to the other. He used the name Bishop Moore because he needed a name for the lease."

"That's where he was murdered," Joshua said. "Whoever killed him knew about that apartment."

"There's another suspect," Cameron said. "One who knew about that apartment."

"Who's that?" Joshua asked.

"Bea Miller."

"Is this a third wife?" Tracy asked.

"No," Cameron said. "Bea Miller used to work at the plant. She filed a sexual harassment complaint against John Davis. Unfortunately, she had a very long history of filing sexual harassment grievances and sexual assault charges against men. For that reason, her allegation went nowhere. She ended up unemployed and lost her house. According to both Davis's assistant and Sherry, he had been receiving threatening phone calls from a woman named Bea for the last four months."

"Wait a minute," Joshua said. "Sherry is married to Shawn Whitaker. How would she know about Bea if Bea is connected to Davis's life?"

"Shawn explained the calls as coming from a warped woman who he had helped after her car had broken down," Cameron said.

"But we found two cell phones on the dresser at the apartment," J.J. said. "It looked to me like he kept his two lives separated all the way down to his phones."

"You're right," Cameron said. "John Davis and Shawn Whitaker had two completely different phone numbers. The only way Bea Miller could have called Shawn Whitaker's phone was if she knew about his alternate life and got access to that phone number." A slim grin crossed her lips. "Bea Miller's last known address is across the street from Davis's safe house."

"There you have it," Tracy said. "This Bea Miller did it."

"I haven't met Bea Miller," J.J. said, "but she sounds like a fruitcake. Would she have gone to the trouble of framing Derek and dumping the body at the Newhart farm?"

"We'll find out," Cameron said. "I'll try tracking her down tomorrow to question her."

"If Kathleen realized her husband was not traveling for work, then it'd be natural for her to follow him, or have him followed, to find out where he was going," Joshua said. "From the looks of it, he'd drive his car to the apartment, change clothes, cell phone, and vehicle, and then assume the other identity. It would have been easy enough for either Sherry or Kathleen to figure it out."

"Ellison's place is not an easy place to find," Cameron said.

"Which means that not only did the killer know about Ellison's threats against Davis, but where he lived," Joshua said. "Unless you can find a way for Miller to get access to that information, I'd say that eliminates her as a suspect."

"Cam, you're going to have to tell the prosecutor about these developments," J.J. said, "because I'm going to have to move to dismiss the charges against Ellison."

"Are you saying you've cleared Derek Ellison for the murder?" Tracy asked, startling them with the reminder that she was still on the phone.

"We can't place him at the crime scene," Cameron said.

"There's a ton of reasonable doubt, Tracy," J.J. said. "We can't allow the prosecution to move forward with the case."

"Sanders will not be happy," Joshua said. "She was looking for a slam dunk for a high-profile murder going into an election."

"I guess that means your first murder case was a winner. Congrats, J.J." Stating that she needed to clean up the kitchen and had an early meeting with a client in the morning, Tracy disconnected the call.

J.J. rose from his seat. "Well, it was fun."

Cameron and Joshua blocked his exit from the study. "There's still the matter of finding out who killed John Davis slash Shawn Whitaker slash Bishop Moore," she said.

"You're a homicide detective," J.J. said. "Investigate."

"Don't tell me you aren't curious yourself," Joshua said. "A man leading a triple life, two wives, two families."

"I'm getting married in less than two months. I'm renovating a mansion, mostly by myself. I've got stuff to do." J.J. gestured at Cameron. "She's the lead detective in this case."

"That's right," she said. "I'm the lead detective. That means that as soon as I show up with my badge and gun, everyone throws up walls and shuts up." She smiled at him. "Whereas you were very close to both families—"

"If I was so close, how is it that I didn't notice that my two girlfriends had the same father?"

"He's got a point," Joshua said.

"J.J., I know that as soon as it does come out, which it will, that Kathleen Davis and Sherry Whitaker were married to the same man, they are both going to claim they had no idea," Cameron said. "Whether they are guilty or not of murder, no one will claim to have known or noticed anything. But with you having a relationship with both Heather and Madison—"

"Today was the first day that I've even seen Heather or Madison since my high school graduation."

"From the way Madison looked at you," she said, "I think she'd be more than open to catching up on old times."

"I'm getting married."

"That's right," Joshua said. "And at practically every wedding, the bride and groom celebrate their first dance as a married couple. Have you and Poppy ever danced?"

"No, but that's okay. I know how to dance. If Poppy doesn't—"

"Nowadays, it's a big show," Cameron said. "I hear a lot of couples pay to have their first dance choreographed."

"You know, Cam, that's not a bad idea," Joshua said. "I hear there's a new dance studio in Beaver Falls."

"It's a wedding reception," J.J. said, "not a Broadway musical."

"Madison owns a dance studio," Cameron said. "She's Shawn Whitaker's daughter. If you and Poppy take private lessons from her, and being an old boyfriend—"

"That will be so awkward," J.J. said. "Me and my fiancé taking dance lessons from my old girlfriend?"

"All you need to find out is if Madison's mother knew about her husband's double life," Joshua said. "You're the best one to find out since you're an old friend of the family. If Cameron goes in to question them, they'll immediately put up road blocks. But you?" He chuckled with a wide grin.

"With Poppy in the same room?" J.J. asked. "She'll never go for it."

"We're not telling you to sleep with them," Joshua said. "Son, when I was married to your mother and working for military intelligence, I used my charm on women to get information all the time. It was one of those tools in my belt."

J.J. shook his head. "I'm not the same heel I was back then. And what about Poppy?"

"Be up front with Poppy," Joshua said. "I was with your mother."

"She trusts you," Cameron said. "Besides, enough time has passed. You've moved on. Maybe they have, in which case all you have to do is be friendly with them—get close. Pay your respect to the families and keep your eyes open to see what their mothers knew when."

"Do you really think their mothers were capable of murder?"

"Our witness heard two women fighting with Davis in his apartment in Calcutta the night he was killed," Joshua said. "It had to be them. Just be your old charming self and Madison will be putty in your hands."

"The last time I was charming, I ended up with broken ribs."

CHAPTER ELEVEN

"The murder weapon was in the defendant's possession. It had his fingerprints all over it. He threatened the victim and had no alibi. Plus, he threatened the detectives with the same knife when they arrived to question him."

Cameron could tell by the set of Seth Booker's jaw, that he was not going to let go of the bone he had been given in the form of what promised to be a high-profile murder case. John Davis, the model husband, father, and grandfather, had been struck down by his drug-crazed son-in-law. It was a senseless crime that promised a lot of press, which in turn promised a lot for Seth's political goals.

Prosecutor Nancy Sanders peered over the top of her reading glasses at Cameron Gates.

"We've identified the crime scene," Cameron said, "and there is no evidence placing the defendant at the scene."

"Because he cleaned it up," Seth said.

"Did you see the defendant?" J.J. said. "He had been wearing the same clothes and hadn't bathed in days when he was taken into custody. The victim had been stabbed thirty-two times. Yet, Ellison didn't have a drop of blood on him."

"Davis's killer would have been covered in blood," Cameron said. "Not only that, but the tire tracks found at the scene where the body had been dumped don't match Ellison's truck." She directed her attention at Sanders. "He didn't do it."

Seth spun around to face Tony, who had been silent during their meeting. "What's your professional opinion, Detective Seavers?"

When Tony turned his attention to Cameron, Seth blocked his view. "Considering that Lieutenant Gates is married to the defense attorney's father—"

"Now that accusation is completely unacceptable," J.J. said.

"It's acceptable when we consider how you landed this case," Seth said. "I talked to the public defender. He said you'd requested it. I also heard that you were at the crime scene before Detective Seavers. What were you doing there? Wiping down your client's fingerprints?"

"I didn't have to wipe down any prints that weren't there," J.J. said.

"Then you shouldn't be worried about Detective Seavers answering my question." Seth turned to face Tony. "In your opinion, whose side had Lieutenant Gates been on during the course of this investigation?"

Tony flicked his eyes from the assistant prosecutor to Cameron.

It was the moment of truth. Cameron had heard murmurings about the young detective. His loyalty lay with those who could best help his career.

Tony cleared his throat. "The truth."

"Yes, Detective Seavers," the prosecutor said. "We want the truth. Answer Booker's question. What have you observed while working with Lieutenant Gates?"

"She's been on the side of truth," Tony said. "That's what I'm saying. It seemed like an open and shut case with the murder weapon being found in Ellison's possession. But there was something that didn't smell right to her." He shrugged. "It smelled okay to me. But it didn't for her. So she ordered me to keep on digging, and we found out that there's a lot more to this case that meets the eye. If she hadn't done that, then we could have sent an innocent man to jail." He glanced at Cameron. "She's the best. That's why I requested to work with her."

"You're only saying that because she's your supervising officer." Seth told the prosecutor, "I want Gates removed from this case."

"You can't remove me from a case that isn't in your jurisdiction," Cameron said.

Seth glared at her.

"The murder happened in Columbiana County, Ohio," J.J. said. "The body was dumped in Pennsylvania."

"I had a long conversation with Herb Clark, Columbiana's county prosecutor, at this sweet little café in Lisbon this morning," Cameron said. "And yes, if you must know, my husband was there. He and Herb go way back. Well, Herb looks at it this way. The murder in Calcutta had happened before the body was dumped in Hookstown, and definitely before the murder weapon was planted in West Virginia. The way he sees it, he gets first dibs on the case and he wants it."

"Figures," Sanders said. "He's up for re-election, too."

"Considering all of the inconsistencies that I plan on throwing at the jury to create reasonable doubt," J.J. said, "you might want to consider letting Clark take it."

"Now, you—"

"Let him take it," Sanders cut off Seth to declare. "It's a dog of a case anyway." She waved both arms in the direction of the door. A sign that they were all dismissed. "Drop the charges and get them out of here. Now."

In the corridor, J.J. shook hands with Tony. "Thank you for your help, Seavers."

"No problem," Tony said.

After J.J. rushed off to meet Poppy, Cameron cocked her head at the detective. "You really know how to shovel it, Seavers. All that crap about asking to work with me. They may have bought it, but don't think I believe it for a minute."

"It's the truth. One day, I intend to become captain of the state police. The only way I'm going to make that is to be the best. Best way to become the best is to learn from the best. That's you."

Cameron spun on her heels and headed down the hall. "Flattery will get you nowhere. If you don't believe me, ask my daughter. Every night, she tells me how beautiful. She still has to be in bed before ten."

John Davis's death had caused a nagging feeling to resurface in Joshua's mind. The facts of Lindsay's death pointed to it being a tragic accident caused by driving while under the influence of drugs and alcohol.

As the county's prosecuting attorney, Joshua would push Sheriff Sawyer and his deputies to keep digging until his gut told him there was nothing more. Yet, John and Kathleen Davis wanted to move on after their daughter's death. Since there was no evidence of foul play, Joshua ignored his gut instinct and let the case rest—until John Davis's murder brought that nagging feeling back with a vengeance.

Joshua waited until he had dropped off Izzy at the middle school and was on his way to his office in New Cumberland before calling Hunter Gardner on his hands-free phone.

"What's up, Dad?" his son-in-law answered.

Joshua grinned. Hunter's father had been a child-hood friend. They'd grown up together. A sheriff's deputy, Hunter's father had been murdered when his son was only five years old. Joshua felt honored that Hunter began calling him "Dad" as soon as he and Tracy had become engaged.

"What's your location?" Joshua asked.

"I'm pulling into the sheriff's office for my meal break. Why?"

"Can I swing by and talk to you?"

"Am I in trouble? Listen, I tried to get to the house to help J.J. sand those hardwood floors, but Tracy needed me to exchange her garbage disposal. She says she needs a bigger one. Can you believe that? The new one is as big as a tank." He sighed. "I'm sorry. I just do what I'm told."

"I want to talk to you about something else."

"In that case, come on over. You'll find me in the break room heating up my breakfast."

In New Cumberland, the sheriff's department was across the parking lot from the prosecuting attorney's office. Joshua parked in his reserved space and jogged to the sheriff's office.

He could smell Tracy's hash browns casserole, stuffed with cheese and homemade sausage, all the way down the corridor. Thinking about the frozen waffles he had eaten for breakfast, he instantly became jealous.

Hunter had set up an elaborate spread across one of the tables in the break room. The microwave was heating up a fluffy three-egg omelet. Two slices of Texas toast rested on a plate next to the hashbrowns that had been prepared in a personal-sized casserole dish. There was also a small bowl of mixed fruit.

"Hungry?" Hunter held out the bowl of fruit.

Joshua broke off a branch of grapes. "Tracy doesn't spoil you, does she?"

"Not at all." Hunter peeled the lid from a plastic container. "Want a brownie? She baked them yesterday."

The microwave beeped.

"How much weight have you gained since you got married?"

"Twelve pounds and counting." Hunter took the perfectly shaped omelet out of the microwave oven and put another plastic container inside. "What's so urgent that you needed to interrupt my breakfast?" He pressed the reheat button and the microwave proceeded to reheat the next item.

"You've become Sawyer's go-to guy for accident reconstruction." Unable to resist, Joshua tore off a corner from a slice of the Texas toast. The bread was warm to the touch.

Shrugging his broad shoulders, Hunter sat at the table. "I like doing it and it's kind of fun trying to figure out how things happened."

"Well, you came to work for the department the year after Lindsay Ellison was killed on Washington School Road." He picked a piece of pineapple from the fruit bowl. "Have you ever taken a look at it?"

"No one ever asked me to." Hunter held out the slice of the Texas toast. "Since you already started, you might as well finish it. Tracy made this with her new bread maker. It's her own recipe."

"Everything is her own recipe." With a smile, Joshua took the slice and broke off a bite.

"She wiped out on that Y where Washington School Road breaks off of Locust Hill. It goes downhill and loops around," Hunter explained between bites of his breakfast. "She had methamphetamine in her system and a point four blood alcohol level. It's a miracle she was even conscious when she took that turn."

"What if she wasn't?" Joshua asked.

"Are you thinking it was murder?" Hunter arched an eyebrow in his direction. "She was knee deep in drugs—hanging out with druggies. That is a high-risk lifestyle. Maybe someone did want her dead."

"It was definitely an accident. The thing is I've always felt like there was something more to it."

"I've been hearing from friends that it was suicide," Hunter said.

"You and J.J. have the same friends," Joshua said. "What exactly do they say?"

"Anything I know is hearsay."

The microwave beeped.

"What else did Tracy pack for you?" Joshua asked while taking in the table filled with food.

"Gravy!" Hunter jumped up to fetch the hot container filled with sausage gravy. He ladled it out across the hash browns and eggs. Pleased with the feast set before him, he retook his seat.

"If I ate all this for breakfast, I'd need a nap within an hour," Joshua said.

"Jealous." Hunter took a forkful of the hash browns and moaned with pleasure. "To get back to Lindsay, most of what I know about that time period, I've learned from Tracy."

"What did Tracy tell you?" Joshua dipped his slice of toast into the gravy.

"She'd made a big mistake throwing her life away on Derek," Hunter said. "She really wanted to be a professional dancer, but she'd figured out that she didn't have what it took to make it. Derek had been pursuing her, so she just gave up. By the time she realized what a mistake she'd made, she was trapped in a loveless marriage to a drunk and stuck with a baby that she didn't know how to raise."

"Do you think that you can tell by looking at the crime scene pictures and accident report, if it was an accident or suicide?"

"Probably."

"How about if the victim had been thrown from the car?"

"What about it?"

"Can you tell if say …"

"If she was conscious?"

"If she was driving or a passenger?"

Hunter stopped eating and sat back in his seat. "What are you hunting for?"

"I don't want to lead you in one direction or the other."

"I understand." Hunter resumed eating. "If I have all the data, I can give an educated guess. What makes you think someone else was driving?"

"Lindsay's body was found in the middle of the road," Joshua said between bites of the toast, while dipping each one in the gravy. "The car supposedly rolled over her. My cousin Tad did the autopsy."

"Did he have an opinion about whether she was conscious or not?"

"He said with all of the drugs in her system that she could have been in a manic state, which could have explained why she took that curve at such a high rate of speed," Joshua said. "She was crushed by the car rolling over her body—before it went over the hill. That bothered me. If she was the only one in the car and thrown out—landing in the middle of the road—then how is it that the car went off the road and rolled down the hill."

"If she had enough speeding going into the curve before losing control, it could happen."

"That's what Sawyer says. Because of all the drugs and alcohol in her system, I just let it go."

Hunter cringed. "With John Davis being murdered, do you really think now is the right time to tell the Davises that Lindsay killed herself if that turns out to be the truth?"

"First, let's find out if my suspicions are right." Joshua tossed the last bit of toast into his mouth. "Then we'll cross that bridge."

CHAPTER TWELVE

Cameron had lived in the Ohio Valley for decades. As a law enforcement officer and then detective, she had traveled over, and believed she knew, every acre of land in her vicinity. Yet, she had been unaware of the mobile park squeezed behind the apartment complex where John Davis rented his safe house and a brush-covered hillside.

Some of the trailers were occupied by lower income couples or families just starting out and working their way up. Others were home to elderly folks on fixed incomes doing the best they could to survive. Then, there were those living in the park who had given up—as evidenced by trash surrounding their living space.

Bea Miller rented a two-bedroom mobile home tucked away in the back corner of the park. A muddy sedan was squeezed into a square that had been carved out of the garbage bags and containers that filled the driveway. When Cameron slid out of the driver's seat of her unmarked cruiser, she saw a rat scurry from a mound of trash and make for the briar thicket on the hillside behind the trailer.

Clutching her service weapon, Cameron made her way up the rickety steps to the door and knocked on it. She heard movement inside the trailer before the door opened a crack.

One magnified eyeball peered out at her through a thick pair of eyeglasses. "What?" its owner asked in a shaky voice.

Cameron held her police shield up for her to see through the screen door. "I'm Detect—Lieutenant Cameron Gates with the Pennsylvania State Police. I'm looking for Bea Miller. Are you her?"

"What do you want?"

"May I come in?"

"No."

Cameron was startled by the abrupt rejection. She took a moment to regroup before explaining, "I'm here to talk to you about John Davis."

"I've done nothing wrong. He's the one stalking me."

Cameron took quick note of her speaking about Davis in the present tense. Possibly, she was unaware of his death, in which case, she didn't kill him.

"Well, if he's stalking you, then maybe I can help you." Cameron took out her notepad. "When was the last time you saw him?"

"I don't know," she said. "Don't have a reason to keep track of the days since Mr. Davis and his influential friends blackballed me so that I can't get a job. He was telling everyone that I'm crazy. They paid all of those men to lie saying that they didn't rape me."

"They bribed *all* of them."

Sensing that Cameron did intend to help her, she opened the door a crack more while using it as a barricade between them. "There was that boy who pinned me down on the bed and kissed me in high school. And then the man at the frat party when I was in my sophomore year in college. They also got that man on the cruise ship."

"And you filed police reports against each of them at the time of the assaults?" Cameron knew that Bea had. It was in her background report. She asked to see Bea's reaction to the question.

"That's what they tell you to do and that's what I did." Bea shrieked, "You have a gun!"

Cameron opened the screen door and stuck her foot in before she could shut the door. "It's for protection. I'm not here to hurt you. Under what circumstance did you see John Davis following you."

"At the grocery store! I swear! He was following me! He's trying to frame me for violating the restraining order! I've seen him at the gas station. He had switched cars. He was wearing a hat and jeans and driving a white truck so that I wouldn't recognize him, but I did. I saw him at the convenience store, too. He's been out to get me ever since I told him that I wasn't going to have sex with him during our interview. As soon as I saw him, I remembered what the judge told me, and I came home and haven't gone back to the store since." She kicked Cameron in the shin and slammed the door shut.

Derek's mother, Sadie, and Joshua waited in the hospital lunchroom for over an hour while Dr. Tad MacMillan, Joshua's cousin, met with Derek and arranged for his medical release. While Sadie ate a sandwich and vegetable soup, her first real meal since Derek's arrest, Joshua noted that he hadn't seen her so optimistic in years.

"I can't thank you enough," she said repeatedly.

"Don't thank me," he said, "thank J.J. He proved to the prosecutor that Derek didn't do it."

"A chip off the old block, huh? Not only can't I believe he took Derek's case, especially after what he had done to his friend in high school, but that he proved he didn't kill John."

"Well, this was the easy part," Joshua said. "The hard part is getting Derek well again. It's going to be a lot of hard work, and it's all going to be on him."

"I hope he listens to Tad." She took a sip of the soup. "Lord knows I've talked to him until I was blue in the face."

"Well, I think Tad may have better luck," Joshua said. "He's been in Derek's shoes. Tad spent many years as the town drunk. Like Derek, for a long time, it seemed like the only one he had left on his side was his mother. Then he had a daughter and he made the conscious decision to be a good father to her. He went through hell, but he cleaned up his act and now he's one of the most respected men in the area."

Squinting at him, Sadie set her spoon down. "I knew Tad's story, but I never realized the parallel between his life and Derek's."

"If Tad can turn his life around, so can Derek."

Beyond her, Joshua saw Tad MacMillan enter the lunchroom. Clean shaven and with auburn hair that had only a touch of gray at the temples, Tad looked much younger than his true age. Dedication to a healthy lifestyle since his sobriety, he was in excellent shape. One would never have guessed that he was quite a few years older than Joshua. Tad gave Joshua a thumbs-up from across the room. Derek had agreed to his offer. "I guess we're on our way to Cleveland."

An hour later, Tad was driving Derek, his mother, and Joshua in his SUV north on the freeway toward a rehabilitation facility on the outskirts of Cleveland.

A sponsor and leader for addiction recovery programs, Tad had been through the routine of delivering guests to the facility multiple times before. For that reason, he was able to remain calm, while Sadie made conversation to ease Derek's nerves where he sat next to her in the back seat.

Several minutes in the ride, Derek asked what day it was. After Sadie answered that it was Tuesday, Joshua asked, "What's the last day that you have a clear memory of, Derek?"

"I dunno," Derek said while staring out the side window at the countryside rushing by. "I remember being in the hospital all weekend. You and Sawyer comin' to the trailer. What day was that?"

"That was Saturday afternoon."

"Lindsay must have visited me the night before that."

Silence fell over the vehicle. It had to have been a drug-induced hallucination of his late wife.

"Does Lindsay visit you often, Derek?" Tad asked.

"No. That was the first time since she'd died," Derek said.

"Are you sure—"

"It wasn't my imagination," Derek interrupted Joshua. "She was real. I touched her."

"And this was Friday night?" Joshua asked.

"I guess." Derek shrugged his shoulders. "I know it was her because I recognized her necklace. Heather gave it to her. Lindsay never took it off."

"Did she say anything?"

Derek shook his head. "I saw her in the kitchen. I thought she was an angel and had come to take me home with her. I went up to her and touched her. She jumped and looked at me. I tried to kiss her, but she shoved me and ran away." A tear rolled down his cheek. "I guess she didn't come for me after all."

Chapter Thirteen

"I've never asked. Do you like dancing?" J.J. looked across the passenger compartment of his truck to Poppy when she didn't answer. They were on their way to Beaver Falls to visit Madison Whitaker's studio. Preferring to make use of the element of surprise, he hadn't called to make an appointment.

Staring straight ahead, Poppy chewed her bottom lip. She picked at the rim of her western hat, which rested in her lap. Why she had taken it with her to sign up for dance lessons, she had no idea. It must have been because she was wearing it while riding Gulliver when J.J. told her it was time to leave. She hadn't even bothered to change out of her riding boots.

"I wasn't planning for us to learn anything too complicated," J.J. said.

"I haven't danced in years." She sighed. "My dad wanted his little girl to be a dancer." She shot a glance in his direction. "A ballerina. I was in dance classes from the time I could walk."

"I pictured you more as a line dancer than a ballerina."

"Yeah, who would've thought. Mom let me continue with the lessons after Dad disappeared. That was only because all of the right people had their daughters in dance." Sadness filled her face. "But then, after …" Her voice trailed off.

"Forget about that." He reached for her hand. "Think about here. Now. Today. You loved dancing. I love to dance. It's something we can love together. Let's have fun with it."

She squeezed his hand. "And drag information out of your former girlfriend."

He smiled at her. "Have I told you today that I love you?"

She brushed her fingers down his cheek and across his jaw. "Maybe not in so many words."

In the middle of the lunchtime rush, downtown Beaver Falls was busy with customers filling the cafes and restaurants, which made it impossible to find available parking in front of the studio. J.J. circled the block twice in search of a space big enough for his truck when he spotted a familiar face behind the wheel of a purple SUV that had scored a spot in front of the dance studio.

Her long dark hair spilled in long waves over her dark cloth coat. J.J. recognized her even with sunglasses covering her eyes. He was so focused on watching her enter the dance studio owned by her rival that the car behind him had to lay on the horn to move him along.

"There's a spot right there." Poppy pointed to the empty space on the next block.

After putting coins in the parking meter, he took her hand and kissed her on the mouth when she stepped up onto the sidewalk. "I saw Heather going inside just now." He led her across the street.

"Why would someone go into a dance studio owned by her archenemy?"

"Good question." He flashed a grin at her. "I intend to use all of my charm to find that out." He grabbed the door handle to open the door for her.

"And I've never seen you charming before," she whispered as she stepped inside.

Dressed in a bright blue wraparound skirt with a long-sleeved ballet sweater, Elizabeth stood up straight from where she had been leaning across the corner of her desk. "J.J.?" Her face broke into a wide grin. "J.J. Thornton!" She turned around to call into the business office behind her. "Maddie! You'll never guess who's here. It's J.J."

To their surprise, a man rose up from where he had been working under the desk. "J.J. Thornton?" The heavy-set man's dirty blond hair was shaggy, his beard equally scruffy. His round face filled with a crooked tooth grin. "Hey, J.J.!" With effort, he rose to his feet. In doing so, his pants fell low on his hips to droop under his beer belly. He pulled up his pants and stuck out his hand. "How ya doin'?"

Shaking his hand, J.J. struggled to place a name with the familiar face. "Fine. How are you?"

"J.J., this is Aaron," Elizabeth said.

"Aaron Collins." J.J. shook his hand with more enthusiasm. "You dated Elizabeth."

Aaron threw his arm around Elizabeth's shoulders and pulled her in tight to give her a hug. "And married her, too. Got married right after graduation. We've got two sweet kids, too. Seven-year-old son and a five-year-old daughter. You?"

"No kids that I know of." J.J. turned his attention to Madison and Heather, who had stepped into the doorway of the business office during the exchange. "This isn't a meeting that I ever expected to walk into."

"You need to get over yourself, J.J." Heather folded her arms across her chest. "Maddie and I have buried the hatchet."

"No one's happier to see that than me," J.J. said.

"Well," Aaron said with a chuckle, "except maybe your health insurance provider."

"Aaron," Elizabeth said, "are you done setting up our public wifi? I have work to do and you need to go pick up Chelsea."

With a grumble, Aaron crawled back under the desk.

J.J. urged Poppy forward. After introductions, Poppy told Heather, "I'm sorry to hear about your father. I know how hard it is."

"Oh, did your father get brutally murdered?" Heather snapped.

"No," Poppy shot back. "Unfortunately, they never found his body. We had to wait five years before the authorities declared him dead."

Heather's face went white. Her hands fell to her side.

"I was a little girl when he went Christmas shopping one morning and never came home," Poppy said. "They found his truck in the mall parking lot. It was one of those cases where everyone knew who killed him and why, but with no body, no one could ever prove it."

"Dang," Aaron said from under the desk.

"Maybe whoever killed him didn't realize what they were doing. Like temporary insanity. They were so enraged ..." Elizabeth's voice trailed off.

"Cameron is still working on locating your dad, Maddie," J.J. said.

Madison's eyes widened. She glanced at Heather, who slowly shook her head.

J.J. went on, "Unfortunately, I'm not privy to any details of her investigation. I'm only Derek's defense counsel. But I can tell you, Heather, that I made a motion to drop the charges against him this morning, and the prosecution is concurring with my motion."

Heather clenched her fists like she wanted to punch J.J.

"I thought Derek had the knife," Elizabeth said.

"The police have located the crime scene," J.J. said, "and there's no evidence to place Derek there. Evidence indicates that he was framed. Heather, don't you want to know who really killed your father?"

"Of course," Heather said miserably. "Where was he killed?"

"I can't be specific because it is an active investigation," J.J. said. "I can tell you that it was in Ohio."

He noticed that Madison and Heather exchanged quick glances before looking away from each other. Madison fought the tears wanting to fill her eyes. In a surprising move, she draped her arm across Heather's shoulders. He cast a questioning glance in Poppy's direction.

"Uh," he began, "I almost hate to ask this but, where were you Friday night?"

Heather's head snapped up. She glared at him.

"When your father was being killed," J.J. asked. "Cameron is going to be asking you. She'll ask everyone."

"I was on a date," Heather said. "If you must know, it was a blind date. In Robinson. I'd met the guy for drinks after work."

"Do you have the guy's name and number?" J.J. asked.

"It didn't go that well," Heather said.

"If it didn't go well, I guess you got home early."

"Are you accusing me of leaving a bad date to go hunt down my father and kill him for whatever reason? I loved my father. Why would I want to kill him?"

"I don't know," J.J. said. "Can you think of a reason?"

Heather grit her teeth. Her jaw muscles tightened to draw her mouth into a tight line.

"The police will want to talk to this guy you went out with Friday night," J.J. said.

"I didn't take his phone number if you must know. But I'm sure I can get it from the friend at work who set us up."

"Do you remember what you were doing Friday night?" J.J. asked Madison, whose eyes grew wide.

"Why would Madison need an alibi for the night of my father's murder?" Heather asked.

"You tell me," J.J. said.

Heather's and J.J.'s eyes locked.

"Maddie was with me," Elizabeth blurted out.

All eyes turned to Elizabeth. Clutching the pendant hanging from the necklace around her throat, she smiled nervously. "Wasn't Friday night our girl's night out, Maddie?"

Her mouth hanging open, Madison said nothing.

"Don't ask us for any specifics though. We got so wasted." Elizabeth rolled her eyes. "We were both so hung over on Saturday."

"I can attest to that," Aaron said from under the desk. "I was stuck taking care of the kids while those two went out right after the studio closed. Elizabeth didn't get home until after midnight."

"You are unbelievable, J.J.," Heather said. "I can't believe I ever even liked you, let alone loved you."

"Ah, man!" Aaron rose up from where he had been working under the desk. His eyes were wide while he took in the stand-off.

"I'm sorry if you think I was betraying you by defending Derek, but I think someone used him as a patsy because he was so damn convenient," J.J. said. "Can you think of any reason someone would have done that?"

"No!" Heather said forcibly before going back into the office. "I need to go back to work." She picked up her briefcase and slung it over her shoulder. "Maddie, I'm going to work on your profile tonight. I'll text you when I'm finished so that you can take a look at it. Okay?"

The two women hugged before Heather rushed out the door.

"Profile?" Elizabeth asked. "What pro—"

"My Instagram profile," Madison said. "Heather's redoing my profile for all of my social media accounts."

Elizabeth's face fell. "I already did those."

"Heather's revamping them to include more search engine key words to drive more traffic to my website. More traffic means more students."

"Well." Muttering, Elizabeth dropped into her chair. "You're the boss."

"Looks like you and Heather have struck up quite a working relationship," J.J. said.

"Heather and I reconnected on a social group for Miss Charlotte's former dance students. I had just moved back to the area after being gone for six years. We met for coffee and realized we had been so immature back when we were fighting over you—and other things. We were jealous, and jealousy can be so toxic for everyone it touches. Heather works in marketing and I own a new business. She volunteered to donate her time to help me with free marketing to help get me started."

"What does she get for her time?" Elizabeth's eyes narrowed. "I'm sorry to sound so suspicious, but I remember. Heather never does anything when she doesn't get something out of it."

"She gets free advertising," Madison said. "A lot of our parents are small business owners—from cosmetics out of their home to Tupperware to construction companies. Heather wants to start her own marketing company. In exchange for helping me, I gave her permission to post an ad on my website and leave brochures here in the reception area."

"There's no better advertising than word of mouth," Aaron said from under the desk. "I've been doing the same thing—trying to start my own computer repair company. It's tough for a small company to get started."

"Good thing the two of you reconnected and became friends when you did," J.J. said. "Considering that you've both suffered trauma involving your father on the same day."

"Eerie," Aaron said. "Kind of like Thomas Jefferson and John Adams."

"Huh?" Elizabeth said.

"Thomas Jefferson and John Adams." Aaron rose up onto his knees. "They signed the Declaration of Independence. They hated each other because one was conservative and the other was liberal. They both became president. Then, afterwards, they became good friends."

With a nod of his head, J.J. picked up the story. "Both of them died on July fourth. When John Adams died, his last words were, 'At least Thomas Jefferson still lives.' Thing was, Jefferson had died hours earlier."

"Like I said. Eerie." Aaron dropped down behind the desk.

"Heather and I are not Thomas Jefferson and John Adams. Is Cameron looking into that woman? Bea. Mom says she was stalking Dad."

J.J. shrugged his shoulders. "I really don't know."

Hoping that Madison would fill the void of silence with useful information, J.J. waited. Madison stared at him while chewing on her bottom lip. He could see her mind working. He felt like she was about to say something more when Elizabeth announced that she had a lesson in five minutes.

Madison uttered a visible sigh of relief.

Inwardly, J.J. groaned.

"Well, it was good to see you again, J.J." Madison moved for the door.

"Would you believe I forgot what we had come in for." J.J. took Poppy's hand. "We would like to schedule some private lessons. As you know, we're getting married at the end of March and I hear a lot of couples have the first dance choreographed for them. I was hoping—" Taking Poppy into a bear hug, he flashed a wide toothy smile.

"You brought your fiancé to your old girlfriend for dance lessons for your wedding?" Aaron asked from under the desk. "Dude! You've got more guts than I ever did."

Madison regarded the two of them for so long that J.J. feared she would refuse and usher them out of her studio with an order to never return. Finally, she asked, "What's your song?"

Unarmed with that information, J.J. paused while Poppy answered promptly, "We want to do the Viennese Waltz to 'Endless Love.'"

Madison took a step back. Slowly, she looked Poppy, dressed in jeans, riding boots, and a western hat in hand, up and down. "The Viennese Waltz?" Her lip curled up. "That's not exactly for newbies. I'm sure J.J. could handle it but—"

"I danced in the children's company of the Rocky Mountain Ballet Theater for five years." Poppy put on her hat and cocked her head to look at Madison out of the corner of her eye. "I can handle anything you throw at me."

Madison let out a sigh. "I'm sorry. I misjudged—"

"That's okay." Poppy winked at her. "You're not the first one to underestimate me."

"Being underestimated is Poppy's superpower," J.J. said.

"Let's take a look at the calendar and get you two set up." Madison led Poppy to the desk. "I can't wait to hear about what it was like dancing with the Rocky Mountain Ballet."

"My schedule is more flexible than yours, darling," J.J. said. "You decide when to schedule our lessons."

Seeing that the two of them were hitting it off, he eased back to angle himself for a view into Madison's office. It was too chancy for him to step inside with Elizabeth at her desk only a few feet away. He wasn't sure what he would be looking for. It was too much to ask for an Internet map up on her computer screen showing the directions to Bishop Moore's apartment.

"I love your red hair," Madison said while daring to touch the ends of Poppy's brilliant red locks.

"Your freckles are adorable," Elizabeth said.

"Ashburn?" Madison said. "That's English isn't it. But your red hair and freckles—"

"Scottish," Poppy said. "My grandmother on my father's side immigrated from Scotland, or so I'm told. She died before I was born. I've seen pictures of her. She's definitely who I inherited my red hair from."

"You have to be more than one quarter Scottish," Madison said. "Have you ever considered sending your DNA to one of those genealogy sites? You'll be surprised by what you find out. My mother told me that I had Native American in me. I sent in my DNA and found out that I had none. I'm more than half Swedish."

"You know, I've been thinking about that. What site did you use?"

Madison grabbed a stickie note and wrote down the website address. Excitedly, she explained the cost of the kit, how to collect her DNA, and how long it would take to get the results, which would break down the percentage of her country of origins.

After several minutes of what J.J. considered to be girl talk, Madison's students arrived. They were an elderly couple training for a tango dance competition.

J.J. slipped his arm around Poppy's waist. "Thank you so much for your time, Maddie. If I hear anything from Cameron about your dad, I'll be sure to let you know."

"Thank you, J.J." She gave him a quick hug and whispered into his ear. "I always knew you'd marry a dancer. I just thought she'd be me."

Out on the street, J.J. flashed Poppy a grin. "Thank you for being a good sport in there. Rocky Mountain Ballet company? Was that the truth?"

Poppy adjusted her hat. "I don't lie. I told you Daddy wanted a ballerina."

They stopped on the corner to wait for the light to cross to the next block.

"Well, hopefully, we'll learn a little bit more than the Viennese Waltz," J.J. said.

"We've already learned a truckload."

"Yes, but nothing conclusive." He led her by her hand across the street. "Maddie and Heather claim they reconnected on social media and Heather is helping her with promotion. That doesn't prove that they know they're half-sisters and told their mothers, which would give them motive to kill their father."

"Oh, but they do know." Poppy took the post-it note from her vest pocket. "Maddie got her DNA tested at this website."

J.J. stopped. He took the note from her. "I heard her tell you that. She got it tested for her genealogy."

"Do you know what else those websites do?"

His eyes met hers.

"They put your DNA into their database and then they do a search for familial matches with other customers. Then, they send you a list of everyone whose DNA matches yours. Now, you only get their site username and a calculation of how closely they are related to you. Second cousin. Third cousin."

"Sibling."

She nodded her head. "Maddie got a DNA test with this site. If Heather did, too, then they would have gotten notices that they had siblings listed in the website's database."

"Now, if I did a DNA test on one of these sites and I got an email telling me I had a sibling I didn't know about, I'd be all over that." He shook his head. "They didn't reconnect over any Miss Charlotte social media group." He smiled. "I guess I owe you."

She wrapped her arms around his shoulders and lifted her face to his. "I think so."

"Dinner?"

"I bust your case wide open and all you can offer me is dinner?" She pushed him away only for him to pull her back into his arms.

"You're right. How about if I offer to marry you."

She pressed her lips against his for a long lingering kiss.

"I'll take that as a yes."

CHAPTER FOURTEEN

In her many years of law enforcement, Cameron had dealt with victims, suspects, and criminal types across the whole spectrum. In doing so, she had learned that different people handle grief or trauma in different ways. Kathleen Davis seemed to handle her grief by burying herself in her work.

At least, that's what Cameron concluded when she arrived at the Davis home after Derek Ellison had been released from police custody. Phone to her ear, Kathleen Davis directed the investigator to the sofa in the living room and took off for the study. After completing a conference call, she went on to another.

Alone in the living room, Cameron examined the array of photographs scattered about. Many were the standard studio shots of the perfect family. Decades old wedding picture of Kathleen in her white gown and John in a tuxedo. Group photo of the entire family, father, mother, and four children, two boys and two girls. The children appeared to be teenagers. The Davis sons were older than their sisters.

Cameron squinted at the girls. Heather and her younger sister Lindsay looked almost like twins with their dark hair and eyes. She recalled J.J. saying that they were only a year apart. How weird, really, it is that two girls from the same family with the same parents and upbringing could turn out so different. One a successful college graduate. The other a high school drop-out and addict who seemingly ended up devoid of hope.

Cameron was startled out of her thoughts by what felt like a pin prick on her ankle. With a jump, she looked down to find Munster, the shaggy little dog, peering up at her. He wagged his tail. "If you wanted my attention, all you had to do was bark."

Munster rolled a small black ball in her direction and barked a demand.

Doubtful that Munster was allowed to play catch in the house, Cameron gave the ball a soft toss, only about a foot off the ground. Munster caught it and scurried out of the room.

Another photograph caught Cameron's eyes. This one was a candid portrait of the two Davis girls posing on either side of their father, who was dressed in a suit. He had an arm around both Heather and Lindsay. The setting appeared to be a restaurant.

Maybe a birthday party?

The Davis sisters were older in this picture. Heather was strikingly beautiful in a green faux leather suit. She wore a gold chain from which hung half a heart around her throat.

On John's other side, Lindsay, clad in torn jeans and over-sized top, had a vacant, almost dead, look in her eyes. She wore a similar necklace around her neck—with what appeared to be the second half of the heart.

With a soft grin, Cameron realized that Heather and Lindsay wore sister necklaces. Also called friendship necklaces, they had become popular among best girlfriends and sisters. Izzy, Tracy, and Sarah, Joshua's third daughter, shared similar necklaces in which each held one third of a heart with a diamond—illustrating a bond of sisterhood. Izzy and Tracy never took theirs off. Not wanting hers to get broken during military activities, Sarah wore hers when she could.

Cameron wondered how long after this picture had Lindsay passed away.

As she returned the picture to the shelf, she noticed Munster standing on the loveseat. His tail wagged while he held the ball in his mouth. "Okay, only one more." She took the ball and bounced it off the floor. Munster gave chase.

Coffee mug in hand, Kathleen hurried out of the study with her cell phone to her ear. Cameron fell in step behind her. Oblivious to the detective on her heels, she breezed into the kitchen.

"Okay, give me a call as soon as you get that done." Kathleen disconnected the call to fill a fresh mug of coffee.

"Ms. Davis, can I have just a few minutes of your time?" Cameron asked. "It's about your husband's murder."

"If J.J. wants to make a deal, I'm not interested." Kathleen brushed past her to hurry into the living room, where she spun around so fast that she almost collided with the detective. "I can't believe J.J, who John and I welcomed into our home when he was dating our Heather, would defend that monster. I really should have known. He blatantly two-timed our daughter. I said at the time that he deserved to be slapped alongside the head, but John kept defending him. He seemed to think J.J. was an honorable young man since he was upfront about being a common hound. And now, how can you, the lead investigator in this case, allow your stepson to—"

"I don't *allow* anything," Cameron said. "J.J. is a grown man. He makes his own decisions."

"What about Joshua?"

"He makes his own decisions, too. The fact is—"

The phone buzzed in Kathleen's hand. Her thumb flew across the screen to answer.

Cameron snatched it from her hand. "She's in a meeting." She disconnected the call and tossed the phone onto the loveseat next to Munster who had returned to chew on the ball.

"You have no right!" Kathleen dove for the phone only to have Cameron push her back.

"Call a cop! Listen, I have news about your husband's murder case. Now, if you cared one ounce about him, then you'll want to know what we've uncovered. If you don't, then you can go back to work, and I can move your name up on my suspect list."

"How dare you!"

"How dare you! Your husband of over thirty years was brutally murdered Friday night and here you're acting like nothing's happened." Cameron pointed in the direction of the state line. "The arraignment for the man accused of murdering him, your grandson's father, was yesterday. Where were you? Probably at a staff meeting."

"You have no right to judge me," Kathleen said in a low voice.

"Do you know why the first suspect we look at when there's a murder is the spouse?" Cameron asked. "Because more often than not, that's who did it. It's sad, but it's the truth."

"Well, good thing you caught Derek with the murder weapon, huh?" Brushing her aside, Kathleen reached for her phone, only to have Munster run off with it.

"Too bad for you that Derek didn't do it."

Before Kathleen could chase after the phone, she spun around to face Cameron.

"It is standard procedure to examine and photograph a suspect and his clothes when he's arrested," Cameron said. "Derek had been on a major bender—"

"He's on a constant unending bender."

"He hadn't bathed or changed his clothes in days at the time of his arrest," Cameron said. "You could tell by looking and smelling him. Your husband's murder was brutally violent. His murderer would have been covered in blood. Derek had no blood on him or his clothes." She added, "He didn't kill your husband, Ms. Davis. Someone else killed him and planted the knife in Derek's trailer to implicate him."

Kathleen lowered herself onto the sofa. "Does that mean the police have released Derek?"

Cameron sat across from her. "Josh and his cousin, Dr. Tad MacMillan, are driving him to a rehab center in Cleveland. It's a residential facility. He'll be there for at least thirty days."

"Who's paying for that?"

"Tad made arrangements," Cameron said. "These types of places always receive donations from benefactors to help guests in dire need of treatment who can't afford it. Derek can stay as long as he needs to in order to get well."

Shaking her head, Kathleen narrowed her eyes. "He'll never change. Leopards can't change their spots."

"I wouldn't be so sure about that." Cameron shrugged her shoulders. "Tad used to be the town drunk. Now he's the county's medical examiner."

Kathleen cocked her head. Her eyes narrowed to slits.

"Unfortunately, in my line of work, I see a lot of folks in grief. I've learned that different people handle it differently," Cameron said. "My first husband died only four months after we were married. I had a promising career in law enforcement. But I basically threw it all away to crawl into a bottle. If I numbed myself enough, I wouldn't feel the pain. That was how I handled my grief." She peered at her. "Luckily, I got the help I needed to turn things around before I lost everything." She leaned across to her. "Some people drown themselves in drugs or booze, or"—she cocked her head at her—"their career."

Kathleen hung her head. Her hands shook as she smoothed her hair. Clearing her voice, she finally said, "Do you have any other information about John's murder besides that you let Derek loose?"

"We're examining the plant's security video for Friday night to see if we can notice any suspicious activity—like someone following him."

"But John wasn't at the plant on Friday," Kathleen said.

Cameron paused. According to the lie John Davis had told Kathleen, he had spent the week in Seattle and was flying in on Friday. "Actually, your husband's assistant told us that he had stopped in at the plant. He was on the phone when she'd left."

That was the truth. Susan Livingston had stated that. Cameron neglected to mention that not only had John Davis been at the plant on Friday, but he had been there the entire week, while Kathleen thought he was in Seattle.

"I guess he stopped in to see what work had piled up while he was traveling," Kathleen said.

"According to your husband's bank records, he had taken ten thousand dollars out of his savings account on Friday." Cameron saw by the way Kathleen had suddenly sat up that this was news to her. "I don't suppose you know what for."

Kathleen shook her head. "John and I always kept our money separate. I liked the independence of having my own money and making my own financial decisions. Maybe he took it out to invest in something. He'd do that once in a while. Or, he'd loan money to the kids to help them out."

"Maybe," Cameron said. "He got it out in cash, and we can't find any way to account for where the money went."

"Are you thinking his killer took it?"

"That's definitely a possibility. What do you know about Bea Miller?"

"Nut case," Kathleen said. "John had to get a restraining order against her after she'd assaulted him in the plant parking lot. She accused him of sexual harassment. You should see that woman. Who would want to sexually harass her?"

"I did try to question her," Cameron said. "She is in need of help."

"Do you think she killed John?" Kathleen asked. "Did plant security let her in to kill him? She'd had her clearances stripped away. If she got to him there—"

"No," Cameron said, "your husband was not killed at the plant."

"Then where?"

"All I can tell you is that he was killed in Ohio. The Columbiana County Sheriff's department and I will work together to investigate his murder." Cameron paused to take in a deep breath. "I have to ask. Where were you Friday night? Between the hours of five in the afternoon to midnight?"

Kathleen sat up straight. Her eyes blazed.

"I have to ask everyone," Cameron said, "including your children."

"I was here waiting for my husband to come home," Kathleen said. "As far as anyone to corroborate, Luke was here, too. We were planning to go out for pizza when his Grandpa came home. When John didn't come home, we left about six-thirty to go to the pizza place in town. We met my sons and their wives and children."

"Did you try to call your husband when he didn't come home?"

"I texted him to meet us at the restaurant."

"What about Heather?"

"She didn't go," Kathleen said. "She was on a date."

"Now, your husband had gotten a restraining order against Bea Miller," Cameron said.

"Several months ago."

"Had she been keeping away since he got that order?"

"I hadn't seen her, but she had been calling him," Kathleen said.

"On his cell phone?"

Kathleen nodded her head. "How she got his number, I have no idea. But she'd been calling him."

"Did she threaten him?"

"Of course, she did," Kathleen said.

"She threatened to kill him?"

"I don't know if those were her exact words. John told me that she said that he knew his dirty little secret and what goes around comes around. If that's not a threat, then I don't know what is."

Cameron cocked her head at her. "Dirty little secret? She actually said she knew his 'dirty little secret'? Did you ask John what she meant by that?"

"I didn't have to," Kathleen said.

"Why not?"

"Don't you get it? My husband? John? Having a dirty little secret? I hate to say it, but John was probably the most boring man in the Ohio Valley." She scoffed. "Believe me, Lieutenant Gates, he wasn't exciting enough to have any secrets."

Chapter Fifteen

That evening, dinner was at the Gardner home. Tracy had invited the family to go over a list of what needed to be completed at the restaurant in time for the wedding and grand opening. The pleasant aroma of cheeses, garlic, and oregano greeted the guests when they arrived.

The Gardners lived in a two-story Tudor home on a four-acre lot in a rural area outside of Chester. Apple trees in their back yard was evidence of the orchard from the subdivision's previous life. The spacious floor-plan had been customized to include a commercial kitchen for Tracy's catering business.

After giving J.J. a hurried hug and kiss, Tracy whisked Poppy away to the study where Joshua had exiled Izzy to work on her science project until dinner. She had put off the assignment for much too long. With a due date of Friday, the project had reached the crisis stage.

"I talked to Jessica," Tracy said with a giggle. "She has a designer friend who thinks she can make your gown."

Izzy bounced off the sofa where she was working. "Can her friend get it done in time?"

"She'll try."

Izzy folded her arms. "'Try' isn't good enough."

Poppy was shaking her head. "Even if she can get it done in time, a custom-made gown, it sounds expensive. I'm not going to blow our budget—not for a dress that I'm only going to wear one day."

"It's your *wedding* day." Tracy's eyes bulged. "This is the most-photographed day of your life. This is your queen-for-a-day day. You're dreaming about this special gown. It's your dream gown. Jessica can get it for you. You have to let her friend make it."

Poppy continued to shake her head. "It won't be the same gown."

"Yes, it will."

"No, it won't," Poppy said. "Jessica's friend will make a gown *like* it, but it won't be *the* gown. Thanks anyway." She turned to leave.

"The wedding is less than two months away!" There was a note of hysteria in Tracy's tone.

"I know. I helped set the date."

"What are you going to do if you don't find this *dream* gown?"

"I'll get married without it." A knowing grin crossed Poppy's face. "But I have faith that it will turn up. Otherwise, why do I keep dreaming about it?" She left to join the others in the kitchen.

Tracy glared at Izzy. "You know she's crazy."

"She hasn't been wrong yet." Izzy frowned. "Except when it comes algebra."

Tracy returned to the kitchen where she found the conversation in full swing about Heather and Madison.

Tracy picked up her cooking spoon and waved it. "I'd love to have been a fly on the wall when Heather and Maddie walked into that coffee shop, or wherever it is they met, and discovered that they were sisters?" With a giggle, she stirred the spaghetti sauce in the slow cooker.

Hunter was brushing garlic butter over the bread sticks. "I can't believe Maddie came right out and told you that she had her DNA tested," he said to Poppy who was sitting at the opposite side of the breakfast counter. Over his shoulder, he told Tracy, "I never did think Madison was very bright."

"Maddie was talking to Poppy about her ancestry," J.J. said while looking over the work drawings spread across the kitchen table. "She didn't think far enough ahead to realize that she was providing us with a clue to connect her and Heather. She always did live in the moment."

"We can't connect Madison to the Davis children until we prove someone from the Davis family submitted their DNA to the same website. Plus, we need proof that the website notified both parties of the familial connection." Joshua sat back in his seat at the table and took a sip from his glass of Chianti. "Good luck in getting a warrant to uncover that evidence. Those ancestry websites hire teams of lawyers whose sole purpose are protecting their clients' privacy. Even if a judge will give you a warrant, the company will fight you all the way to the supreme court."

"Your father's right," Cameron said. "Right now, we don't have enough probable cause to get a warrant."

"You've been married to Josh too long," Hunter said. "He's usually the one saying we don't have probable cause."

Tracy dropped the spaghetti noodles into the boiling water and stirred them. "Let's just suppose Heather and Maddie don't know that they're sisters. I mean, the Miss Charlotte former dance students' social group does exist. I belong to it and I've seen Heather and Madison on the website. They could have reconnected, buried the hatchet, and become friends just like they said."

Considering her theory, they all exchanged glances.

Turning his attention to J.J., Hunter slowly shook his head. "Sorry, I was at the Christmas formal when Maddie hurled that punch bowl at Heather. If J.J. hadn't pushed her out of the way, it would have been her who got hit in the face instead of him."

"You're such a gentleman." Poppy hugged J.J. and rested her head on his shoulder.

J.J. kissed the top of her head. "I try."

Shaking his head, Hunter put one last swipe of butter on the bread sticks. "Nope, I just can't visualize those two being friends."

"Have you eliminated their mothers as suspects?" Poppy asked.

"I talked to Kathleen this afternoon." Cameron shook her head. "She claims she took Luke out for pizza and met her sons and their families there. I talked to both of Davis's sons and the restaurant. They were all there from like seven o'clock until close to nine."

"And the time of the murder?" Tracy asked.

"Between eight and ten," Cameron said. "So Kathleen has an alibi for half of the kill time."

"Where was the restaurant?" Joshua asked.

"Calcutta." Cameron arched an eyebrow when she answered. "Basically, around the corner from the crime scene."

They exchanged long questioning glances.

"The witness overheard Davis arguing with two women and saw them leaving his apartment," Joshua said.

"But," Cameron said, "Davis's sons said Kathleen arrived with Luke and left with him. Would she really have taken her seven-year-old grandson to Grandpa's safe house to meet with his other wife to confront and murder him?"

"Maybe she left him in the car while she committed the murder," J.J. said.

"And dump the body?" Cameron asked. "And plant the murder weapon at his father's house?"

"Recently, there was an abduction and rape case where the perp snatched his victim and stuffed her into a box in the back of his van," Joshua said. "He was a construction worker. He had padded the inside of the box with carpeting so that it would be sound proof. Then, he went home, picked up his family, and took them out to dinner in the wife's car. Then, he took his family home and told his wife that he'd gotten a call to go out on a job. He got into the van in which he still had the victim locked in the box and took her to a motel where he raped her. After he was done, he put her back in the box and drove her to the edge of town where he dumped her. She went to the police and reported it. They found a witness in the parking lot from where she had been snatched. Based on his description, the police tracked down the van to the suspect."

"But he had an airtight alibi because he had been having dinner with his family right smack in the middle of the time-frame for when the crime had been committed," Cameron said.

"The victim had fibers from the carpet used to line the box on her clothes," Joshua said. "The rapist had dismantled the box by the time the police caught up with him, but they found the fibers matching the carpet in the van. They got other physical evidence, too. If they didn't have the physical evidence, they would have dropped him as a suspect because of this alibi. My point is this. He had used his family to create an alibi to conceal his crime. I mean, what kind of man takes his family out for a wholesome dinner while he's got a rape victim locked up in the back of his van?"

"A very sick man," Cameron said.

"You're going to need to find out if Kathleen had made any detours on her way home after the pizza place," J.J. said.

"I know," Cameron said. "I also need to find out where wife number two was at the time of the murder."

"What about Heather and Madison?" Joshua asked J.J. "The witness could have seen Davis's daughters confronting him about betraying their mothers."

"No." Tracy placed her hands, encased in oven mitts, on her hips.

"Why not?" Joshua said. "We know they're connected. Wouldn't be the first time siblings joined forces to take out a parent who'd betrayed their family."

"Heather claims she was on a date the night of the murder," J.J. said. "But she said it wasn't a good date and ended early. She didn't get the guy's phone number. I told her to ask the person who'd set it up to get that information for us. Maddie was having a girls' night out with her office manager."

"Are you talking about Elizabeth?" Tracy asked.

"Elizabeth Collins," J.J. said. "Used to be ... I can't remember her maiden name. She's married to Aaron Collins."

"She works at the dance studio," Cameron said.

"Maddie went for a girls' night out with Elizabeth?" Tracy asked.

"Aaron said Elizabeth got home really late and they had gotten very drunk," J.J. said.

"Does that seem odd to you, Tracy?" Cameron asked. "Madison did hire her to manage the office at the dance studio. I got the impression that they were friends."

"Elizabeth says," Tracy said. "She has a tendency to exaggerate her own importance. I don't know if Madison's Dance Studio is big enough to need someone to *manage* it. She only just opened it in August."

"Elizabeth seemed kind of put out when Maddie said Heather was redoing portions of the studio's website," J.J. recalled.

"Elizabeth is a strange bird," Tracy said. "I always felt torn between feeling sorry for her because she never quite fit in anywhere and trying to keep my distance."

"Are you saying she could be lying about going out with Madison Friday night?" Cameron asked.

"Aaron confirmed the alibi," J.J. said. "He took care of the kids."

"Madison did claim to have a sinus headache Saturday morning," Cameron said. "She could have been hung over."

"No, that was Heather," Tracy said.

"Madison had a headache," Cameron said. "Remember when we ran into them outside the bridal shop? Elizabeth offered to get aspirin for her."

"Because she had a migraine," Tracy said. "That's different from a sinus headache. Heather had a sinus headache. Madison had a migraine."

"Both of them had headaches on Saturday morning?" Joshua asked.

"Where did this girls' night out take place?" Cameron asked. "Beaver? Chester? Hookstown?"

"Calcutta?" Joshua asked.

J.J. cringed. "I didn't ask."

"If they have just recently found out that their father was a louse, then maybe they went out to vent and get drunk," Tracy said.

"And invited Elizabeth, the odd one along?" Hunter asked.

"She is a girl," Poppy said.

"Why lie about it if they did nothing wrong?" J.J. asked.

"Because they're not stupid," Poppy said. "They're smart enough to know that if you found out that they know about their relationship that they'll become suspects."

"She's got a point," Hunter said.

"But there's still another angle to look at," Cameron said. "Both Sherry and Kathleen have stated that John was receiving threatening phone calls. Now Kathleen assumed they were from Bea Miller, a former plant employee who has definite mental issues. Sherry believed they were from an obsessive woman also named Bea who her husband, Shawn, had helped when her car had broken down."

"Do you think they're one and the same?" Tracy asked.

"They have to be," Hunter said.

"What are the odds that the same man would be getting threats from two separate women named Bea?" Joshua asked.

"But that doesn't make sense," J.J. said. "Davis had two separate cell phones. One for each family. If he was getting threatening phone calls from the same woman on both phones, then that meant whoever was calling him knew about his two lives."

"And had the numbers for both phones," Joshua said, "which means whoever it was had to have known the location of his safe house. That's the only place she could have accessed both phones to get the numbers."

"Is it any wonder that the safe house happens to be the crime scene?" J.J. asked.

"Digital forensics is examining the phones to see if they can trace those calls to see if they came from the same caller," Cameron said. "If we're lucky, the caller didn't use a burner phone. At the very least, we can locate the general area from where the calls were made. Also, Kathleen said John told her that the caller claimed to know his 'dirty little secret.'"

"A disgruntled former employee would have the motive and opportunity to learn about Davis's double life if she followed him from the plant to Calcutta where he'd switch from one life to the other," J.J. said.

"Especially if she lived directly behind the apartment complex," Cameron said. "I tracked down Bea Miller today.

She rents a trailer in a park within walking distance of Davis's apartment."

"And you said she's mentally unstable," Tracy said. "Maybe, this Bea Miller went in and committed the murder after the fight the witness overheard."

"But my gut tells me it's not Bea Miller," Cameron said. "She's obviously paranoid. She'd seen Davis around—at the gas station and store. She assumed he was stalking her. I don't think she had any idea that he had an apartment across the road from where she was living."

"Paranoia would give her motive to kill Davis if she believes he's out to get her," J.J. said.

"He gets a restraining order against her and then stalks her to provoke her into reacting so that he can have her arrested," Joshua said. "At least, that's how it looks to her. So she kills him in what she views as self-defense."

"My gut is saying she didn't do it," Cameron said.

"She has motive and she has means," J.J. said. "Does she have an alibi?"

"I couldn't get that far in the interview," Cameron said while taking her vibrating cell phone from her pocket. "Did I mention that she's paranoid?" She put the phone to her ear. "Lieutenant Gates here."

Across the kitchen, Tracy was shaking her head. "It can't be Heather and Maddie. It can't be."

"You should have seen Heather this afternoon," J.J. said. "She can be pretty aggressive."

"Yeah," Hunter said. "Remember when she punched J.J. in the face and gave him that black eye?"

"He wouldn't have gotten that black eye if Maddie hadn't ducked." Tracy dumped the pasta into the strainer.

"Dancers can be wickedly fast on their feet," J.J. said.

Cameron stuffed her phone into her pocket. "Well, it looks like we just got a break in the case. An anonymous tip.

A witness saw Heather Davis and her SUV in the apartment complex at the time of the murder, and it was used to dump his body at the Newhart farm."

CHAPTER SIXTEEN

On the outskirts of Chester, Locust Hill Road led up a hill and through the valley to Route 8 on the other side of the county. Once out of town, Locust Hill split at a fork in the road. The left branch offered a steady incline through the valley. The right branch dropped down and around a sharp hairpin curve before snaking through the countryside. The inner portion of the curve was home to a steep hundred-foot drop-off into a ravine.

The next morning, Joshua arrived to find that Hunter had set up flares at the beginning of Washington School Road and on the other side of the curve. He parked his SUV behind the police cruiser, as far off the road as possible.

Dressed in his uniform, Hunter had opened the rear of his cruiser to make a workspace. He had spread out reports and photographs of the accident. Leaning against the open compartment, the deputy studied the results from an accident reconstruction program on his laptop.

"I guess I got you curious." Joshua sauntered over.

"Tracy says you're a bad influence on me." Hunter tapped the laptop's keyboard. "I've entered all of the data that I could find." He gestured at the pictures of the skid marks on the road. "These are really helpful. Sawyer did a good job with taking everything down—most importantly, the measurements." He nodded at the laptop. "I'm not as brilliant as you may think."

"I won't tell Tracy that," Joshua said with a grin.

"This program that I use takes the data and creates a visual reconstruction of the accident. That way we get a visual of how the accident happened. Granted, there's still some things that we need good old fashion gumshoe work to find out—"

"Like what was happening inside the car."

"But, we can still see how it happened." Hunter took a stack of the accident photos and led him around the curve and halfway up the hill toward where the road split. He handed the pictures off to Joshua.

"This is where it started." Hunter pointed to the gravel on the shoulder of the road. "You can see in that picture where there's a skid mark along the edge of the pavement and the gravel has tire marks in it. Sawyer was swift enough to notice it. That's where the car first went off the road."

"The car swerved to the right, but the driver corrected it before going down the hill." Joshua referred to the pictures and the accident report. "But there's no brake marks until the car hits the bottom of the hill and the curve."

"The driver overcorrected." Hunter led him back down the hill and across the road to the outer rim of the curve. "The tire marks and metal and damage to the car paint a pretty clear picture when you get down here. I'd say the driver was going fifty miles an hour when the car crossed the center before hitting the brakes. The car was on the opposite shoulder before the driver was able to make the turn. At that point, the driver had to have panicked. He or she turned too sharp and the car shot across to the other shoulder on the inside of the curve."

"Which drops off into the gully." Joshua pointed to the drop-off while crossing the road.

"The driver spun the wheel again to avoid going into the ravine," Hunter said. "Suddenly, the car was spinning in the other direction. The passenger door opened and Lindsay went flying."

"Out the passenger side door?"

Hunter handed Joshua the medical examiner's report. "You had to have seen this already. Lindsay had gotten run over."

"Tad said the car had rolled over her. It wasn't the wheels that crushed her, but the car itself."

"Did you see the gas cap on her back?"

Puzzled, Joshua flipped through the medical examiner pictures. Unable to see what Hunter was talking about, he handed the stack to the deputy who took out a picture that Tad had taken during the autopsy. Among the bruises and broken bones, there was a circular bruise in an outline on Lindsay's shoulder blade.

"The gas cap on this car was on the passenger side," Hunter said, "which means the car rolled over her from that side over the top to the driver's side." He pointed to the steep hill on the inside of the curve in the road. "That means she was thrown from the passenger side of the car."

Hunter took the pictures of the totaled car rammed up against a thick tree at the bottom of the ravine. "This car rolled down rear first. The driver spun around to avoid going down the gully front ways. However, at that point, the car had so much momentum, and he spun it around so fast—"

"The driver ended up doing a donut."

"Between the speed that the car was traveling when it hit the curve, and angle of the road, we had a perfect storm," Hunter said. "The car rolled sideways over Lindsay. Then, the rear tires went onto the shoulder and down the ravine. The car then went down the ravine end over end."

"How positive are you that someone else was driving?" Joshua asked.

Hunter dug a picture from the bottom of the pile and showed it to Joshua. It was a picture of a skid mark. To Joshua, it looked almost like a half moon.

"After Lindsay had been thrown out, after she had been rolled over, the driver turned out of the skid with their foot on the gas. He or she was still fighting to keep from going down the hill. Lindsay was already outside the vehicle when that happened."

"What happened to the driver?" Joshua asked. "How is it possible that someone was in this accident and walked away?"

"If they were drunk or high enough, they may have been so relaxed that they didn't get hurt." Hunter pointed at the gully. "That's a long hill. Maybe they bailed out when the rear wheels started going over—before the car started rolling end over end."

"And walked away," Joshua said, "leaving Lindsay lying in the middle of the road like roadkill."

"Bishop Moore got what he had comin' to him." Brenda Bayles glared up at Cameron from her motorized wheelchair.

The detective reconsidered her decision to step into the managers office, out of the cold, to wait for Ross Bayles to return from a maintenance job in one of the apartments. Something told her that the freezing temperatures outside were warmer than the bitter woman inside.

Brenda was clad in a housedress with an afghan wrapped around her to keep her warm. She wore slippers on her feet. Her swollen legs, marked with varicose veins, were bare. She tapped an open pack of cigarettes to extract one while eyeing Cameron, who watched through the window for Ross Bayles's arrival.

"What did Bishop Moore do to deserve being murdered?" Cameron regarded her out of the corner of her eye.

The old woman lit her cigarette and took a long drag on it. She blew smoke out of the corner of her mouth. "Bishop was a selfish bastard. Using his good looks and charm to suck the living daylights out of women. Then, after he'd sucked them dry, he'd throw them away like yesterday's garbage and start on a fresh piece of ass." She pointed out the window. "I saw his last two victims coming out that night."

Cameron peered up at the breezeway where John Davis's apartment was located. While the window provided a clear view of the walkway from the parking lot, one couldn't see the apartment itself—especially from the lower angle of a wheelchair. "You saw them? There were two of them?"

"Couldn't miss them," Brenda said. "One was hysterical."

"Can you describe them?"

"A blonde and a brunette. Pretty. Of course. Bishop wouldn't be caught with an ugly woman. Young enough to be his daughters."

"What time was that?"

Brenda shrugged her shoulders. "About ten minutes before eight. I remember the time because I'd run out of cigarettes and sent Ross out to get more. I was waiting for him to come back. He took forever."

"You were watching the clock because you were afraid of going into nicotine withdrawal."

"I love my cigs." Brenda took another long drag on her cigarette. "I've been smoking since I was a little girl. They give me pleasure—what little I have in this life."

"You saw the two women leaving at ten minutes to eight," Cameron said while peering out the window. "They were young and pretty. They were hysterical."

"*One* was hysterical. You're not listening. The blonde was freaking out and her friend was consoling her."

Cameron squatted and looked out the window—trying to envision what Brenda could have seen. From the wheel-chair, she could not have been able to tell which apartment the two women had been visiting. "Are you certain they were coming from Bishop Moore's apartment?"

"I heard them before I saw them," Brenda said. "They were yelling awful things at him. I opened the door to see where the fight was and saw them leaving his apartment."

Cameron opened the door. As Brenda had said, upon stepping outside, there was a view of Bishop Moore's apartment door, which was still blocked off with yellow crime scene tape. Yet, the view was only clear enough to see the edge of door, not into the apartment.

"One of them was telling him that he was going to pay for what he'd done," Brenda said. "I heard the door slam shut. The blonde was shrieking like her guts were being ripped out. She said she didn't know how she was going to tell her moth-er." She giggled. "I'll bet he got her pregnant. The brunette hugged her and said that she'd take care of everything. I guess that means she knows a good doctor to give her an abortion. They had their arms around each other when they walked down to the parking lot. They got into a purple SUV and left. I told Ross about what had happened when he finally decided to come home." She shook her finger at Cameron. "About time someone taught that man a good lesson."

"Would you recognize those two women if you saw them again?"

Brenda stubbed out her cigarette. "Fraid not. My eyesight ain't what it used to be." She did a u-turn with her wheelchair and went into the living room to resume watching a talk show hosted by a psychiatrist talking about the risks of hatred to our health.

Cameron saw Ross Bayles racing toward the office across the complex grounds in an ATV with a cart hooked behind it. As he drew near, the roar of the ATV's engine sounded like a lawnmower on its last legs.

"Detective Gates?" Ross blurted out upon seeing her waiting for him. He took his tool chest out of the cart and carried it inside. "I hope you weren't waiting long." He dropped the tool chest onto the table and stepped into the living room doorway.

Cameron followed him.

Brenda Bayles had wheeled her chair to the lift recliner. She pushed herself up out of the chair and shuffled to turn herself around—positioning herself in front of the seat. Then, she dropped her great weight down into it. She landed with such force that the recliner was propelled into the corner. Ross went behind the chair to shove it out from the wall to allow room for it to recline.

Brenda seemed oblivious of her husband's presence while she lit another cigarette and hit buttons on a remote to lift the footrest and drop the back into position. She didn't acknowledge him until he turned to join Cameron in the kitchen. "Ross, get me a beer."

Ross grabbed a can from the fridge and hurried into the living room. Upon returning, he told Cameron in a low voice, "I know you have a job to do, but, if possible, can you not come to the office when I'm not here? As you can see, my wife has some serious issues."

"I understand," Cameron said. "She seems to have had very strong feelings about Bishop Moore."

"She didn't know him."

"She knew him well enough to hate him. She knew which apartment was—"

"Only because a ton of cops were here the other night searching it."

"Does Brenda ever talk to the tenants?"

"Only when she absolutely has to," he said. "She's not a well woman. She's been dealing with addictions her entire adult life. It's done something to her brain. The only exposure she had with Moore was maybe when he came into the office to pay his rent at the first of the month. Otherwise, she'd have no reason to even know who he was."

Staring at him, Cameron considered his excuse. Beads of sweat formed on his upper lip and forehead. "None of these cameras in this apartment complex work?"

"Not a one."

"It'd be worth the investment to get them fixed," Cameron said. "Once word gets out that they don't work, the crime rate will go through the roof."

"I can only do so much with what the owners give me to work with," he grumbled.

"Where were you Friday night?"

"I rarely saw the guy." Ross flapped one of his arms. "I told that other detective and a uniformed officer and—"

"Now you're going to tell me," Cameron said. "I want to hear it in your own words."

"I got off work at five o'clock and cooked dinner. I was cleaning up afterwards and just getting ready to sit back and have a beer when Brenda discovered she was out of cigarettes. She blew her top and I knew that if I didn't go get another box that there'd be hell to pay. So I got in the van and went to the store to get a box."

"What time was that?"

"It was seven o'clock." He shrugged his shoulders. "I got back around eight-thirty."

"It took you ninety minutes to go buy a carton of cigarettes? The convenience store is around the corner."

Ross shot a glance in the direction of the living room.

Cameron lowered her voice. "Did you stop in on a friend while you were out?"

His mouth curled up. "You see what I have to put up with."

She sighed. "I'm not judging you. I'm just trying to find out what happened."

"I barely knew the guy."

"I need to ask everyone," Cameron said. "Where did you go?"

"She lives in the building around back. Building D. Apartment Three-B. Third floor. I parked in the lot in front of her building and went up to see her after I got the cigs. I came back here at eight-thirty."

"And your wife didn't suspect anything?"

"I told her that I ran into a friend." He shrugged his shoulders. "It isn't like she cares any."

"Did you see anyone around the Moore apartment when you got back?"

"Nothing," he said in a firm tone. "Everything was quiet. His friends' car and truck were here. I figured he was on a layover or whatever it was. Didn't know anything was up until the cops started asking questions on Monday."

"Why did your wife hate Bishop Moore?" Cameron asked.

"She didn't know Bishop Moore," he said with a growl.

"Maybe she didn't know him, but she certainly hated him. Why is that?"

Ross glanced over his shoulder into the living room.

"Kill the bastard!" Brenda yelled at a woman being counseled by the talk show host about her serial cheating husband. "The only good cheat is a dead one!" With a cackle, she took a drink from her can of beer. "Slash that pretty boy's face. That'll teach him a lesson." She took a long drag on her cigarette.

"Can't you see? My wife is not a well woman."

Cameron took note of Brenda's face pinched with hatred as she focused her tiny eyes on the cheating spouse on the television screen. Slowly, she nodded her head in agreement.

Later, on her way to her cruiser, Cameron texted Tony: "Want full background check on Brenda Bayles."

CHAPTER SEVENTEEN

"You know I'm going to have to come clean with the wives eventually," Cameron told Joshua.

It was in the sheriff's office in Lisbon, Ohio, that Cameron and Joshua stood behind the sheriff deputy's chair to watch the traffic camera footage from the intersection of Route 170 and Dresden Avenue, one of Calcutta's two major crossroads.

"Bruno's Pizza is less than a mile away," Cameron noted while watching the traffic flowing through the traffic lights. "Kind of ironic that the Davis family was dining right around the corner from their patriarch's secret apartment."

"Ironic or suspicious?" Lieutenant William Parks said while watching the recording through his small eyes. The mountain of a man was built like a tank. He stood with his muscular arms crossed. His face seemed to be in a permanent scowl. Cameron couldn't decide if he was scowling or squinting because of bad eyesight.

Next to her, Joshua pointed at a cream-colored SUV that sped through the intersection. "That's Kathleen's car. I recognize the gold trim."

The deputy took the recording back thirty seconds and replayed it at a slower pace. The luxury SUV with gold trim traveled in the direction of the freeway to East Liverpool and the Chester Bridge. They could see Kathleen at the wheel and a child in a car seat in the rear section.

"She's heading away from the apartment complex," Joshua said, "and she has Luke with her. Unless she looped around and came back, I'd say this can clear her."

Her eyes still on the recording, Cameron grasped the deputy's shoulder. "Hold it right there."

The deputy hit the pause button. The image froze with a purple SUV turning right onto Route 170. The street light overhead beamed onto the windshield.

"Isn't that Heather's SUV?" Cameron asked.

"Pennsylvania tags." The deputy compared the registration number they had for Heather's vehicle. "The plates are a match."

Cameron and Joshua moved in to peer at the woman driving the vehicle. They both recognized Heather Davis behind the steering wheel.

"There's a blonde in the passenger seat," Joshua said.

"Oh, yeah," Cameron said. "That's Madison Whitaker. Her sister."

"Two witnesses saw a blonde and a brunette leaving the crime scene," Joshua said. "Our anonymous tipster says Heather's SUV was used to transport Davis's body."

"We can't stall any longer," Parks said. "We've got what we need to get a warrant to search Davis's SUV."

"I don't like anonymous tips," Cameron said. "Been my experience that they always have their own unscrupulous agendas."

"I don't like it any more than you do," Joshua said. "But right now, the tipster's agenda is irrelevant." He pointed at the paused image on the monitor. "The point is Heather, and it looks like Madison, too, were in the vicinity of the murder and lied about it. We need to search Heather's SUV."

"I'll call Clark to get moving on a warrant," Parks said.

"I'll go talk to Madison to see what she has to say," Cameron said.

Sherry Whitaker bred her Bichon Frise dogs at her home on the outskirts of Monaca, Pennsylvania. Full grown, the little white dogs were no more than eighteen pounds, which meant they didn't require a lot of space. Cameron discovered during her investigation that Sherry Whitaker was noted in dog circles for being an accomplished dog trainer. This required room for working with her clients' championship dogs, as well as caring for them. It would not be a good thing if one of Sherry's charges were to get out onto the road and be hit by a car. For that reason, the Whitakers lived and worked in a red-brick ranch style home on four heavily fenced acres.

After turning off the two-lane country road, Cameron lowered the window to her cruiser to press the security button on the gate, which slowly rolled open to allow her to drive up the long driveway to a detached garage. She noticed a spacious back yard that included numerous obstacles of various shapes and sizes with which to exercise and train the dogs.

A compact red SUV with a magnetic sign on the side panel reading "Madison's Dance Studio" was parked in front of the garage. The sign included the address, phone number, and website.

"Have you found Shawn?" A tiny pup in each arm, Sherry Whitaker rushed out onto the side porch to greet Cameron when she slid out of the driver's seat of her cruiser.

Behind her mother, Madison chewed on her bottom lip. Her long blond hair blew in the chilly breeze. Her cheeks and the tip of her nose turned bright pink in the cold. She was dressed in rose colored leggings with a matching wrap-around sweater.

"We're following up some leads," Cameron said.

"You'd think you would have found his truck by now," Sherry said. "We're talking about an eighteen-wheeler with a sleeper cab. It should be easy enough to spot."

"Did Shawn keep his rig here?" Cameron asked.

"Oh, no," Sherry said with a laugh. "His truck is bigger than our driveway. Noisy, too. Some of my clients' dogs can be pretty high strung. They'd have a nervous breakdown after hearing Shawn start that baby up. He kept it at the dispatch office up in Austintown. Did you talk to them?"

Behind her, Cameron noticed that Madison's eyes were wide with what looked like fear. Slowly, she shook her head.

"I've tried to find the name and phone number of the guy who ran the office," Sherry said. "Shawn told me never to call them because they didn't like personal phone calls. So, he would call me when he stopped at night—until we got cell phones. Then, he was able to call me from the road."

"We've talked to the dispatch office," Cameron said.

"And what did they say?" Sherry asked. "Have they heard from Shawn?"

Cameron could see Madison holding her breath. "I'm sorry. They don't know anything."

It was the truth. The dispatch office that Sherry stated her husband worked out of did not know anything about any trucker named Shawn Whitaker.

Sherry slumped.

Madison grasped her mother by the shoulders. "Mom, it's cold. Why don't you take the pups inside so they don't get sick? I'll talk to Cameron. Maybe together we can figure something out."

Sherry rubbed her face into the fur of the two pups while making her way into the house. Once her mother was inside, Madison turned to Cameron. "Let's talk in the garage." Without waiting for a response, she led the detective through a side door into the two-car garage, which turned out to be a workshop filled with woodworking tools.

"Dad loved to work with his hands," Madison said with a sweep of her arm at the workbench that took up the width of the building. Tools littered the bench. "There was nothing he couldn't do. He and Mom put up that security fence by themselves."

"Your mother is going to have to be told," Cameron said. "Sooner rather than later."

Madison shivered in the cold.

"How long have you known?"

"Only a few weeks." Madison shrugged. "Not even a month." She looked up. Her blue eyes met Cameron's. "Was he killed at his apartment in Calcutta?"

"Yes."

Madison blinked her eyes. Unable to stop the tears, she grabbed a rag from the bench and wiped her nose.

Cameron patted her shoulder. "You connected with Heather through the ancestry website, didn't you?"

Madison nodded her head. "Heather did the test a couple of years ago as part of a research project she was doing for a class. I did the DNA test when I came back home from New York out of curiosity about where my ancestors had come from. Dad never really told me very much and Mom didn't even know when her family came here to America. Heather and I got the notifications about there being enough markers for us to be siblings right before Christmas. But all they gave us were user IDs. We emailed each other for a couple of weeks. I couldn't believe it when I found out she lived in the same area. It was so nice having a sister. We decided to meet the day after New Year's." She let out a deep breath. "It blew both of our minds."

"Didn't you exchange names in the emails?"

"Even though we were sisters, we didn't know if the other one was a psychopath," Madison said. "We exchanged first names only. I'd known Heather all through school. I'd never realized in all those years that I'd never met her father. I'd met her mother, but never her father. Same with her. He never came to one of my recitals. He was always on the road. Now I know why." She let out a chuckle. "Do you want to know how good he was?"

"Tell me."

"Heather and I were born one day apart—luckily it was in different hospitals. He never would have managed to pull it off with two different names and two different mothers at the same hospital."

"What happened to all the hatred between the two of you when you realized—"

"It went up in smoke." Madison threw up her hands. "Suddenly, every fight, every nasty trick, slight, snub, it was all so trivial compared to what Dad had done not to us—but to our mothers." She looked up at Cameron. "My mother adores that man. Same with Heather." A tear rolled down her cheek. "He'd betrayed both of our mothers, we …" Her voice trailed off. Hugging herself, she shrugged her shoulders.

"You found common ground by virtue of a shared trauma," Cameron said. "You joined forces."

"We didn't join forces to kill him!"

"Heather's SUV was seen in the area. Security cameras recorded you riding in the passenger seat. Witnesses saw a blonde and a brunette leaving his apartment after a loud argument. Are you telling me that you didn't confront him?"

"Yes, but we didn't kill him!" Madison ran her hands through her hair. "Heather and I got together quite a few times to talk about what we were going to do. For all we knew, Dad had a few more wives stashed away somewhere. So we investigated. We snatched his cell phones. He had two different phones—one for each family."

"What did you find?"

"Some calls from a woman named Bea on both phones. Heather asked her mother and she told her that Bea was a loon who Dad had gotten a restraining order against. Well, my mom said Bea was a fruitcake who Dad had helped when her car broke down. Obviously, this Bea, whoever she really was, was stalking him and must have killed him."

"She was calling him on both phones," Cameron said, "which means she had knowledge of his two families. Did either you or Heather tell anyone about your father?"

"No!" Madison shook her head.

"What about Heather? Didn't she tell her brothers?"

"She didn't know how. She said if she did that they'd kill—" Blubbering, Madison shook her head. "No, they wouldn't have really killed him. I mean—"

"I know what you mean," Cameron said. "Madison, your father had withdrawn ten-thousand dollars from his savings account on that Friday. One that he had under John Davis. He got it in cash. We haven't tracked it down. Did he say anything, or did you see a lot of money when you went to his apartment?"

Madison's mouth dropped open. "I saw a big brown envelope on the kitchen counter when we first got there. While we were fighting, he picked it up and folded it in half and shoved it inside his jacket pocket." She let out a breath. "So maybe it was a thief who killed him. Maybe this had nothing to do with Dad being a cheat."

"We're wondering if maybe he was being blackmailed because he was a cheat," Cameron said. "Tell me about Elizabeth Collins?"

"What about her?" Madison scrunched up her face. "She was a good friend back when we were in school."

"Why the look? It's like you're trying to convince yourself that she's a good friend."

"Elizabeth is a little … I guess needy is the word. When I came back home, I ran into Elizabeth at the mall. We chatted a bit and I mentioned opening the dance studio and she just latched onto me. Calling me. Offering suggestions. Doing stuff. I couldn't get rid of her." She lowered her voice. "To tell you the truth—I can't afford to have an employee, even if she is only part time."

"She claims the two of you went out Friday night. Obviously, that's not true."

"J.J. told you." Madison let out a breath. "I wish Elizabeth had said something to me about that. She lied to protect herself. She had told Aaron that she was going on a girls' night out with me so that she could go meet some guy at a bar. The dummy should have told me that to give me a heads up. Aaron has been working on our computers at the studio. What if he had said something to me and I had no idea what he was talking about? I didn't know a thing until J.J. asked what I was doing Friday night and Elizabeth jumped in to say we were together."

"When in actuality, you were with Heather."

"She did have a blind date, but it was just for drinks after work," Madison said. "We started texting each other about which family Dad was with when. After a few weeks, we figured out his pattern. We knew he had to have a halfway place where he changed his clothes and phones and vehicles. He had spent the week here when he was supposed to be in Seattle. He was supposed to return to Chester on Friday. So, I followed him in the morning, and he went to that apartment complex in Calcutta. I knew that had to be where he switched from Shawn Whitaker to John Davis. Then, I followed him to the power plant. Heather had that date and couldn't get out of it. So, I had to follow him from the plant. He went back to Calcutta. I met Heather at the Time Out Bar and Grill in East Liverpool to have a couple of drinks and work up our nerve to go confront him. I was so nervous, Heather had to drive."

"What time did you go back to confront him? What did he say?"

"I think we got to his apartment right before seven o'clock." Madison shook her head. "The rest of the night was a blur. I remember ..." She sighed. "He didn't deny it. Actually, I think he looked a little relieved that we knew. He said—he said that he loved both of our mothers and that he couldn't decide between the two of them. So, he decided to have both families. That he loved all of us equally. Have you ever heard such a thing?"

"What did Heather and you say to that?"

"I cried like an idiot. I just stood there and bawled. Heather, she let him have it. The harder I cried, the madder she got. When we left, we told him to stay away from our families—stay away from our moms—I remember Heather said that if he came near her mom again that she'd kill him."

Cameron cocked her head.

"But I know Heather didn't mean it that way. She'd never—"

"Are you sure?"

"She couldn't have."

"What time did you leave your father's apartment?"

"I have no idea. I remember walking past the apartment manager's office. There was a woman in a wheelchair sitting outside watching us. She was a very unpleasant woman—scowling at us like we'd done something wrong."

"Where did you go?"

"We had to go back to the Time Out Bar for me to get my car," Madison said. "We were so upset that we were shaking. So, we went inside to have a couple of drinks to calm our nerves." She sighed. "The next thing I remember is waking up here at home the next morning. My car was still in East Liverpool. I had to ask Elizabeth to take me back to the bar to pick up my car."

"That's why you had a headache when we saw you at the dance studio," Cameron said. "You were hung over."

"I've never blacked out before," she said. "Really. I have no idea how I got home."

"Did you ask Heather?"

"Heather said the bartender called an Uber to take us home when the bar closed at midnight. She paid for it."

"Do you remember the two of you being together the entire evening?"

Madison nodded her head. "Heather and I were together the entire time."

"But you just said you blacked out and can't remember how you got home," Cameron said while digging her vibrating cell phone from its case.

"I may not remember how I got home, but I'd certainly remember killing my own father, wouldn't I?"

With a shrug, Cameron read the text from Joshua: *Parks got the warrant to search Heather's house and SUV.*

"Anonymous tip?" Heather Davis blew her top when Cameron and Lieutenant William Parks met her at her single-family home in Shippingport after she had arrived home from work with a search warrant. Uncertain of who to stop first, she followed the uniformed Columbiana sheriff's deputies searching through her things.

"What anonymous tip?" She glared at Joshua, who had met them to offer what support he could. "Why would I kill my father?"

"We know, Heather," Joshua said.

"Madison! I should have known!"

"No," Cameron tried to explain as Lieutenant Parks stepped through the open door. "Lieutenant Gates, you're going to want to see this."

Cameron hurried out the door with Heather directly behind her. In the driveway of the small house, the rear compartment of the purple SUV was open. Lieutenant Parks and two deputies parted to make room for Cameron. The spare wheel cover had been removed. A dish towel was spread out across the spare tire. The white towel was marked up with brownish splotches that Cameron recognized as dried blood. One brown mark was a streak across the towel in the unmistakable shape of a knife blade.

"I never saw that towel before in my life," Heather said.

"That's what they all say," Lieutenant Parks said with a chuckle.

"That bitch!" Heather said. "I'm gonna—" Realizing what she was about to say, she stopped. "I want a lawyer." She turned to Joshua. "What's J.J.'s number?"

CHAPTER EIGHTEEN

While the Columbiana Sheriff's cruiser took the freeway to transport Heather Davis to Lisbon, Cameron, with Joshua in the passenger seat, took Dresden Avenue out of East Liverpool. A few miles along the two-lane road took them to the Time Out Bar and Grill. In the evening hours, after dinner, the sports bar was moderately busy with regulars.

When Cameron stepped in with her badge clipped to her belt next to her service weapon, the crowd took notice to watch her and Joshua approached the bar. The bartender was quick to ask them what they wanted.

"Just answers to a couple of questions." Cameron brought up Heather Davis's and Madison Whitaker's drivers' license pictures on her tablet.

"Were you tending bar Friday night?" Joshua became aware of a heavyset man eyeing Cameron with a salacious smile on his face. He sat on the stool next to where she leaned against the bar.

With a quick glance around the room, he saw that his wife, as usual, was the prettiest woman in the bar. Cameron's good looks were not glossy like that of a fashion model. She didn't color her cinnamon color hair, which she wore in layers to the bottom of her neck. Makeup amounted to a bit of mascara. Usually, she ditched lipstick in favor of chapstick.

The bartender took his time trying to recall which day was Friday.

"Yeah, Butch," the guy on the stool said. "Friday night. You were here." He smiled at Cameron. "I was here, too."

"Norm is here every night," Butch said.

Cameron showed Butch the pictures. "Do you recall seeing either of these two ladies here Friday night?"

"Yeah, they were here. Drank martinis. Lots of martinis."

Norm made no pretense of looking over Cameron's shoulder. "The blonde came in first—by herself. She was upset. I tried to talk to her, but she wanted to be alone. I thought maybe her boyfriend'd dumped her."

"She drank two martinis before her friend came in," Butch said. "The brunette. They had another round of martinis. The brunette paid their bill and they left."

"About what time?" Joshua asked.

Butch shrugged his shoulders. "Have no idea."

"They weren't gone very long," Norm said. "They came back. They came in together that time. The blonde was even more upset than she was before. The brunette was comforting her."

"Do you remember what time they came back?" Joshua asked.

While Butch shook his head, Norm answered, "Close to eight because I left at eight after the soccer game was over. They were sitting in the booth over there and had put in an order for a pitcher of martinis. Butch was serving them when I left."

"Are you absolutely certain about that?" Cameron asked.

"I make it a point to always keep track of the lookers." Norm grinned.

"He means hit on them," Butch said.

"I don't always hit on them."

With a smirk, Butch shook his head while mouthing. "Always."

"You make it sound like I don't have discriminating taste," Norm said. "I do have standards."

"Name the last looker, who wasn't a regular, who walked through that door that you didn't hit on," Butch said.

"Me," Cameron said.

"You haven't walked out yet. Give him time."

"There was that strange bleach blonde who came in Friday," Norm said. "I didn't hit on her."

"I know the one you're talking about," Butch said. "She doesn't count."

"She was a looker and she wasn't a regular."

"She was also weird."

"Not that weird," Norm said.

"She had a huge dark cloud hanging over her head."

"Which is why I didn't hit on her," Norm said. "But you can't deny she was a looker and she wasn't a regular and I didn't hit on her. That means she counts."

"Gentlemen," Joshua said in a sharp tone. "to get back to the two lookers drinking martinis in that booth on Friday night—"

"I never hit on the brunette either," Norm told Butch.

"Only because you had to go home to your wife before you had a chance."

"Excuse me," Joshua said. "To get back on the two ladies. Since Norm went home to his wife at eight. I guess it's up to someone else to tell us what time they left after coming back."

"Now that I can answer," Butch said. "I called them an Uber to take them home at midnight. When they came back, they were really upset about something. We were pretty busy, but I remember they had several rounds of martinis." He shook his head. "I'm not setting myself up to get sued. I arranged an Uber to take them home at closing."

"And you close at midnight," Cameron noted.

"Did either of them leave between eight when Norm saw them come in and midnight?" Joshua asked.

Butch shook his head. "They sat there in that booth the whole time. Neither of them left until the Uber car arrived and I helped pour them into the car. I even had to search their wallets to give the addresses to the driver."

"Who paid for the drinks?" Cameron asked.

"The brunette paid from her phone before we took them outside," Butch said. "She held her liquor better than the blonde."

"That means there will be a digital record of the time," Cameron told Joshua.

"She paid with her phone both times," the bartender said. "You'll find a digital record of what time they left the first time, too."

"Hey, what did they do?" Norm asked.

"Looks like nothing since you two can testify to their whereabouts Friday evening," Cameron said.

"Do you mean we're busting whatever case you're working on wide open?" Norm asked.

"Pretty much," Cameron said.

"Guess that will make you pretty grateful, huh?"

"Pretty."

"Grateful enough for a kiss?" Norm tapped his heavily stubbed cheek.

"Told you he'd hit on you if you gave him enough time," Butch said.

"Just one more kiss, and then you can go." J.J. pulled Poppy in close and covered her mouth with his.

She wrapped her arms around his shoulders. Hoping to prolong the kiss, J.J. held her as tight as he could. He savored the taste of her mouth—until he felt a pair of thick, soft, furry lips on the back of his neck.

The magical moment broken, he opened his eyes.

The thick furry lips continued to nuzzle on his coat collar and work their way down to his shoulder.

Poppy giggled.

"Gulliver, you're not my type," J.J. told the Appaloosa gelding who had let himself out of his stall after finishing his dinner.

With a "baa" Ollie hopped into Gulliver's open stall to check for any potential leftovers. The rooster, Charley was directly behind him.

"I should be going." Poppy escorted the horse back into his stall.

"Fifty-nine days from now, you won't need to go home. We'll just say good night to all of the animals and go into our home together and—" He cleared his throat.

"And what?" Shooting him a wicked grin, she shooed Ollie and Charley out of the stall.

He chuckled. "Whatever you want."

"As long as it doesn't involve algebra." She closed the stall door.

He gave her a long lingering kiss on the lips. "I assure you," he said with his lips close to hers, "algebra is the last thing on my mind right now." He groaned when the phone in the case on his hip buzzed. He released his hold on her to take the phone out of its case. Seeing his father's ID, he sighed. "What now?"

While he spoke on the phone, Poppy went to check on the new pregnant mare at the other end of the barn. Pilgrim was still in quarantine.

"What's up, Dad?" he asked while admiring the way her jeans hugged her toned figure.

Between the experiences of her traumatic adolescence and their spiritual beliefs, they had decided to wait until their wedding night to become intimate. It was a decision the two of them had made together and not discussed with anyone, including their closest friends and family. After all, that part of their relationship was really no one's business. Since their engagement, the couple had become increasingly amused by how everyone assumed Poppy had taken up residence in J.J.'s home and that they spent their evenings exploring various sexual activities.

Two months seemed like an eternity. As the days stretched to weeks and then months since their engagement, J.J. began wondering why he hadn't suggested they elope. *Is it too late to run off to a justice of the peace?*

"Am I interrupting something?" Joshua asked after J.J., caught up in a fantasy, didn't respond to his question about if he was busy.

A master escape artist, Gulliver strolled past J.J. and down the center aisle to where Poppy was checking on Pilgrim. Upon seeing the open stall, Ollie scurried inside with Charley riding on his back. Once there, they embarked on what resembled a dance in the fresh hay to send straw everywhere.

"We're just bedding down the animals for the night and the dynamic duo are acting like a couple of two-year-olds on a sugar high." J.J. ushered Ollie out of the stall, but Charley would have none of it.

"I've got another client for you," Joshua said.

"What's the charge?"

"Don't you want to know who it is first?"

Staking his claim on the stall, Charley rose up on his legs, flapped his wings, and shrieked.

"You have the whole rest of the barn to play in!" J.J. swung his arms toward the stall doorway. "Get out of here!"

"What's Charley doing now?" Joshua asked.

J.J.'s answer was drowned out by Captain Blackbeard, their prized stallion, whinnying his objection of Gulliver, a mere gelding, being allowed to roam free while he was locked in his stall. Gulliver made a habit of antagonizing the stallion by releasing the mares, three of whom were pregnant with Blackbeard's colts, but leaving Captain Blackbeard locked up.

"It's okay, Captain," Poppy said in a soothing tone while leading the Appaloosa back to his stall. "Gulliver's going to behave himself. Aren't you, handsome?" She gave the horse a loving pat on the rear as he went back into the stall. She then shooed the rooster out. "Pilgrim is doing great. Her eyes are clear and even have a healthy sparkle to them."

"Pilgrim is doing great," J.J. told Joshua.

"Glad to hear that," Joshua said. "Do you feel like driving out to Lisbon to sit in on an interrogation?"

"Who's the client and what's she accused of?"

"Heather Davis," Joshua said. "Traffic cams show her in the area at the time of the murder, two witnesses place her in the apartment complex, and a bloody towel was found in her SUV."

"But you don't think she did it."

"We know she didn't do it."

CHAPTER NINETEEN

"Sorry to interrupt your evening." Cameron met J.J. in the corridor outside the interrogation room when he arrived at the sheriff's office.

"It was a hard decision. I had a choice between interviewing a murder suspect who's innocent in a nice warm conference room or sanding hardwood floors in a cold farmhouse. Why did you call me? If you know she's innocent…"

"Because you already have a relationship with her." Joshua leaned against the wall with his arms folded.

"Back when I was a cad."

"I'm always going to be her boyfriend's father," Joshua said. "Cam is the enemy police detective. She'll open up to you."

"Besides Heather requested an attorney," Cameron said, "and she asked for you."

"She slapped me just a couple of days ago."

"She'll forget all about that once you flash those dimples at her," Cameron said with a grin.

"If you don't think she killed her father, then why is she here?" J.J. asked.

"We're trying to figure out who the anonymous tipster is," Cameron said. "I believe Heather and Madison know. Problem is, they most likely don't know they know."

J.J. narrowed his eyes. Knowing now that it was unlikely his client was going to be charged, he wished he had stayed comfortable in his jeans and warm plaid shirt instead of changing into slacks and a sports coat.

"The tipster said Heather had been at John Davis's apartment and fought with him on the night of the murder," Cameron said. "This female tipster also claimed that she saw Heather leave the apartment with what looked like a bloody knife wrapped in a dishtowel. That knife was planted in Derek Ellison's trailer, and the dishtowel was planted in Heather's SUV."

"Derek told me on the drive up to the rehab center that he saw an angel who he had believed in his stoned state to be Lindsay," Joshua said. "Of course, his timing would be a giant question mark, but he said he found the knife the next morning. Suppose this angel was actually the killer planting the murder weapon to implicate him."

"When that frame fell apart, she decided to plant the bloody dishtowel in Heather's SUV and call in an anonymous tip," Cameron said.

"How did Heather not notice the bloody towel?" J.J. asked.

"It was concealed in the spare tire compartment," Joshua said. "When was the last time you looked in your spare tire compartment?"

"John Davis was stabbed thirty-two times," Cameron said. "Even though the killer wrapped him up in a comforter, there had to be blood all over the place. Forensics found no blood in the back of Heather's SUV and it hasn't been cleaned recently."

"This anonymous tipster had to know about Derek's threats and that Heather had gone to her father's apartment on the night of the murder," J.J. said. "That means she's the killer."

"Right now, the only suspect who meets both of those conditions is Madison," Cameron said.

"Heather claims it was Madison," Joshua said.

"But Madison is Heather's alibi," Cameron said. "The two of them were getting drunk after confronting Davis at the Time Out Bar and Grill. Both the bartender and a customer can vouch for them being there during the kill window."

"Elizabeth Collins claimed to be with Madison that night," J.J. said.

"That was a lie Elizabeth had fed to her husband," Cameron said. "She was out cheating on him and she used Madison as her cover. When you asked Madison where she was—"

"Aaron was there," J.J. said with a nod of his head.

"Elizabeth had to jump in to say Madison was with her to cover for herself."

"They didn't do it," Joshua said.

"Heather now thinks Madison, her sister, is the anonymous tipster," Cameron said. "Those two enemies had set all differences aside to become sisters and now this happens."

J.J. turned around to look at the door where Cameron was looking over his shoulder. Clad in a royal blue fur trimmed coat, Madison shivered.

"Oh," J.J. said, "I get it. You're asking the former lover and cheat to play big brother and arbitrator to bring these two sisters back together again."

"I'm more interested in finding out who anonymous is so that we can find a killer," Cameron said, "and I think these two have to work together to help us find her."

"What are we going to do if the killer ends up being one of their mothers?" J.J. asked.

"What's she doing here?" Heather charged at Madison as soon as she saw her enter the interview room ahead of J.J.

"Just give her a minute to explain!" J.J. threw himself between the two women who went at each other.

"You set me up!" Heather tried to reach around J.J. to get at Madison.

"I tried to help you!" Madison replied.

"By telling them that we were there? I told you to tell the police that you were working at the studio alone."

"Yeah," J.J. said with sarcasm. "Never tell the truth when you can come up with a nice lie."

"You should know, J.J.!" Heather said.

"I never lied to either of you and you know that!"

"I never should have trusted you!" Heather said to Madison. "You probably planned on setting me up from the very instant you got that notification from the website. I'll bet you knew all along that Dad was a cheat and when you found out I was your sister, you figured you'd have your cake and eat it too by killing him and framing me. You always were jealous of me."

"Me? Jealous of you? Give me a break!" Madison said. "How do I know you didn't set me up? Getting me good and drunk so that I would pass out. Then you went and killed him."

"And then call in an anonymous tip on myself?" Heather's eyes were wide.

"Heather's right," J.J. said. "That wouldn't be a very good plan."

"Unless she made it look like she was being framed to take suspicion off herself so that you'd think I was framing her."

"That doesn't even make sense," Heather said.

"People saw us at Dad's apartment," Madison said. "Remember that old woman in the wheelchair?"

"The one smoking up a chimney in twenty-degree weather?" Heather shuddered.

"She saw us there."

"When Madison threw you under the bus, she threw herself under the wheels as well," J.J. said. "The fact is neither of you set the other up. Neither of you killed your father."

"Then why are we here?" Heather asked.

"Because apparently your father's killer knew the two of you were at his apartment that night," J.J. said. "They knew enough about Derek to frame him by planting the murder weapon in his trailer and had access to Heather's SUV to plant the dishtowel." He urged them to sit at the table. "In order for us to track down his killer, you both need to come clean with everything that you can remember about that night. Exactly where you were, what was said, who was around to witness it. Everything you can think of."

Seeing that the fight between the two women was over, Cameron and Joshua entered the interrogation room.

"Do you think that maybe the two of you can trust each other enough to work together?" Joshua asked.

Madison and Heather's expressions were filled with an equal mixture of distrust and guilt.

J.J. pulled out two chairs, set next to each other, from the table. "Something I learned growing up is that with family you have everything. Without it, you have nothing. You two need to work together to get justice for your dad—who, in spite of being a bigamist, did love both of his families."

"Sit down," Cameron said.

Madison and Heather sat at the table.

"I didn't call in the tip," Madison said.

"I guess I knew that all along," Heather said. "I just couldn't think of who else could have planted that dishtowel."

They dared to smile at each other.

"Madison," Cameron said, "you told me that you waited for your father to leave Shippingport after work on Friday. What time did he leave?"

"It was close to six when he left. I had parked in the visitors' lot at five o'clock and waited for him to leave for like an hour."

"I couldn't follow him because I had that stupid blind date," Heather said. "One of my co-workers had set it up a couple of weeks ago."

"But you have the dance studio, Madison," Joshua said. "Did you have to contact any students to reschedule lessons?"

"Luckily, I didn't have any scheduled," Madison said. "My studio is still working on getting students."

"Did you just close up shop?" Joshua asked. "I mean—"

"Elizabeth worked the office in case someone walked in for information," Madison said. "We close at five o'clock on Fridays—unless I have lessons scheduled."

"What excuse did you tell Elizabeth for leaving early?" Cameron asked.

"I just told her I was meeting someone for drinks and left," Madison said. "She's my employee. I don't have to report to her."

Cameron noticed Heather roll her eyes in J.J.'s direction. "What was that about, Heather?"

"What?"

"You just rolled your eyes like my fourteen-year-old. What was that about?"

"It has nothing to do with Dad."

"Let us decide that," Joshua said. "Why did you just roll your eyes when Madison mentioned not having to report to Elizabeth? What were you thinking?"

Heather chewed on her bottom lip. "Truthfully?"

"No, I want a bold-faced lie," Cameron replied.

Heather uttered a sigh. "Elizabeth and my sister became friends after I went to college." She told J.J., "You were gone by then. Things were rough for Lindsay—having a baby, being married to a loser, being broke all the time. Her real friends had left the area to get jobs and go to college. Turns out Elizabeth got pregnant about the same time and married Aaron. They moved into the trailer in the lot behind Lindsay and Derek. Their babies were the same age. They were both broke and lonely. I guess, at first, it was nice having a friend stop in to keep her company, but after a while…" She turned to Madison. "Lindsay couldn't get rid of her."

"She did kind of force her way into the job at the studio," Madison said. "I really wasn't ready to hire anyone yet. I'm still trying to get on my feet."

"I've always felt like she killed Lindsay."

Joshua sat up in his seat. "What do you mean? She killed Lindsay? Wasn't it an accident?"

Heather's usually confident demeanor fell. "Lindsay and I had a fight that night. Luke's birthday was coming up. I had an opportunity to go to a conference in Colorado. It was a fabulous networking opportunity. I couldn't pass it up. Lindsay took it personally. To make it worse, she blabbed to Elizabeth about it. The last time I talked to my sister, she'd called me on the phone from Chester Park where she and Elizabeth were drinking and doing Lord knows what."

"Lindsay was at Chester Park that night?" Joshua asked.

Heather rolled her eyes. "That was her and Elizabeth's favorite hang out spot. They'd get pizza and booze at the drive-thru and then go to the park to eat and drink and do heroin. Lindsay got good and wasted. She called me to cuss me out saying that if I was a real sister I'd be there for Luke's birthday. I could hear Elizabeth in the background egging her on."

"Do you know for a fact that Elizabeth was with her?" Joshua asked.

"Of course. At one point, Elizabeth grabbed the phone from her said that Lindsay had fired me as her sister. *She* was now Lindsay's sister." She stopped to catch her breath. Her face contorted with emotion. "They disconnected the call before I could say anything."

Madison draped her arm across her shoulders.

"A couple of hours later, my sister was gone," Heather said in a soft voice.

Exhausted, Cameron went straight to bed as soon as they had gotten home from Lisbon. Thankfully, Tracy and Hunter had offered to allow Izzy to sleep over at their place since they suspected it would be a late night of interrogations. Joshua had given strict orders that Izzy work on her science project instead of bridal shower stuff. Tracy had promised that she'd make sure Izzy stayed focused.

Feeling a dire need for ice cream, Joshua went into the kitchen to find Admiral and Irving sitting side by side.

The animals looked up at him as if to demand an explanation for why Izzy wasn't there for them to sleep with. Her bed was cold and lonely without her. If they had arms, they would have been folded across their furry chests.

"She'll be back tomorrow."

Both cocked their heads at identical angles.

Joshua gave them each a treat and patted them on the head to send on their way. In the refrigerator, he discovered a pan of brownies—a little goodie left by Tracy when she had picked up Izzy.

"What a woman," he mused.

He placed two brownies on the bottom of a big bowl, topped them with two scoops of ice cream, hot fudge, whipped cream, and two cherries. With a wicked grin, he took his concoction upstairs to present to his bride.

Cameron was already undressed and in bed. With the comforter pulled up to her shoulders, she lay on her back with her fingers laced behind her head. Deep in thought, she stared up at the ceiling. He recognized the far-away look in her eyes.

Playful, he bent over at the waist and followed her line of sight to the ceiling. "What are you looking at?"

"My case."

"And what do you see?"

"I see ice cream." She sprung upright and held out her hands. In doing so, the comforter fell to reveal her naked bosom.

"I see your girls."

"Wanna trade?"

He handed the treat to her. "I don't think those will look as good on me." He proceeded to undress. "What are you in such deep thought about?"

"Why did John Davis go back to his apartment in Calcutta?" she asked around a mouthful of ice cream and a brain freeze. "Madison and Heather had been keeping tabs on him and figured out his routine. Knowing that he would be returning to the Davis family on Friday, Madison followed him from the Whitaker house in the morning. He went to Calcutta where he switched from the downhome trucker who did woodworking—"

"Woodworking?" Joshua tossed his clothes in the hamper.

"You should see his workshop." She let out a moan of pleasure upon discovering the brownies on the bottom. "You do love me."

He slipped into bed next to her. "Don't thank me. Thank Tracy. She left them for us."

She spoon-fed him a taste of ice cream coated with hot fudge and a bite of brownie. While he enjoyed it, she said, "Madison says he does beautiful woodwork."

"I've never known John to do anything with his hands. He doesn't even mow his own lawn."

"I'm beginning to suspect John Davis and Shawn Whitaker were two sides of the same man," Cameron said.

"Do you mean like a split personality?"

"I wouldn't go so far as to call it a mental illness," Cameron said. "I get the sense that Kathleen is a very controlling person."

"I couldn't live with her."

"People like Kathleen are usually the way they are because they have to be," she said. "They're the adults in the room. Every room needs an adult—someone to keep things in order—otherwise you have chaos. But sometimes, when you control someone too much, you can end up stifling who they really are."

"Like a corporate vice president who has a secret love for woodworking," Joshua said.

"Would Kathleen have let John set up a workshop in their garage?" She handed the bowl, with a generous share of ice cream left, back to him.

"The John Davis I knew may have assumed Kathleen would have considered it pedestrian and disapproved." He dug into the last of the brownies.

"Would he have even asked?"

"Maybe he was afraid of disappointing her by revealing that side of him," Joshua said. "He told Madison and Heather that he loved both of his wives. I think he was telling them the truth. In all the years that I knew them, I never saw any clue that John did not adore Kathleen."

"But there was this side of him that he feared she would not approve of," Cameron said.

"A side that loved working with his hands and driving a manly truck. That side fell in love with Sherry Whitaker."

"Is there a secret side that you're afraid to show me?" she asked.

Looking at her out of the corner of his eye, he set the bowl on the night table.

"I know, your smartass side. I know that side all too well." Seeing a small mound of ice cream left, she reached across him to pick up the bowl and finish off the treat. "To get back to my point. On Friday morning, Shawn Whitaker turned into John Davis. Suit and tie. Audi. Cell phone. He went to Shippingport and worked all day. About six o'clock, he left the office. Madison followed him to the apartment in Calcutta." She tapped his chin with the bottom of the spoon. "He had his clothes, phone, and Audi—everything he needed to be John Davis. Why didn't he go straight to Chester? Why go back to Calcutta?"

"Good question. Maybe he forgot something. Maybe he picked up the wrong phone."

"I think he went to pay someone off," she said. "He had that ten-thousand-dollars in cash, which he had withdrawn that afternoon. Madison told me she saw a thick brown envelope on the counter when they had confronted him. He'd folded it up and put it in his jacket pocket. He had no brown envelope on him when we found his body. Sometime between eight o'clock, when the daughters left the apartment, and midnight when Davis's body was found, someone took that money and killed him."

"Who?"

"Whoever it is knew about Davis's double life." Cameron put the empty bowl on her nightstand. "It was a woman and she'd called him on both phones. He called her Bea."

"Bea Miller?"

"I think Bea Miller is too paranoid to go anywhere near him."

"We both know of murders committed by paranoids who have been so deluded that they think they're killing in self-defense."

"I think Bea Miller is too paranoid to leave her house, but I could be wrong." She wrapped her arms around him and rested her head on his chest. "She wouldn't be asking Davis for money anyway. Money would be of no interest to her."

Joshua reached up and turned off the light on his nightstand. "Maybe the old woman smoking up a chimney saw who went in after Madison and Heather had left."

Cameron sat up and turned on the light on her nightstand. "What did you say?"

"The old woman smoking up a chimney in twenty degrees. Didn't you hear that part of the fight between Madison and Heather this evening?"

"How did I miss that? It had to be Brenda Bayles. She saw them leave the apartment. I got her statement today. She was waiting for Ross to come back after sending him to get cigarettes. She told me that she was watching for him because she was on the verge of nicotine withdrawal."

He sat up on his elbows. "Are you sure she was out of cigarettes? Maybe she was just low."

"Ross told me that it was an emergency because she went to get a cigarette and had none."

They stared at each other with realization.

Joshua broke the stunned silence. "If she was out of cigarettes, how could she have been smoking up a chimney while watching Madison and Heather leave Davis's apartment?"

"B! Brenda Bayles!" Cameron frowned. "She wasn't waiting for her husband to come back with cigarettes. She'd sent Ross out so that she could go pick up her extortion money."

"As apartment manager, they have keys to all of the apartments," he said. "She's sitting there in that wheelchair all day watching people come and go. She had to notice that Davis was coming in an Audi and leaving in a truck. She noticed the change in his clothes and styles. She got nosy and searched his apartment. She figured out that he was a bigamist and saw a big payday."

"She blackmailed Davis," she said. "He went back to Calcutta to pay her off, but when Heather and Madison confronted him, he saw that it was out there anyway. Would you have paid the extortion money then?"

"No way."

"Brenda must have lost it when he refused to pay up and stabbed him to death."

"In that wheelchair?" Joshua shook his head. "Her husband must have been in on it. Do you even know if he actually did go out to get cigarettes?"

"She can get out of that chair," Cameron said. "I saw her. I'm willing to bet if she was mad enough, she could have flown out of it to stab Davis if she wasn't getting her payoff. Then, Ross went in to clean up and dump the body. That has to be it. They killed him."

CHAPTER TWENTY

The next morning, Cameron decided to finish her first pot of coffee before nagging Tony about the whereabouts of Brenda Bayles's background check. She was preparing the second pot when she felt like she was being watched. Hand on her weapon, she turned around to see two pairs of eyes filled with angst.

"I fed you two."

Admiral's eyes flicked in the direction of the biscuit jar. Irving uttered a low growl in his throat.

With a sigh, Cameron punched the button on the coffee-maker to set the pot brewing and reached for the biscuit and the cat treat jars. After handing them out, Admiral and Irving remained in their spots—still gazing up at her.

"I'm sorry. Did I forget to sprinkle them with the extra special love spice that Izzy uses?"

With another growl, Irving stood up, turned around, hitched his tail up at her, and walked away. Admiral, how-ever, was willing to give her another chance to get it right. She tossed a second biscuit in his direction.

She found Tony in her phone's contacts, pressed the button to call him, and focused on willing the coffeemaker to brew faster.

The speaker uttered the sound of the phone ringing when Irving scurried out the back door as J.J. opened it. Holding the door open, he jerked his chin at the wraparound porch. "Dad was supposed to leave his floor sander for me."

"Hey, Gates," Tony said from the other end of the call. "I assume you're wanting to hear what I found out from Brenda Bayles's background check."

"Where's Dad?" J.J. asked her in a low voice.

"He's got a meeting this morning," Cameron said hurriedly. "Tony, what did you find out about Bayles?"

"Oh, she's a real piece of work," Tony said. "I'll start with the highlights."

"He said he'd leave it out here for me to pick up." J.J. went back out onto the porch.

Tony continued, "She'd spent seven years in prison for second-degree murder. That was forty years ago. I found that under her maiden name of Jarvis."

"Bingo!" Cameron felt like jumping up and down. With a sense of satisfaction, she poured a fresh cup of coffee.

J.J. returned and went into the pantry to search there.

Tony went on. "She and her boyfriend shot and killed a clerk while robbing a convenience store in Canfield."

J.J. stepped out of the pantry to listen.

"He was sixteen. She was eighteen," Tony said. "He said she'd pulled the trigger. She claimed it was him. Since he was a juvie, authorities took his side. He testified against her and got two years in juvie detention. She got seven years in prison."

"This was in Canfield?" J.J. asked.

"That's where the robbery happened," Tony said. "She and Ross Bayles moved here from Youngstown four months ago."

"Davis started getting the phone calls from someone he called 'Bea' four months ago," Cameron said. "Since he had been harassed by Bea Miller, he may have assumed the calls were from her. Or, Brenda could have given him her first initial. Whatever it may be, the time period between when the Bayles moved here and the phone calls started is a match."

"Brenda has been arrested numerous times for DUI," Tony said. "She's also had a few arrests for bar fights. A few years ago, she got into a car accident. This time, her husband was driving. She broke her back in three places. I read one statement that said she didn't do the physical therapy. That's why she's in a wheelchair."

"I saw her get out of that wheelchair," Cameron said.

"She's probably able to get up and down, but not necessarily walk," J.J. said.

"Her rap sheet certainly got quieter since she landed in the wheelchair," Tony said. "Probably because she can't get out to drink and cause trouble like she used to."

"Bishop Moore is from Canfield," J.J. said.

Cameron shook her head. "His last known address was North Jackson."

"Bishop Moore was run over in Austintown thirteen years ago," Tony said.

"Ross Bayles told us that Bishop Moore was from *Canfield*," J.J. said. "The day that we went to Moore's apartment and he let us in, he told us that Moore was from Canfield."

"That's right," Cameron said. "How did I miss that?"

"I missed it, too. In the office, Bayles told me that he didn't know that much about Moore."

"But he did know that Moore was from Canfield," Cameron said, "which he isn't."

"Maybe it was on Moore's rental application," Tony said.

"The convenience store that Brenda Bayles and her boyfriend robbed was in Canfield," J.J. said. "The boyfriend testified against Brenda to send her to jail for seven years. Ross says Bishop Moore is from Canfield, when there's no paper-trail to indicate that. Maybe Ross said that because Moore is the one who sent his wife to prison."

"Can't be," Cameron said with a shake of her head. "Bishop Moore is nothing more than an identity that John Davis stole. The real Bishop Moore was killed thirteen years ago."

"Run down in a bar parking lot," Tony said.

"Brenda Bayles went to jail for murder forty years ago," J.J. said. "Since that time, she'd done a lot of drinking and drugs. Anyone can see that her brain has fermented. John Davis was about the right age—using Bishop Moore's information—"

"Tony, what's Brenda Bayles's age?" Cameron asked.

"She's fifty-eight," Tony said. "According to the records we have for Bishop Moore, based on the social security number …" there was a long pause. "Fifty-six."

"The same age as Brenda Bayles's juvie accomplice," J.J. said.

"What previous address did he list on his rental application?" Cameron asked Tony while keeping an eye on J.J.

"The same address Bishop Moore was living at when he was killed," Tony said. "North Jackson. Not Canfield."

"Did your background check show where Moore graduated from high school?" Cameron asked.

There was another silence while Tony checked his records.

Cameron said, "If he was sentenced to a juvie deten—"

"Nothing in his records about ever graduating from high school," Tony said.

"If Bishop Moore testified against Bayles to get her sent to prison," Cameron said, "that would give her real motive for stabbing him thirty-two times. It would also explain why she hated him so much."

"But the real Bishop Moore is dead," Tony said.

"Brenda Bayles is an insanely bitter woman," Cameron said.

"After forty years of bitterness, she's at rock bottom," J.J. said. "It must have eaten away at her every time she saw him attractive and seemingly successful."

"She even told me that he used his good looks to suck the life out of women."

"That's probably what the guy who testified against her to send her to jail did," J.J. said. "At least from where she sat."

"She sees a man who is approximately the same age by the same name from the same area as the guy who had sent her to jail," Cameron said. "It probably never occurred to her that it wasn't him. She spies on him and gets some goods to blackmail him. If Bayles was blackmailing Davis for being a bigamist, why would he still pay it after Madison and Heather confronted him?"

"I wouldn't have," J.J. said. "If it's out there, what's the point?"

"And that's why Brenda killed him," Cameron said. "He still had the blackmail money when Heather and Madison confronted him. After they left, he told Brenda to take a hike. She refused to let this opportunity for payback slip by, so she released all the fury that has built up and stabbed him to death."

"Excuse me." Tony's voice uttered from the phone's speaker. "Do you have any evidence of that? Remember, this guy is not the real Bishop Moore. Even if we get the juvie file opened and find that the Bishop Moore from North Jackson was the guy who'd sent Brenda Jarvis to jail for murder, the guy in Calcutta didn't. So she has no motive to kill that guy."

"Unless you can prove that Brenda Bayles *believed* the victim was the same Bishop Moore who had sent her to jail," J.J. said.

"And that she took the ten thousand dollars that he withdrew from the bank on the day of the murder," Cameron said. "Tony, did you get a report back from the phone records?'

"There's one phone number that made regular calls on both Shawn Whitaker's and John Davis's phones," Tony said. "That call came from a pre-paid burner phone."

"Of course," Cameron said. "Tony, call Lieutenant Parks at the sheriff's department to get working on a search warrant for the Bayles office and apartment. If we find that phone and the money, then we'll have them."

After disconnecting the call, Cameron looked at J.J. who was still glancing around the kitchen. "I'm going to catch a killer today." Mug in hand, she ran up the back stairs to get dressed.

J.J. heard a long mournful whine next to him. Admiral gazed up at him, then looked over at the biscuit jar, and then back again. "Don't they ever feed you?" He gave the dog a biscuit. With a sigh, he petted the grateful dog. "I don't suppose you know where Dad put the sander."

After finishing the biscuit, Admiral looked up at J.J. and licked his chops. He wasn't talking.

"Check out ur website."

Madison smiled upon reading Heather's text.

At the kitchen table, she brought the cup of herbal tea to her lips while swiping her thumb across the screen of her phone to open the website. To her surprise, Heather had uploaded a video of Madison dancing at the state competition from years before. She had placed it on her homepage. Madison was so enthralled by the video that she didn't notice the three puppies chewing on her bare toes under the kitchen table.

"Where did u get that?" she texted Heather before picking up one of the pups, who squeaked at her.

"Found it on the state competition's website archives. Downloaded it. Great promotion potential."

"What are you smiling at?" Sherry Whitaker asked.

Madison felt like her bottom had left her seat when she jumped upon hearing her mother's voice from behind the chair. She placed the phone face down on the table and sipped her tea.

Squinting at Madison's flustered state, Sherry set down the cocker spaniel she was carrying and held up her hand in a signal for the dog to stay. "Are you okay?"

"You scared me. I guess we're all on edge."

"I know I certainly am." Sherry strapped a fanny pouch in which she carried training treats around her waist. "I haven't slept in days. The only thing that keeps me sane is working with these dears. It takes my mind off of what your father may or may not be going through. Or, worst case—" She broke down.

Madison draped an arm across her shoulders. "I miss him, too."

Sherry took the pup that Madison held and sighed. "I'll be okay."

"I know you will. We both will."

"I'm going to tell you a little secret," Sherry said in a low voice. "One I've never told anyone."

Fearful that her mother was about to make a confession that would move her to the top of the police's suspect list, Madison held her breath.

"One of the things I loved most about your father was"— a slim smile crossed her lips—"him being gone all the time."

"You loved Dad most when he was gone?"

Sherry giggled. "I loved him. He loved me. I had no doubt about that. But he let me be who I am"—she gestured at the puppies littering the kitchen—"puppies and all. I always knew I was a little weird."

"Mom, you're not weird."

"Yes, I am." Sherry rubbed her face in the puppy's fur. "I love my dogs—being outdoors working with them. I don't like worrying about my weight, drinking a beer at the end of the day, and dancing to Keith Urban. I am who I am and that's who I am. And you know what? Your father said he loved that the most about me. He accepted who I was, and I accepted him the same way." A tear traveled down her cheek. "When he was gone, I didn't have to take care of any man. And I didn't have to do it when he was back. We just accepted and loved and appreciated each other the way we were." She sighed. "There will never be another man like him."

"That's for sure," Madison said.

"But I'll be okay." Sherry patted her hand. "Because I've learned through the years, I don't need a man. I wanted your father. I loved your father. I so enjoyed being with him. But I never *needed* your father." She put the puppy down. "He was a nice-to-have. And *you* don't need any man either." She snapped the leash onto the cocker spaniel. "Oh, I heard from Lieutenant Gates this morning. She'd like for us to meet her at her house later on today to update us on what she has."

Madison's stomach twisted as she thought about how heartbroken her mother was going to be upon learning of her father's betrayal. "In Chester?"

"She'll call later on with the time." Telling the cocker spaniel to heel, she headed out the back door. "That's the worst thing. Not knowing. Even if it's bad news, I just want to know what's happened to my Shawn."

"So do I," Madison said as her phone buzzed.

"Even if she's found your father with amnesia in a small town in Montana married to another woman with a bunch of children, at least I'll know and we can move on from there," Sherry said on her way out the door with the dog. "Come along, Allister."

"That sounds totally plausible." Madison groaned when she read the caller ID. It was Elizabeth.

In an instant, she recalled Heather's account of how Elizabeth had sucked the life out of Lindsay. There were times when she felt the same way—like Elizabeth was a leech who had latched onto her and was sucking the life out of her. She considered letting the call go to voice mail, but instead answered.

"Hey, Maddie, what are you doing?"

"I'm helping Mom with the puppies." Madison took in a deep breath. "I was going to call you."

"I guess great minds think alike."

"I only have one lesson scheduled for today. J.J. and Poppy this afternoon. How about if you take the day off and spend some time with your little ones?"

"But you need me."

"Mom needs me," Madison said. "I've been so focused on the dance studio that I've been leaving Mom to handle Dad being missing all on her own. She just broke down here. I should be here for her, and you know what, you need to be there for your family. So, I'm just going to go into the studio this afternoon to work with J.J. and Poppy. Then, I'll come home."

"I'll come over, too."

"What?" Madison felt her heart skip a beat.

"I'm your best friend," Elizabeth said. "I need to be there for you."

Panic set in as Madison listened to her.

"What kind of friend would I be if I abandoned you in your time of need? I'll come over and—"

"No!"

Elizabeth paused before asking, "What?"

"Mom really doesn't feel like company right now."

"I'm not company. I'm your sister."

Madison felt her mouth drop open. Her head spun while she thought of how best to respond. "Mom and I just want to be alone in our grief right now. Bye, Elizabeth."

"That sounds pretty final, Maddie." Elizabeth's tone shifted. Her voice was low—even threatening. "What did Heather tell you about me?"

"Nothing. What would she have to tell me? She barely even knows you."

"Then why are you blowing me off?"

"Seriously? I thought we were out of high school." The phone chimed in her ear to signal an incoming call. Madison checked the screen to see that it was Heather. "I have to go. Heather's calling me." She regretted saying it as soon as the words exited her mouth. Elizabeth was cursing when Madison disconnected the call.

"Hey, did your mom hear from Cameron?" Heather asked. "She wants to meet at the Thornton house later on this afternoon. Are you going to be there?"

"I think I should. Don't you?"

"Yeah. It will help to cushion the blow. Mom's head is going to explode."

"Heather," Madison said, "what kind of marriage did Dad have with your mother?"

"If you want to call it that?" Heather laughed. "Well, Dad was gone half of the time. You already know that. It isn't like it was all Dad's fault. I don't know if you ever noticed, but Mom is OCD. Don't get me wrong. I love my mother and I know I am a lot like her, but everything has to be her way or she'll freak out. Dad once pointed out that she went through five vacuum cleaners in four years because she couldn't handle a speck of dirt. It would drive her nuts. Dad learned to just go along with it."

Madison looked down at the shredded newspaper that the puppies had thrown about the kitchen. "He wouldn't have stayed if he didn't love her. He told us. I was freaking out so much when we talked to him, but now I remember him saying that he loved all of us equally."

"I know," Heather said. "Listen, are you going to be at the studio this afternoon? I have some logo samples I want to show you. We need to get working on your brand if we want you to stand out."

"Lunch."

"Coffee shop."

"See you at noon, sis!"

They giggled. It was their first term of endearment as sisters.

"See you, sis," Heather replied.

CHAPTER TWENTY-ONE

Hunter Gardner was nervous. Joshua could see his leg shaking where he was sitting across from Sheriff Sawyer, who was reading the accident report that his deputy had put together.

When he'd finished, Sheriff Sawyer placed the report down in the center of his desk. "You're telling me that your computer program says Lindsay Ellison wasn't driving at the time of the accident."

"There's no way the wheels could have been turned out of the skid after Lindsay had been thrown from the car," Hunter said, "unless someone else was behind the steering wheel to do it."

"Not only that, but Lindsay was thrown out of the passenger side of the car," Joshua said. "That's how she ended up with a bruise outlining the gas cap door on her shoulder."

"And for some reason you believe it was Elizabeth Collins driving? Her best friend—"

"And drinking buddy," Hunter said. "I've talked to quite a few witnesses who claim those two were tight, and they saw them together the night of the accident."

"I'd interviewed witnesses at the time of the accident, too," the sheriff said. "They told me that the two of them had been eating pizza and drinking down in Chester Park. I've talked to Elizabeth myself."

"I saw your notes in the file, sir," Hunter said.

"Elizabeth told me that Aaron, her husband, had picked her up at the park about eleven o'clock," the sheriff said. "Aaron had offered to drive Lindsay home because he saw that she was under the influence. She'd refused and they'd left her there alone with a bottle of vodka."

"Maybe it was one of her other friends from the park who'd driven her home," Hunter said.

"No," Joshua said. "It had to be Elizabeth."

"But Aaron says—"

"Aaron is lying to cover for his wife," Joshua said. "The Collins home was less than a mile from the accident."

"The Collins lived in the trailer behind the Ellisons," Hunter said. "Even highly intoxicated, Elizabeth could have walked it."

"Could have," Sheriff Sawyer said. "'Could have' doesn't mean she did."

"Heather Davis told us last night that she and Lindsay had a fight that night."

"That's in my report, too," the sheriff said. "That's why Lindsay went out drinking."

"With Elizabeth," Joshua said. "The Collins lived in the lot behind the Ellisons. Elizabeth was there all the time. Heather told me that Elizabeth fed the fight and got Lindsay all worked up. The last time Heather talked to Lindsay, Elizabeth got on the phone and said that Lindsay had fired her as her sister. A couple of hours later, Lindsay was dead."

"I admit that's an awful last conversation to have with your sister before she's killed," Sheriff Sawyer said, "but it was a couple of hours before the accident. Aaron apparently picked Elizabeth up right after that call."

"I've raised daughters," Joshua said. "These two were teenagers at the time. Teenaged girls. They were drinking and doing drugs. We're talking about a cocktail of hormones and booze and chemicals. That creates drama." He leaned across Sheriff Sawyer's desk. "My gut is telling me that even if Aaron did swing by to pick Elizabeth up, she and Lindsay would have been too worked up to stop."

"Josh," the sheriff said, "you're the prosecuting attorney. It's your decision about picking up Elizabeth Collins. Are you really going to sit there and tell me that if I went to you with this"—he held up Hunter's report—"that you'd go for it?"

Joshua shook his head.

"Do either of you have any proof, evidence, that Elizabeth was the one behind the wheel to turn the tires out of that skid?" Sheriff Sawyer asked. "Anyone see her get behind the wheel of Lindsay's car on the night of the accident?"

Both Joshua and Hunter were silent.

"I didn't think so." Sheriff Sawyer handed the report back to Hunter.

"Is the Ellison car still around?" Joshua asked.

"If it is, it's probably out at the impound yard," the sheriff said.

"Maybe if we take a good look at it, we'll be able to find some—" Hunter said.

"Elizabeth stated that Lindsay drove her to the park that evening," the sheriff said. "So if you find any evidence that she was in the car, she'll simply say she left it there on the way to the park."

"You'll never know what you might find if you don't look," Joshua said.

"Knock yourselves out," Sheriff Sawyer said.

Cameron turned into the apartment complex directly behind Tony's cruiser. They parked next to each other in the visitors' lot. Lieutenant Parks's car and an additional marked sheriff deputy's cruiser took up two other spaces.

Cameron greeted Tony with a nod of her head. Beyond him, she saw Ross Bayles strapping down a rolled up carpet in the bed of his pickup truck.

When the apartment manager saw the police, he waved to them. "Back again?"

Lieutenant Parks took the search warrant from his coat pocket as the group made their way toward him. "Mr. Bayles, we've got a warrant to search your office, apartment, and vehicles." He held the warrant out for him to examine.

Ross took the papers. "Why would I have wanted to hurt Moore?"

"Not you," Cameron said. "Your wife. Brenda. Back forty years ago, her sixteen-year-old boyfriend and she robbed a convenience store in Canfield. One of them shot and killed the clerk. Her boyfriend testified against her—saying that she pulled the trigger. Because of him, she spent seven years in jail for second-degree murder."

"We got the court to unseal the records," Lieutenant Parks said. "Her boyfriend's name was Bishop Moore."

"But then, you already knew that," Cameron said. "The night we searched Moore's apartment, you told us that Bishop Moore was from Canfield. Yet, nowhere on his apartment paperwork did Bishop Moore indicate that he was from Canfield. Your wife recognized the name and she told you that he was the one who sold her out forty years ago."

"Yeah, I knew all about Bishop Moore." Ross jerked his thumb in the direction of the apartment where Davis had been killed. "But that guy wasn't the same Bishop Moore. That bum was killed years ago. Some drunk ran their truck over him."

"Maybe she didn't know her former boyfriend was dead," Tony said.

"Nah, she knew. She was the one who told me about it."

Lieutenant Parks gestured for Ross to open the office door. "We'll be wanting to interview your wife."

Ross's face turned red. "She's gone. Had a doctor's appointment this morning."

"If she's at the doctor's office, what are you doing here?" Cameron asked. "She certainly couldn't have taken herself."

"A friend." Ross cast quick glances at Tony and one of the deputies moving toward the back of the truck. The deputy carried a forensics kit to search for physical evidence.

Cameron bit her tongue to keep from expressing doubt about Brenda Bayles having a friend to take her to the doctor's office.

Ross wiped his brow, which was drenched in sweat despite the bitterly cold day. "Listen. I'll be the first to admit that my wife is a psychopath. She killed a man and spent time in prison. She came out crazier than she was when she went in. Whatever she did to Moore, I had no part of. I work hard to make an honest day's pay. I have to get this carpet over to a unit on the other side of the complex now or the installers are going to leave and then it'll be a bear trying to get them back."

"You can leave after we search your truck." Lieutenant Parks instructed the deputy to start with the bed of the truck.

"For what?"

"Whoever dumped the victim's body in Hookstown left tire tracks in the mud. Forensics cast impressions of them." Cameron circled the truck while examining the tires. "Based on the tread marks, our forensics people told us that we're looking for a full-sized truck or SUV." She rounded the front of the truck.

"Okay, if you insist. I need my phone to call the tenant to let him know that I'm gonna be late." Ross yanked open the driver's side door.

Cameron stepped toward the open driver's door. As she approached, she saw Ross reach under the seat. She noticed that his phone was in a case on his belt. She saw the handle of the pistol as he pulled the weapon out. "Gun!" she screamed while yanking her weapon from the holster on her hip. She jumped back, brought her foot up and delivered a kick to the door. The door slammed against Ross Bayles.

Before he was hit against the door frame, Ross managed to fire one shot at the sheriff deputy crouching in front of his open forensics case. The deputy went down with a bullet to the chest. Tony ducked behind the rear of the truck.

The door was still between Cameron and Ross Bayles. Stunned, he fumbled on his knees to get a firm grip on the gun. He intended to go down fighting. She threw her full weight against the door. The door hit Ross in the head. As he fell, Cameron held him against the door frame.

Seeing that Cameron had him pinned, Lieutenant Parks ran around and aimed his gun at Ross's head. "Drop the gun, Bayles!"

Wedged between the door and the seat of the truck, Ross seemed to consider firing his weapon again.

"I said drop it! I will shoot you!" the police lieutenant shouted at him.

His eyes wide, Ross dropped the pistol to the ground.

While Cameron kicked the dropped weapon out of reach, Parks shoved Ross to the ground and handcuffed him.

"How's the deputy?" Cameron ran over to where Tony was knelt over the deputy sprawled out on the ground.

"Wind was knocked out of him," Tony said. "The ballistics vest took the full force of the bullet.

Gasping for his breath, the deputy peeled his hands away to reveal the bullet hole. "That's gonna leave a mark."

"If you weren't wearing that vest, it would have left a whole lot more than a mark," Cameron said.

Lieutenant Parks joined them once his other deputy took charge of placing Ross Bayles in the back of their cruiser. "I guess we finally got our man."

"He didn't want us searching this truck." Cameron looked in the back of the truck. The only thing inside was the rolled-up carpet.

"Because he used this truck to dump Davis's body and knows that we'll find forensic evidence to prove it once we examine it," Tony said.

"I don't believe Brenda Bayles has any friends." Cameron tested the weight of the carpet and found it extremely heavy. "Help me pull this out."

Together, the three of them pulled the carpet from the truck and unrolled it. As they did so, Brenda Bayles's lifeless body tumbled out.

CHAPTER TWENTY-TWO

Madison arrived at the old-fashioned coffee-shop before Heather. Unlike the trendy crowded one on the other side of the shopping plaza, they preferred the one that was inexpensive, something the two young women just starting out needed. The diner had greasy food, plastic booths, and fast service.

She took a corner booth and ordered two bottled waters and grilled chicken Caesar salads. While waiting, she recalled a previous lunch at the same diner.

Was it really less than a month ago?

She was the one who had suggested to the mysterious sister that they meet there. It would have been too easy for them to miss each other in the crowd at the other coffee shop.

Madison was surprised that her sister knew precisely which diner she was suggesting. "I don't live far from there at all," she had written in her email.

The thought had crossed Madison's mind that she could have met her sister without knowing it. It was definitely a possibility in the rural tri-state area.

She racked her brain trying to figure out not only who her half-sibling could be, but also her mother's identity. The existence of a half-sibling meant her father had been unfaithful to her mother. That reality rendered Madison numb.

After getting over the initial shock, she thought over what she had seen of her parents' marriage. They were a loving family. Physically demonstrative of their affection. Madison's memory was filled with images of her parents constantly hugging and kissing each other. When in a room together, her mother always had a hand on her father, stroking him. Holding his hand. Sometimes, she would simply rest her hand on his arm.

During her adolescence, Madison would be embarrassed by how affectionate they were in public.

Maybe, Madison concluded, they had been in the middle of a trial separation during which her father had a brief relationship with another woman.

Discretely, Madison had asked her mother if she and her father ever had any problems during their marriage. After a hearty laugh, Sherry replied with a firm, "No. Why do you ask?"

Madison said she was just wondering what the secret was to a happy marriage.

"Trust," her mother answered. "Complete trust."

At that all-important meeting, Madison instantly recognized Heather Davis when she walked in.

Figures, my archenemy shows up just as I'm about to meet dad's love child. What a sure way for it to get all over the Ohio Valley.

Heather recognized her, too. Seeing Madison, she came to a halt and looked around the diner. Madison prayed she'd sit on the other side of the restaurant—far out of earshot.

It seemed like an answer to her prayers when Heather turned on her heels and went to a booth in the opposite corner. With her back to Madison, she faced the door.

They sat—both staring at the door.

The minutes ticked by.

With dread, Madison recalled that the Heather in the email had said that she had long brunette hair.

Heather Davis had long brunette hair.

Her half-sister was the same age as she.

Heather Davis was her age.

Their meeting was twelve noon.

Heather Davis came in at twelve noon on the dot.

The flush rose from her chest, up her neck, to her cheeks.

Is it possible? No, it can't be! Heather's dad is a big shot at the nuclear power plant. Her mother is a refined lady—super mom. Dad have an affair with Kathleen Davis? In his dreams!

"Excuse me."

Madison jumped in her seat.

There she was. Heather Davis standing over her. That arrogant expression that Madison recalled from years before was gone. It was replaced with—what?

"Madison,"—she paused to lick her lips—"are you here to meet …"—she swallowed—"your sister?"

"Are you …"

Yep, it was humility on Heather Davis's face. It looked so strange there.

Madison nodded her head. "That would be me. You?"

Heather nodded her head.

Together they regarded each other in silence—their memories flooding with slights, insults, and fights over clothes, boys, and dance competitions from long ago.

"Now what do we do?" Heather asked.

Madison slipped out of the booth. "We hug it out and start all over, sister." She wrapped her arms around Heather and held her tight until she relented and hugged her back.

From that moment on, the past was gone.

A new relationship of sisterhood was born.

If they had been shocked numb by the news that they were half-sisters—the shock was heightened with the realization that their relationship was not so much the result of infidelity on their father's part but a seemingly well-organized life of bigamy.

"Hey, sis!" Heather snapped her fingers in front of Madison's face to jolt her out of her memories. "You were a thousand miles away." She slid into the other side of the booth and took her laptop out of her briefcase. "Wait until you see what I've done." She opened her laptop.

When the server arrived with their lunch. Madison waited for her to leave before she said in a soft voice, "I was just thinking about Mom and Dad. She's still hanging onto the hope that he's alive. It's going to be bad enough finding out that he's been murdered, but to find out that he had a whole second family …." Her voice trailed off. "She's going to be heartbroken."

"Dad loved your mom," Heather said in a strong voice. "He loved you."

"You say that like he didn't love your mom."

"He did go off and marry another woman and start a family with her," Heather said.

"Why would he have stayed with your mom and go to all that trouble of setting up a half-way place and going back and forth if he didn't want to be with her," Madison said. "He told us. He loved both families the same amount and couldn't leave either one."

"Even if Mom is OCD." Heather dragged her eyes from the laptop to look at Madison. "Everyone loves your mom."

"That's not true. Mom is loud and uncouth."

"You could hear her laugh all throughout that dance studio when she was there."

"Like I said, she's loud. I could be so mortified by her."

"We were both mortified by our mothers," Heather said. "Your mother just naturally makes everyone smile when they're around her." She pointed to herself. "My mom scares the crap out of them. The woman goes through three admin assistants a year."

"Maybe she's tough because she feels like she has to be," Madison said. "Obviously, Dad needed someone to keep him in line. That someone definitely isn't my mom. Every year, she has to file for an extension on her income tax because she forgets to do them."

"I remember once when Mom and I walked into Miss Charlotte's studio. Your mom was in the middle of singing with—what was her name?" She snapped her fingers. "Rosie! Linda's mom. Remember that! Your mom was cleaning up some sort of mess that some kid had made in the reception area. She had the vacuum cleaner and was singing that song from *Mrs. Doubtfire.*"

"That scene where Robin Williams was dressed up like Mrs. Doubtfire and vacuuming the floor to Aerosmith's 'Dude Looks Like a Lady'!" Madison laughed.

"Everyone was doubled over crying they were laughing so hard! Rosie and your mom were dancing with the vacuum cleaner! I thought it was so cool that your mother knew all of the words to that song."

Madison sighed. "I was horrified."

"My mom thought it was disgraceful that your mother dancing and singing *that* song in front of *innocent children*."

"Why would she think that?" Madison asked.

"Our family had a certain reputation to maintain," Heather said. "I think Dad liked being with your mother because she allowed him to take off his mask—to be who he really wanted to be. He could enjoy life." She sighed. "There isn't a lot of joy in our house—especially since Lindsay ..." Her voice trailed off.

Together, they ate in silence. Madison studied Heather's sad expression. She always turned quiet when Lindsay came up.

"Why did you take dance lessons?" Madison asked.

"Why not?"

"You were already a cheerleading captain," Madison said.

Heather corrected her. "Co-captain. Mom was very disappointed that I had to share that with Tracy Thornton."

"Student council. Newspaper. All of these things—and always at the top. You didn't need dance for your college resume. Why take it?"

"Because I like to dance," Heather said. "How's that for a reason?"

"Did you really? Do you dance now?"

"I haven't danced in years."

"At what point did it stop being fun?"

"When you started beating my butt in competition."

"Dancing isn't meant to be a competitive sport," Madison said. "Dancing is about letting the music take over your body to move you—like the way Aerosmith took over my mother that night. When you allow that to happen—then it can create a complete feeling of joy like no other. That's not competition. That's art."

Heather stared at Madison, who turned her attention to her salad. "I don't remember ever feeling anything like what you're describing."

"Because everything in your life has always been about being number one. That makes it work," Madison said. "That's why you kept coming in second in dance competitions. Your technique was perfect—every time. Every step. But you were so focused on technique that you weren't enjoying it—and the judges could see that. I heard the judges say time and time again that your technique was perfect, but there was something missing. They couldn't see what it was, but I could. You

were missing the joy that comes with loving what you're doing. If you had just loosened up to enjoy the routine, then you
would have blown me out of the water."

"Is that why you left New York?" Heather asked. "The
competition took the joy out of dance?"

"I can't even say when it started. I was living in a dumpy
apartment with five other dancers. Everyone was taking pills
to keep their energy up to take lessons all day long. Waiting
tables or tending bars at night—all so that we could be professional dancers. It was all about the dance. Then, one day, I
was at yet another audition. I had danced my heart out that
day. The choreographer told me that everything was perfect.
My leaps were the highest. My turns were right on point."
She kissed her fingertips. "Perfect-o!" She uttered a sarcastic
giggle. "Then, he told me that my breasts were too small." She
took a bite of her salad. "I was out."

"You didn't get the job because your breasts were too
small?"

"A few minutes later, I got a call from my agent. He said
this was not the first choreographer who had said that. He
suggested that I get implants. Told me that I would be guar-
anteed to get more jobs if I did that. He knew a doctor who
could do it right away and give me an artists' discount."

Heather glanced at Madison's slender frame. "Obviously,
you didn't take him up on that."

"I was hiking back to my apartment—because I didn't
have enough money for the bus—when it hit me. I thought
back—trying to remember the last time I had fun dancing.
I'd spent every waking hour trying to please agents, choreog-
raphers, dance instructors, directors, and producers. I realized
I was dancing for them—and they didn't appreciate it. Even
when I was dancing in competitions here, I danced for myself. I've always danced for myself—to bring joy to myself—
and I was lucky enough that others found joy in it, too." She

stabbed the salad. "Five days later, I was home. Never again will I dance for anyone but me."

"I wish I could learn how to do that," Heather said.

CHAPTER TWENTY-THREE

Handcuffed to a table in the interrogation room, Ross Bayles sat with his head in his hands. After being transported to the sheriff's department in Lisbon, he had been left to wait for hours. He could assume that the police were searching his office, apartment, and truck with a fine-tooth comb.

He jerked upright when Cameron breezed through the door and dropped an evidence bag containing a thick brown envelope onto the table. Reddish brown splotches marked up the envelope.

"Where did you get the ten-thousand dollars, Ross?" She dropped into the chair across from him.

Lieutenant Parks stepped into the room. His massive arms crossed, he leaned against the wall.

"Don't tell us you never saw that money before," Cameron said. "We found it in a duffle bag next to the door in your office. It was filled with your clothes and toiletries. I'm assuming you were using that for getaway money after dumping your wife's body."

"I did not kill Moore," Ross said. "Brenda did that."

"Good idea," Cameron said. "Blame the dead woman. The dead woman you killed."

"I didn't kill her," Ross said. "I found her dead this morning. I knew you guys were closing in and how it would look. I panicked. I decided to dump her where no one would find her and get the hell out of Dodge."

"And why would we be closing in if you were innocent?"

Ross let out a deep breath. "I came back from getting her cigarettes that night and Brenda was in a rage. Now, she'd fly off the handle on a regular basis, but I had never seen her like that. That was when I found out that she had tried to blackmail Moore—one of our tenants. Like I wasn't going to get fired if he ever reported that to the owners!"

"And that's why you killed her," Parks said.

"I didn't kill her!" Ross said. "You have to believe me. She must have taken too many of her pills—she's got them all over the house. That's why we're broke all the time."

"What happened Friday night?" Cameron asked.

"I had told Brenda about my noticing Moore coming and going, looking like two different people. One week, he'd be driving the burgundy Audi. The next week, he'd be wearing jeans and driving the truck. I'd made a joke about him having a split personality. Suddenly, Friday night, Brenda announces she has no cigarettes and she's beating on me to go get her cigs. So I go out."

"And stop in to see your mistress before coming back," Cameron said.

Ross raised his eyes to hers. His face hung in sadness. "The woman I married thirty years ago disappeared a long time ago."

Cameron felt a tug of sympathy. "Go on. What happened when you got back?"

"I told you. She was like I've never seen her before. Practically wrecked the place. Cursing up a storm. She ran her wheelchair over a chair and crushed it. That was when I found out that she had let herself into Moore's apartment and went snooping. She found out that he had two women. She'd gotten the phone numbers for both of his phones and had been harassing him. She ordered him to give her ten thousand dollars or she was going to blow the whistle on him to his women. She sent me out to get the cigarettes so that she could collect the money."

"And then he didn't pay," Cameron said, "you went to collect it."

"No, I did not!" Ross pounded his fists on the table. "That's why I was running. Because I knew that was what it looked like." He rubbed his face with his hands. "When I got back and found out what she'd done, I lost it. I admit it. I had given up so much for that woman. I moved her down here to get her away from her druggie friends in Youngstown. We were on our way again. But she had ruined everything. It seems Moore didn't know who was blackmailing him. He didn't know until Brenda showed up at his door. Then, he put it together. He realized that she had let herself into his apartment with the master key and snooped through his stuff. Not only did he refuse to pay her the money she demanded, but he was going to call the owners."

"Which would get you fired," Cameron said. "When you found out, you went to talk him out of it, but things went south."

"You're only half right," Ross said. "I did go to talk him out of contacting the owners, but I found him dead already. Obviously, Brenda had lied. She told me that it wasn't her, but who else would have done it? That woman was a pathological liar. I saw how mad she was. There was blood everywhere. I checked to see if there was any hope of him being alive and I found the money in his jacket pocket. I thought he didn't really need it, so I took it. I didn't even tell Brenda that I had it. I was going to stash it away in a rainy-day fund. Then, when I found her dead this morning ..." He shrugged his shoulders. "What's the use? There's no way you're going to believe me."

Cameron wondered if she was getting soft. Not only did she almost believe the guy, but she felt a tinge of sympathy for him. She was grateful for the knock on the door.

"You're not going to believe this," Tony whispered to her once she stepped into the corridor.

"Try me."

"The medical examiner says her cursory exam of Brenda Bayles indicates that she died of a massive heart attack," Tony said. "She found no obvious signs of murder."

"How about poison?"

"No obvious signs," Tony said. "The ME told me that Brenda Bayles was in obviously poor health. A broken back that never healed right and arthritis all throughout her body, which is why she couldn't walk. Swollen feet."

"Her hands were swollen, too," Cameron recalled.

"ME is going to run a tox screen, but off hand, she believes it was a heart attack."

Cameron's instinct kicked in. "She died of natural causes."

"But wait. There's more," he said. "The treads on Bayles's truck don't match those left at the Newhart farm."

"Which means Bayles didn't dump Moore's body," she said.

"Unless he has another vehicle stashed away," he said, "but DMV records don't show any."

"He didn't do it," she muttered on her way back into the interrogation room.

Ross was sitting with his head in his hands. Lieutenant Parks even appeared to have softened.

She slipped into the chair across from him. "How did Brenda seem when you got back from picking up the cigarettes?"

"I told you," Ross said. "She was crazy mad."

"You said there was blood everywhere in Moore's apartment."

"Yeah. Someone had done a real number on him."

"Did your wife have any blood on her when you got back from the store?"

Ross's face went blank. He blinked several times before saying, "No."

"Was she wearing the same clothes that she had been wearing when you'd left?"

"Yeah." He nodded his head.

"Had she bathed?"

He shook his head.

"I noticed that her hands were swollen—"

"Arthritis. She had it really bad. That's why she was collecting disability. She couldn't walk."

"I'm willing to bet she didn't have any strength in her hands," she said.

"None."

"She probably wouldn't have been able to grasp a knife in order to stab someone several times?"

In silence, Ross shook his head.

"Which means you killed Moore," Lieutenant Parks said. "After all, you had the money."

"But the tire treads on his truck don't match those found at the dump site," Cameron said in a low voice before turning back to Ross. "You've only been in the area four months. Are you familiar with Hookstown?"

"Heard of it," Ross said. "Drove through it, but don't really know where anything is."

"What did you do when you found Moore's body?"

"I told you. I took the money, but I left the body as it was and waited for someone else to find it and report it. Maybe one of his friends would come looking for him when he didn't show up at the travel agency where I thought he worked."

"Why didn't you report finding the body?"

"Because I thought Brenda had done it and I knew you'd be asking why I had gone to talk to him and then it would all come out about Brenda being a murderer."

"Your wife went to jail for murder forty years ago," Cameron said, "but that wasn't the only murder she'd committed. That's why you jumped to the conclusion that she'd killed Moore so fast. You completely knew that she was capable of it."

Ross looked at her from out of the top of his eyes.

"What are you talking about, Gates?" Lieutenant Parks asked.

"Bishop Moore," Cameron said. "The real Bishop Moore. You told us earlier that Brenda told you that he had been run down by a truck at the bar he tended in Austintown a dozen years ago. I checked. Yes, he was run over. That was reported in the news. But it was never made public that evidence indicated that the police were looking for a truck. That's what ran him over. Now, how would Brenda have known he was run down by a truck unless she was the one who did it?"

Ross clenched his fists.

"While cruising bars, Brenda ran into the old boyfriend who had sold her out and ruined her life all those years ago, didn't she? She got her revenge. She waited for him to leave the bar after it closed and ran him over. Then, she backed up over him again, just to make sure."

"You want to know the really crazy thing?" Ross said. "When we ran into this Bishop Moore here in Calcutta, she was convinced it was the same guy. I told her that she'd killed the guy already, but she didn't believe me. That crazy old bat had killed a man and forgotten all about it."

CHAPTER TWENTY-FOUR

"We don't have to do this now," J.J. told Poppy after parking his truck one block from the dance studio. "Now that Heather and Madison admit to having known for weeks about their father."

Poppy threw her head back and laughed. "Too late to turn back now, J.J. We're here. Besides, I went out and got a ballet skirt and dance shoes." She threw open the door and scrambled out of the truck. "First, we're going to learn the Viennese waltz. After that, the mambo."

J.J. grinned softly. It was plain by the bounce in Poppy's step that she was looking forward to dancing again. Most of the time, she dressed in jeans, riding boots, and skipped makeup. When working with the horses, she would braid her hair or pull it back into a ponytail. On Sundays, she would dress up in dresses, style her hair, and touch up her emerald eyes with mascara and color on her lips.

For their first dance lesson, she wore her hair up in a bun on top of her head and had put on black tights and leotard with a wrap-around skirt and sweater. She made him feel out of place in his running pants and sneakers.

They walked hand in hand down the street to the dance studio. As they drew near, they passed Heather's purple SUV.

"It isn't like it's not out in the open anymore." J.J. slowed down.

"They need to tell their mothers," Poppy said. "Better for them to hear from their daughters than the news media. You know once the media finds out, and they will, it will be all over."

"Cameron and Dad invited both families to their place tonight," J.J. said. "They think it's best to break the news on neutral ground."

As they neared the store front, a top-forty tune floated out into the street. J.J. opened the door and held it for her to step through.

"That doesn't sound like 'Endless Love,'" Poppy said.

"Where's Elizabeth?" J.J. asked as they went through the empty reception area into the studio.

They stopped when they saw Heather and Madison dancing from one end of the studio to the other. While Madison wore yoga pants and dance shoes, Heather was dressed in slacks and button-down shirt. Her feet were bare.

"Don't look in the mirror!" Madison chastised Heather while doing a jump and landing in front of Poppy. "Your form is perfect! Don't worry about it! Just feel the music and move with it. Do what your body tells you to do."

Heather stopped. "Anything?"

Her arms spread out wide, Madison spun around on her toes. "Anything!"

Heather backed up against the far wall. "You asked for it!" She took off at a run down the length of the room, took a flying leap, somersaulted, and ended with a spin on her back.

Poppy let out a gasp. Madison shrieked and clapped. J.J. was speechless. He'd halfway expect that of Madison, but not

242

Heather. By the time Heather stopped spinning, she was giggling like a maniac.

"I've *always* wanted to do that," she said while Madison pulled her up onto her feet. "I practiced for years in high school but was afraid people would think I'd lost my mind."

"You're right about that," J.J. said.

"But I had fun." Heather hugged Madison. "Never did I ever have so much fun dancing. For once, it was what I had imagined when I signed up for lessons."

Madison and Heather were giddy.

"I didn't know we were having a party."

Madison jumped at the sound of Elizabeth Collins's voice from the doorway.

With a tight grin, Elizabeth regarded them. She took off her parka to reveal that she was clad in blue dancing tights with a matching wraparound skirt. Her eyes were heavily made up with bold blue coloring and dark eye-liner. Her lips were painted bright red.

"Elizabeth," Madison said, "I thought I told you that you didn't need to come in today."

Elizabeth went behind the reception desk. "I know, but I need to work on the newsletter for our students. We need to send those out regularly if we want to keep them engaged." Grasping the medallion around her neck, she dropped into her chair.

Madison looked back and forth between Elizabeth and Heather.

J.J. opted to ease the awkward moment by suggesting that they get started on their lesson.

Heather went to put on the high-heeled shoes she had removed for dancing. "I should go. I want to see Mom before the meeting tonight."

"No, stay," Madison said. "Poppy and J.J. want to do the Viennese Waltz for their wedding. You used to do it so beautifully. Remember when you did it for the competition in our junior year? I'm sure you'll have some suggestions." She winked at her. "It'll be fun."

"Fun can be addictive." Heather dropped her bag.

"This isn't going to end in a cat fight, is it?" J.J. asked with a sly grin.

"Not unless Poppy starts it," Heather said with a giggle.

At the impound yard located in a back corner of New Cumberland, Hunter studied the vehicle number listed in the case file and compared it to the numbers on the tags glued to the windshields. Searching for the dark blue 2002 Chevy Impala, Joshua made his way up and down the rows of vehicles, many wrecked, some simply taken in for evidence in crimes.

"Even if we do find it, it's been sitting out in the elements for three years," Hunter called out in a loud voice so that Joshua could hear him wherever he was. "What makes you think there will be any viable evidence inside that car that we can use?"

"Over here!" Joshua called out to him. "I found it."

Not knowing where Joshua was, Hunter jogged down the main roadway, searching the side aisles until he found his father-in-law peering through the driver's side window of a mangled dark blue sedan.

"Sawyer's right," Hunter said. "Any evidence we find of Elizabeth being in this car, she can claim happened on the way *to* Chester Park."

"We'll never know if we don't look." Joshua pried open the driver's door and bent over at the waist to examine the inside. "There's yet another avenue we can travel."

"What's that?" Hunter went around to the other side of the car.

Joshua squatted to examine the dashboard and steering wheel. "We can talk to Aaron." As the odor of mildewed body fluids assaulted his nostrils, he grabbed his nose and stood up.

Hunter chuckled. "I told you it's been sitting out in the elements for three years."

"Smells like an old diaper pail." Joshua frowned.

"I don't have that much experience smelling diaper pails."

"Yet." Joshua bent over and put his face close to the driver's seat cushion. The strong odor of mildewed urine made him want to wretch. Once again, he covered his face and stood up.

"You look like you've found something."

Joshua rested his arms across the smashed top of the car. "Say you've been drinking. Your bladder is full, and you get behind the wheel of a car. Suddenly, you get into an automobile accident. What other type of accident are you likely to have?"

"Are you sure that's what you smell? Wouldn't it have stopped smelling by now?"

"The car's been closed up all this time," Joshua said with a shrug of his shoulders. "It's had time to ferment."

"It's been sitting in that seat cushion for three years. The car has been sitting out in the open. Even if forensics can extract DNA from the urine, most likely it's going to be so degraded that it won't be usable."

"Deputy Gardner, stop being such a pessimist. We'll never know unless we try."

"You need to point your toes more," Elizabeth said while J.J. helped Poppy into her coat.

Startled by her comment from behind the reception desk, J.J. was uncertain what to say.

As Madison had thought, Heather had some wonderfully imaginative suggestions in choreographing the waltz that they couldn't wait to try. J.J looked forward to practicing with Poppy alone—especially the dips and lifts, which they had practically nailed down by the end of the lesson.

After an hour of working hard with Madison and Heather, J.J. felt danced out. He was on dance overload and ready to go home.

Elizabeth moved on to Poppy. "You should arch your back during the fleckerl."

Poppy glanced up at J.J. "I'll keep that in mind. Thank you, Elizabeth."

Talking in low voices on a far corner of the studio, Madison and Heather cast furtive glances in Elizabeth's direction. Concerned, he went over to them and asked in a low voice, "Is everything okay?"

"I can't afford to keep Elizabeth on," Madison said. "To tell you the truth, I didn't want to hire her in the first place. We ran into each other at the mall. It was nice seeing an old friend. We met for lunch and I mentioned that I was going to open a dance studio. Next thing I knew, I couldn't get rid of her."

"Money that you spend on her wages is money that you could invest in the studio," Heather said.

"You're going to have to tell her the truth," J.J. said. "I know it's hard. I've had to let people go at the farm, but it's all part of being a business owner."

Madison frowned. "This is not fun."

"Think of it as the grown-up part of dance." Heather patted her on the shoulder.

"J.J., are you going to be at the meeting tonight?" Madison asked.

"I wasn't planning to. Cameron has no intention of charging either of you. Derek has been cleared. I've got work to do at the old farm house." Seeing their wide blue eyes boring at him, he sighed. "Do you want me to be there?"

"We could use the moral support," Heather said while putting on her coat. "Mom is going to freak."

"Your mother never did like me," J.J. said. "How would my being there help?""

"But my mom always liked you," Madison said.

"Has your mother met anyone she didn't like?"

"I see your point." With a laugh, Madison escorted the three of them toward the front door.

As they passed in front of the reception desk, Elizabeth looked up from her computer screen. A tight grin crossed her face. She slid the heart-shaped medallion back and forth on the gold chain around her neck.

Heather slowed down.

Looking up at her, Elizabeth released her fingers from the medallion to let it drop against her chest.

Heather stared at her.

J.J. opened the door. A frigid breeze rushed into the reception area and whipped around them while he held the door open. "Heather, are you coming?"

J.J.'s voice startled Heather out of her thoughts. Turning her back on Elizabeth, she hurried out onto the sidewalk.

"Are you all right, Heather?" J.J. asked while zipping up his coat.

Nodding her head, she stared straight ahead. "Is your dad going to be there tonight?"

"I assume so. It's his house. Why?"

"I need to talk to him." Heather trotted to her SUV.

"Did I miss something?" Poppy grasped J.J.'s arm. "She looks like she saw a ghost."

With a shrug, J.J. took her hand and ushered her up the street to the truck. "We need to get back home. You know how testy Ollie and Charley get when we leave them alone too long."

A few minutes later, they found themselves traveling behind Heather Davis's purple SUV on Midland-Beaver Road, a four-lane stretch between Beaver and Shippingport, at which point the road split with two lanes crossing the Ohio River and the other branch traveling on to East Liverpool.

"It's nice to see that Madison and Heather have become friends," Poppy said.

"Nice but strange. You didn't see how those two used to fight."

The SUV in front of them swerved, almost weaving into the next lane. Slowing down, J.J. wondered if Heather was distracted by something—like a text on her cell phone.

"Elizabeth doesn't seem to be too keen about their friendship," Poppy said. "She's jealous."

"I can certainly see that." .

Heather swerved again—this time in the other direction. She corrected her course, but the vehicle continued to weave back and forth.

"What's going on?" Poppy asked.

Tapping his brakes, J.J. checked his rearview mirror to change lanes and pull up alongside her. Possibly, he could see what was causing her erratic driving.

Suddenly, the rear driver's side wheel spun off the SUV's axel and flew back to hit the hood of J.J.'s truck.

Before J.J. could react, the airbags deployed. Unable to see where he was going, and aware that the SUV was directly in front of him, all J.J. could do was hit the brakes and spin the steering wheel.

The airbags deflated a split second before the truck was hit in the rear.

J.J. saw stars burst before his eyes when his forehead connected with the steering wheel.

They were then propelled backwards when the front of the truck collided with what they knew had to be Heather's

SUV. In the next beat, they were hit on the passenger side by a car that didn't have time to avoid the truck pushed into its lane by the van that had collided with its rear.

Trapped in his seatbelt, J.J. felt like he was sinking into a tunnel as the horns and tires squealed around him. Poppy's scream echoed in his ears. "Poppy?" J.J. reached for her hand. He felt her fingers wrap around his. "Are you okay?"

He heard nothing as he drifted into nothingness.

Chapter Twenty-Five

"Wake up, J.J." Poppy's voice drew him out of the depths of unconsciousness.

Beyond her strong voice, he could hear the murmurs of various people. His nostrils picked up the scent of antiseptic. With a shudder, he opened his eyes to see her smiling emerald orbs gazing down at him. Her freckled nose crinkled.

"You had me worried there for a second." She kissed him on the cheek. "Maybe you just felt like taking a nap." When she pulled back, he saw that her right arm was in a sling.

"How bad is it?" he asked, referring to her arm.

"Only a slight concussion." She brushed the fingertips from her good hand across his cheek down to his chin. "We're at Beaver Valley Hospital." He realized that he was on a gurney in an examination room. "You've been drifting in and out of consciousness since the accident."

The reminder of the accident caused J.J. to reach up to his forehead. He recalled hitting his head on the steering wheel. His fingertips felt the smooth tape holding a bandage in place.

"The doctor assures me it will be healed in time for the wedding."

He reached out to her. "What happened to your arm? Is it broken?"

"My shoulder." She adjusted the sling. "No heavy lifting for a month."

"I could have lost you," he whispered.

She stroked his face. "You'll never lose me." She kissed him softly on the lips. "When you truly love someone, they are with you always, even when they're gone."

He took her hand and kissed her fingers. "We are forever."

She let out a heavy sigh. "We're both better off than Heather."

The reminder of what had caused the accident prompted J.J. to try to sit up. She eased him back down. "Tell me she's not ..." He was unable to say the word.

"She's in a drug-induced coma," Poppy said. "Swelling of the brain. It could have been a lot worse. The airbags saved her life."

"What made her wheel come flying off her car?" J.J. asked.

"We had a four-vehicle accident on Midland-Beaver Road," Cameron told Tony while feeding a five-dollar bill into a vending machine for a soft drink. "Two of the drivers were treated and released at the scene. J.J. and Poppy were brought here by ambulance. They're being treated and will be released tonight. Heather Davis's injuries are more serious. She's in a drug-induced coma. We won't know more until tomorrow."

The detective was puzzled about why he had been summoned to Beaver Valley Hospital to investigate a car accident. After all, they were homicide detectives.

Cameron bent over to retrieve her change and drink from the vending machine. "The accident was caused by a wheel flying off an SUV. That SUV was being driven by one of the daughters of our murder victim John Davis."

Realization came to Tony's eyes.

"But wait. There's more." She took a sip of the soda. "The towing people stated that when they lifted Davis's vehicle onto the tow truck, a second wheel fell off. That got them curious. They checked and found that the two remaining wheel were both missing a lug nut and the lug nuts left on were loose." She eyed him over the top of her drink. "This was no accident. Someone was trying to kill Heather Davis." She tapped him on the chest. "That makes this our case."

"Do you think the two are connected?" Tony asked while following her through a pair of double doors to the waiting area.

She narrowed her eyes and shot him a glance over her shoulder, which prompted him to stop.

"I guess that means you do."

She led him into the waiting room where Kathleen Davis was slumped in a chair. Her usually sophisticated demeanor had been replaced with grief over her murdered husband and worry for the only daughter she had left.

Izzy was reading a children's book to Luke on a sofa across the room.

"Where's Josh?" Cameron asked as she saw him walking through the double doors with Madison and Sherry Whitaker. She opened her eyes wide and tossed her head in the direction of Kathleen Davis. "Do you think now—"

"It has to be done," Joshua said as he showed the Whitaker women into the waiting room.

Madison paused in the doorway to compose herself. "I'll tell them."

Recognizing another former dance mom, Sherry hurried across the room. "Kathleen, Madison told me about Heather's accident. We came as fast as we could." She took the chair next to her and clasped her hands. "I hadn't realized that the two girls have become friends."

The touch of her hands drawing her from her grief, Kathleen looked from Sherry to Madison and back again. Her face contorted while she tried to figure out who they were. When she did, she said, "I didn't realize they were *friends* either." She focused on Madison. "Weren't you the one who shredded Heather's homecoming gown?"

"You do remember me. I was afraid you wouldn't."

Kathleen slowly shook her head. "You aren't Heather's friend. You never were her friend."

"I had the same reaction," Sherry said. "But after Joshua Thornton called to tell us what had happened to Heather, Madison explained that they'd reconnected a few weeks ago. They patched up their differences and are BFFs now. Madison insisted that I come here with her to offer our support." She smiled comfortingly at Kathleen.

"This is some sort of trick." Kathleen pointed at Madison while slowly raising to her feet. "*You* must have done this to Heather. Somehow, you caused this accident. You probably killed John, too."

"No, that's not true."

"Kathleen, I understand what you're going through," Sherry said.

"Has someone brutally murdered your husband?" Kathleen asked.

"My husband is missing, but I have this sick feeling that something awful has happened to him."

"You have no idea what I'm going through! Your daughter is standing here before us looking healthy and well. She always was jealous of my daughters."

"Jealous?" Sherry's hands were on her hips. "Who's the one with all of the dance trophies?"

Cameron fired off a glare at Joshua for allowing this to happen. Catching her silent message, he suggested that Izzy take Luke to the cafeteria.

Once Izzy had hurried Luke out of earshot, Cameron stepped into the middle of the brewing skirmish. "Wait a minute, ladies!" She held both arms out to push the two women as far apart as possible. "We've been doing a lot of investigating this past week and you two are going to want to sit down to hear what we've uncovered."

Fear crossed Sherry's and Kathleen's faces. Hesitant, they took seats across from each other.

"Now, this is not easy to say," Cameron said.

"Shawn's dead." Sherry hung her head.

Cameron paused.

"Shawn?" Kathleen repeated the name. "Your last name is Whitaker, isn't it?"

"Yes, my name is Sherry. Shawn Whitaker was my husband."

"Shawn Whitaker was my brother's name."

"My Shawn was your brother?" Sherry asked.

"No." Madison stepped forward. "Mom, Dad was her husband."

"No, my husband was John Davis."

"Yes, Ms. Davis," Cameron said, "your husband was John Davis. Sherry Whitaker's husband's name was Shawn Whitaker. We've discovered that John Davis was also Shawn Whitaker."

Kathleen and Sherry sat up straight. With wide eyes, they stared at each other. In unison, they shook their heads.

"That's not possible." Kathleen looked up at Cameron. "This girl is pulling some sort of scam."

"It's true," Cameron said in a soft voice. "Your husband was killed in an apartment he had been renting in Calcutta under the name of Bishop Moore for the last twelve years. We found evidence that he had been living under three identities. John Davis, which is his original true identity. Shawn

Whitaker, the identity under which he married Sherry. Madison here is his daughter from that marriage."

"That makes her Heather's half-sister." Joshua slipped into the seat next to Kathleen. "They found out through one of those ancestry DNA websites and have become good friends. That's why Madison came here. She wants to be here for Heather."

"But they used to fight like cats and dogs," Kathleen said. "They both dated J.J."

"That's ancient history," Madison said with a wave of her hand. "Heather and I love each other—as sisters. We call each other. We text. She's working on my dance studio website. I taught her how to make dancing fun again."

Breaking out of her stunned stare at the wall, Sherry stammered. "I had no idea ... I don't understand. How? Why?"

Madison sat next to her. "Dad said he loved both families equally and couldn't leave either one."

"You talked to him about this?" Sherry asked.

"Heather and I confronted him about it at his apartment last week," Madison said.

Kathleen pointed a finger at Madison. "So *you*—"

"Both Madison and Heather have airtight alibis for the time of the murder," Cameron interjected.

"I'm going to be sick!" Covering her mouth, Kathleen ran from the waiting room.

Cameron started to give chase but found Sherry's hand on her arm.

"Allow me." With a soft smile, Sherry trotted down the hall after Kathleen.

"Should they be left alone?" Tony asked Cameron in a low voice. "What if they kill each other?"

"That's why you might want to go with them."

"To the *ladies'* room?" Tony grasped his service weapon and looked around for help in the form of a volunteer to go for him. "But there are *things* in there."

"You don't have to go in. Just wait outside the door. If you hear gunshots, then you can go in."

"Go in?"

"Keep your eyes closed so you don't learn our secrets."

His eyes wide with terror, Tony hurried after them.

"Kathleen! Are you in here?"

In the ladies' room, Sherry bent over and peered under the stall doors until she located Kathleen Davis's legs.

After having become physically ill with the news, Kathleen flushed the toilet and opened the door to find Sherry Whitaker standing before her.

Concerned filled the other woman's face. "Are you okay?"

"No!" Kathleen brushed past her to go to the sink. "My cheating husband is dead."

"I guess that's a good thing," Sherry said, "because if he was alive, we'd kill him and then we'd spend the rest of our lives in jail. I wonder if they would have allowed us to be cellmates." She shrugged her shoulders. "I mean, since we shared a husband, we might as well share a jail cell."

"Once the jury found out what he did to us, then they'd refuse to convict." Kathleen took a small bottle of liquid soap from her purse, squirt a generous amount into her hand, and rubbed them together. She studied Sherry's reflection in the mirror. "I can't believe you didn't know he was married."

"I can't believe you were married for over thirty years without noticing that he spent half of his time with another family." Sherry squinted at the Kathleen scrubbing the soap over every inch of her hands, wrists, and up her arms—not unlike a surgeon getting ready for an operation.

"How could he resist?" Kathleen stuck her hands under the hot running water. "I can just see him melting like butter with you seducing him away from our family with your come-hither bedroom eyes."

"That is not—" Realizing what she had said, Sherry studied her image in the mirror. "Do you really think I have bedroom eyes?" She batted her eyelashes.

"It's plain to see what he saw in you." Kathleen bent over to stick as much of her hands and wrists under the water as possible. "You were the fun wife. The one he could go running to when he got sick of my nagging."

"I'm sure you weren't a nag."

Kathleen spun around to face her. "Of course, I was a nag. I had to be. Someone had to run the household. Keep the budget to buy a lovely home. Keep the kids on track for their scholarships. If it weren't for me, John would have been content to sit in middle management. I made him the man he was."

"Oh, so you're the one who made him a bigamist."

Kathleen threw back her head and let out a wail. Sherry caught her as she dropped to her knees. On the floor, Sherry held her while her heart broke.

The bathroom door flew open. Covering his eyes with his hand, Tony raced in. "Is everything okay in here? Should I call for backup?"

Izzy returned from the cafeteria with Luke. "He's hungry and I don't have enough money to buy him anything."

Madison reached into her bag. "Luke, do you like apples and cheese sticks?"

"I'm not allowed to take food from strangers," Luke said.

"Well, I'm not a stranger." Joshua took the plastic bag from Madison.

"No, Gram said you were a good guy."

"You can have some of this to hold you over until we get you some dinner." Joshua took an apple slice for himself and held out the bag to the small boy. "Luke, this is Madison. She's your aunt. Madison, this is your nephew Luke."

"Nice to meet you, Aunt Madison." Luke held out his hand to her. As they shook hands, he asked, "How come I never met you before?"

Madison became misty eyed. "I'm new to the family."

"Do you like dogs? I have a white one. Gramps gave him to me. His name is Munster. Gram calls him a filthy beast."

"Madison, thank God I found you!" Elizabeth rushed into the waiting room and ran up to Madison. She was in such a state that she almost knocked Luke to the floor.

Frightened by the strange woman, Luke hid behind Joshua who sheltered him.

"I went by your house and you weren't there," Elizabeth said while looking at the assortment of people gathered around the waiting room. "I've been calling your cell and you didn't answer. Then, I heard on the news about the accident and I was afraid that somehow you got mixed up in that."

Joshua and Cameron stared with interest at the wild-eyed woman shifting from one foot to the other. She was dressed in blue dancing clothes under her heavy winter coat. Her eyes darted around the room—stopping to study each one of them.

"I had turned off my phone because I had personal family business to take care of," Madison said.

"What business?" Elizabeth grasped the necklace. "Did your dad's murderer come after your mom, too?"

"No," Madison said. "Elizabeth, I don't really want to talk about it. You should be home with Aaron and your kids right now."

"But you're my best friend," Elizabeth said, while staring at Cameron who was focused on her. "Best friends don't have secrets from each other."

"We're in the middle of an active police investigation," Joshua said. "Madison isn't allowed to talk about it."

"She's allowed to tell her sister," Elizabeth said.

"Did Davis marry her mother, too?" Izzy asked Joshua in a low voice.

Cameron asked Elizabeth, "Does your sister tell you everything?"

"I don't have a sister, unless you want to count Madison. We're as close as sisters."

Cameron shot a glance at Joshua, who rose to his feet.

"Elizabeth, maybe you can help us," Joshua said. "Madison needs a break. How about if the four of us go get a bite to eat."

A wide grin crossed Elizabeth's face as she trotted toward the door. Once her back was turned, Joshua whispered into Madison's ear.

Madison let out a deep sigh. "You're right, Josh. I didn't realize how hungry and tired I was. I could use some dinner."

"Wait for me outside. I just need to talk to Izzy for a minute. Dinner is on me."

"What are you up to?" Cameron asked him in a low voice.

"Hunter and I have reopened the investigation into Lindsay Ellison's accident," Joshua said. "We believe Elizabeth was driving during the fatal wreck. We need her DNA to prove it though. I can get that sample during dinner."

"Be careful. You'd be surprised what comes out of those DNA tests."

Joshua got dinner orders from Luke and Izzy, while instructing them not to go anywhere. "If they release J.J. and Poppy before we get back, text me. They're going to need a ride home."

Izzy noted that the sun had set during the hours of waiting in the emergency room. "The horses are going to be hungry." She never forgot about the critters at J.J.'s farm. "And Ollie and Charley don't like it when they're left alone for too long."

Joshua took out his phone. Luckily, he had the contact number for the farm's foreman. "I'll send someone to take care of them. I hope Charley doesn't give them too hard of a time." He escorted Cameron toward the emergency room exit with his hand on her back. "What made you think Elizabeth had a sister?"

"Haven't you noticed that necklace she keeps playing with?" Cameron said. "That's a sister medallion."

"Like the ones Izzy, Tracy, and Sarah have," Joshua said.

"Hers is half a heart," Cameron said while zipping her coat. "Which means there's a sister who has the other half."

"But she has no sister." Joshua grasped her arm and stopped. "Lindsay's angel was wearing a necklace."

"Lindsay's angel?"

"The angel Derek saw in his trailer on the night of the murder. The one who planted the murder weapon to frame Derek for Davis's murder. Derek told me that he knew it was Lindsay because she was wearing a sister's necklace that Heather had given to Lindsay. She never took off."

"Was Lindsay's necklace found after the accident?"

"We'll have to ask the family."

Cameron stopped. "She knew Shawn Whitaker was dead."

Joshua had taken a couple of steps before he realized what she had said. He turned and cocked his head at her.

"Until this evening, as far as anyone knew, Shawn Whitaker was only missing," Cameron said. "The only ones who actually knew he was dead were those of us involved in the investigation, Heather, and Madison."

"Yet, just now, Elizabeth asked Madison if whoever murdered her father came after her mother," Joshua said. "She may have overheard Heather and Madison talking about it."

"In light of what you suspect about Lindsay's accident, do you really believe that?"

They broke into a run through the double doors leading out to the parking lot. Expecting to find Madison and Elizabeth waiting next to his vehicle, Joshua ran across the lot. As they neared the SUV, they discovered that neither Madison nor Elizabeth were waiting.

Joshua stopped in the middle of the roadway. "Where did they go?"

Cameron turned around to search for any sign of the women in the shadows scattered around the darkened lot. In the early evening, many of the hospital's employees had left for the day.

A pair of headlights flashed on. The car tore out of a space at the far end of the lot. The tires squealed as the car spun out of its slot and sped toward Cameron—caught in the glare of its high beams.

As the car raced toward his wife, Joshua dove for her. He grabbed her around the waist and together they landed on the pavement between two ambulances.

They heard the blare of horns as the car cut off other vehicles in its escape onto the street and into the night.

CHAPTER TWENTY-SIX

"I can't believe you didn't get the license plate number," Cameron told Joshua after snapping orders at Tony to go with the chief of hospital security to find out what their cameras may have captured in the parking lot.

Anxious to talk to Sherry Whitaker to find out what she knew about Elizabeth Collins, Cameron spun on her heels to go into a meeting room where John Davis's wives were waiting in private.

"Excuse me for keeping you from becoming roadkill," Joshua yelled at her back before returning to his attention to Sheriff Sawyer on his cell. "Get a team out to the Collins place. Cameron will meet you there. We're taking J.J. and Poppy home. I'll get there as soon as I can."

Sitting side by side in a couple of padded chairs in the corridor, Izzy told Luke, "They do this all the time. It takes some getting used to." She jumped out of her seat when she saw J.J. being wheeled toward them. She cringed when she saw a big bandage across his forehead. "That looks like it hurts."

"It does." J.J. told the orderly to stop and pushed up out of the chair. To his surprise, his legs felt wobbly. Poppy grabbed his arm to ease him back into the chair. Seeing Joshua on the phone, he said, "It looks like Dad got a break in the case."

"Sort of." Lowering her voice so Luke wouldn't hear, Izzy said, "Some crazy lady kidnapped Madison."

"Elizabeth," J.J. said. "She must have tampered with Heather's car, too. Why?"

"Jealousy," Poppy said. "I told you. Didn't you see it? She was very threatened by Heather, and Heather didn't like her much either."

"Women notice those types of things," Izzy said. "We've got an instinct that you men don't."

"Where's Luke?" Kathleen demanded to know after she and Sherry learned that Madison was missing.

Cameron had ushered Sherry and Kathleen into a small meeting room where doctors would meet with patients or their family members in private. Upon learning the news, Kathleen hugged Sherry, a move that surprised Cameron. They continued to comfort each other while Cameron dug for information to help her find Madison.

"Luke's with my husband," Cameron said. "We'll keep him safe until one of your sons can take him home. Right now, we need to figure out why Elizabeth would do this. I'm hoping that the two of you, since your children have had some sort of relationship with her both in the past and the present, would maybe remember something that—"

"Elizabeth always got on Heather's nerves," Kathleen said. "I told Lindsay that she was odd back when they became friends after high school. She should have listened to me."

"I warned Madison about hiring her to work at the dance studio. With it being a new business, it's not smart to expand too fast." Sherry turned to Kathleen. "Shawn taught me that when I set up my business."

"I taught John that when we were studying business in college."

"Then I guess that advice came from you."

"Excuse me, ladies," Cameron said. "Madison is missing. The first few hours are the most crucial."

"Do you think it was Elizabeth who tampered with Heather's SUV?" Kathleen asked.

"We have detectives looking at the security videos for the business's around the dance studio to see if they can find evidence of her tampering with it."

"She was such a strange bird back when the girls were in dance," Kathleen said with a frown. "She latched onto Lindsay when they ended up living next door to each other. I always blamed her for dragging Lindsay down even further into drugs."

"Elizabeth had problems fitting in," Sherry said. "I saw that at the dance studio. She'd try to make friends with the other students, but she tried too hard. She'd become clingy."

"That's exactly what she'd do."

"I think it had to do with her being a foster child."

"She was a foster child?" Kathleen asked. "How would you know that?"

"Her foster mother told me," Sherry said. "I talked to all of the parents. You'd be surprised what they told me."

"Elizabeth was in the system?" Cameron made a note to check with child services for Elizabeth's background information. "Elizabeth wears a sister's necklace. Did she have a sister?"

"Maybe a foster sister. The foster mother who brought her to Miss Charlotte's had a couple of other foster children." Sherry shrugged her shoulders and shook her head. "I did notice Elizabeth wearing the necklace when Madison hired her. She didn't wear it back when they were in high school."

"Is the medallion a half-heart?" The color drained from Kathleen's face.

"Yes," Cameron said. "I saw Heather and Lindsay wearing necklaces like it in a photograph at your home."

"Heather and Lindsay got them for Valentine's day shortly before Heather's graduation," Kathleen said. "Lindsay never took hers off. We couldn't find it after she'd died. We tore that trailer apart. We wanted her to be buried with it."

"Elizabeth was with Lindsay the night she died," Cameron said. "Witnesses saw them together."

"Lindsay's death was particularly hard on Heather. She was her baby sister. Heather felt like she failed to protect her. Then, not being able to find the necklace—that devastated her. We assumed Lindsay threw it away after their fight because she was so mad at her."

"Maybe she didn't," Sherry said. "Maybe she gave it to Elizabeth."

"Or Elizabeth took it," Cameron said as she rose to answer a knock on the door. "What is Elizabeth's maiden name?"

"I don't know," Kathleen said as Sherry answered.

"Gallagher. The foster family's name was Fletcher."

"How do you remember that?" Kathleen asked.

"It's a gift," Sherry said with an arched eyebrow.

Cameron found Tony in the hospital corridor. "Security camera got it all," he whispered to her.

Cameron ordered a uniformed officer to stand guard outside the meeting room while she followed Tony through the reception area to the security office. A quick glance out the window revealed that Joshua's SUV was gone—meaning that he had taken J.J. and Poppy home.

Tony opened the door to the security center. The chief of the hospital's security wore a starch white shirt with a gold badge on his chest. Standing behind one of his staff's chair, he waved to them.

The security video was paused to show the emergency room entrance. The downward angle of the shot provided a view of the entrance and two rows of parking spaces which ended at a heavy hedge and fence that bordered the lot.

The video was frozen with Elizabeth and Madison in mid-stride exiting the hospital.

The officer pressed the "play" button.

The two women stepped to the end of the walkway and stopped. Madison turned to look toward the door—assumingly in anticipation of Joshua joining them.

Cameron realized that the women did not know which vehicle belonged to Joshua.

Her back to the camera, Elizabeth spoke excitedly to Madison. She gestured toward the far end of the lot.

"She's asking Madison to go to her car with her." Cameron pressed her finger on the image of the car in the last space. "That's the car that almost ran us down."

Madison hesitantly followed Elizabeth, who continued urging her. Twice, Madison stopped to look back at the entrance.

"If we had just come out one minute earlier," Cameron said.

"It's not your fault," Tony said.

Upon reaching the car, Elizabeth opened the rear passenger door and pointed inside. Madison stepped around the door and bent over to look at something inside the back compartment. Close behind her, Elizabeth stepped forward. Madison jerked before Elizabeth shoved her into the backseat.

"She tazed her," Tony said.

"That's what it looks like to me," Cameron said.

Elizabeth looked around to make sure no one saw what she had done. Then, she climbed into the backseat. It was unclear in the security video what she was doing.

Cameron assumed she was securing Madison—possibly drugging her or bounding her. After a short time, Elizabeth got out and went around to the driver's side. She climbed into the driver's seat as Joshua and Cameron ran into the parking lot. As they stopped to look around, Elizabeth's vehicle started. Abruptly, the lights turned on, and Elizabeth raced toward Cameron, who escaped only when Joshua tackled her.

"Looks like your husband saved your life," the chief of security said.

"I married well," Cameron said.

CHAPTER TWENTY-SEVEN

"I guess we can assume my truck is totaled."

J.J. waited until they had crossed the West Virginia state line before breaking the silence inside Joshua's SUV. He sat in the front with Joshua driving. Strapped into his booster seat, Luke sat in the back with Izzy and Poppy.

Everyone was lost in their thoughts with worry about Heather's injuries, Madison's abduction, and how much worse things could have been. One minute they were dancing. The next, disaster struck.

"You and Poppy being treated and released after a four-vehicle accident. Heather ending up in serious condition with a head injury." Joshua shook his head. "Things could have been a whole lot worse."

"I could have lost Poppy," J.J. said in a voice barely above a whisper.

Joshua shot a reassuring grin in his direction. "But you didn't."

"I'm worried about Heather," Poppy said. "I've only just met her this week, but I like her." She tapped the back of J.J.'s seat. "I can see why you dated her, J.J. Why you dated

Madison, too. They're so much fun. I could see us all being friends. We need to invite them to the wedding."

"You want to invite J.J.'s old girlfriends to the wedding?" Izzy asked. "Wouldn't that be awkward?"

"Why would it be awkward?"

"I guess not," Izzy said with a roll of her eyes.

"Heather wanted to talk to you tonight, Dad," J.J. said.

"When did she say that?" Joshua shot a glance across to J.J. in the passenger seat.

"At the dance studio when we were leaving," J.J. said. "I was holding the door open for her to walk out, and she was staring at Elizabeth."

"I remember that," Poppy said. "She and Elizabeth were staring at each other like two cats wanting the same mouse. I was afraid J.J. was going to have to break them up."

"Interesting comparison," Joshua said.

"When we got out onto the sidewalk," J.J. said, "Heather asked me if you were going to be at the meeting tonight—you know at the house with Kathleen and Sherry? She wanted to talk to you."

"And she was staring at Elizabeth right before that?" Joshua turned left onto the long lane leading to J.J.'s farm house.

Three vehicles were parked next to the house. Tracy's SUV, and Hunter's and the sheriff's cruisers. Poppy's truck was parked in its usual spot in front of the barn.

Ollie shot out of the pet door, bounced across the porch and down the steps to greet them. His wings spread wide, Charley screeched from where he was perched on the porch railing. The dogs gathered together to welcome their masters.

Tracy opened the door and hurried out. Sheriff Sawyer and Hunter followed her.

"Dogs!" Luke pointed out the window. "Lots of dogs. All different shapes and sizes. I like dogs."

"Wait until you see the horses," Izzy said while helping him out of his seat.

Joshua hurried around to help J.J. when he saw Izzy and Luke taking off for the barn. Ollie and a trail of dogs followed them. "Don't go too far. Luke's aunt is on her way to pick him up."

Joshua turned the corner of the SUV to find Sheriff Sawyer, his hands on his hips, standing before him. His crisp uniform was adorned with white feathers of various sizes.

"That rooster is crazy." The sheriff jabbed a thumb over his shoulder at where Charley stood guard on the porch railing.

"Tell me something I don't know," Joshua said.

"Charley's not crazy," Poppy looped her arm through J.J.'s "He's very protective of those he loves."

"Loves?" Sheriff Sawyer asked. "That mutant vulture is about as loving as a badger."

"Actually, badgers have gotten a very bad rap," Poppy said while keeping J.J. steady on his feet through the front door, which Tracy held open for them. "They're basically shy. All they want is to be left alone. They get cranky when humans back them into a corner."

"First time I ever heard of a badger described as being 'cranky.'"

"One man's 'vicious' is another man's 'cranky,'" Joshua said while trotting up the steps to the front door.

As Sheriff Sawyer passed him, Charley rose up onto his feet, spread his wings and let out a screech as if to remind the lawman that he oversaw the farm's security. The sheriff paused to fire off a glare at the bird, who, refusing to back down, returned it.

The pleasant scent of pot roast wafted through the house. Bread was baking in the bread maker. Tracy had also delivered an extra cheesecake that she had made while cooking for an event the next day. "After the day you two have had, you deserved it more than I do," Tracy said while giving J.J. a hug.

"But—" A sharp look from Tracy silenced Hunter's objection.

"Hunter, see what you can do to help J.J.," Tracy told her husband from over her shoulder as he followed her into the kitchen to plead his case for the cheesecake.

"He's got my cheesecake. What more does he need?" Hunter grumbled.

Poppy entered the kitchen as Hunter left. "Do you need any help?"

"Asked one of the patients," Tracy said with a laugh. "I'm fine. This is what I do. Go rest with J.J."

"I should go out to the barn to check on Pilgrim."

Tracy cut her off before she could go out the back door. "Izzy is out there. You know she will check on each critter and let us know if there's any problem."

Poppy cringed. "Pilgrim is still adjusting and I'm afraid she'll have a difficult birth."

"She's not due for another two months." Tracy guided her toward the hallway leading to the living room. "We're here if you need anything. I suggest you take a break from the farm animals and focus on finding that wedding gown."

"You still don't have a gown?"

Joshua's voice startled both women. They turned around to find Joshua at the refrigerator with a glass in hand. He had been fetching a glass of water for J.J. to wash down a pain pill.

"Don't tell J.J." Tracy warned.

"Don't you think he'd notice if Poppy came down the aisle in her birthday suit?"

Poppy giggled at the visual.

"She has a very specific gown in mind, and we can't seem to find it. I think she needs to give up," Tracy said with a roll of her eyes. "They just don't make wedding gowns with gold lace overlay."

"Maybe they don't make gowns like that," Poppy said, "but there is one out there that I'm meant to wear. Just give it time. It will find me."

"Hey, Josh, have you got that water?" Hunter called to him.

"I need to help J.J." Poppy took the glass of water from Joshua and hurried into the living room.

"Gold lace overlay?" Joshua murmured.

Hearing him, Tracy nodded her head. "I've never seen a gown like that. Have you?" Without waiting for his response, she followed Poppy.

J.J. insisted on resting for a while in the living room instead of going to bed and resting like the doctor had ordered. "It's just a mild concussion," he said to the room full of family and friends staring at him. "Don't worry about us. You need to get out there and find Maddie."

"I never dreamed Elizabeth would do this type of stuff," Tracy said. "She did some nasty little things in high school but—"

"What kind of nasty little things?" Joshua had kept his and Cameron's suspicion about Elizabeth murdering John Davis to themselves until they uncovered a clear motive.

Tracy shrugged. "Stealing stuff. Little things. Jewelry. Hairclips. MP3 players. At the dance school, we all knew that she was a kleptomaniac. We'd just be careful not to leave things laying around. It was like she couldn't help herself. We felt sorry for her." She let out a gasp. "Now that I think about it—"

"Think about what?" Sheriff Sawyer asked.

"It was during our senior year, Heather had gotten really sick on the day of the championship competition." Tracy told J.J., "This was after you had gone off to Penn State."

"A.J.J," Hunter said with a chuckle. "After J.J."

"It was bad. Heather got really sick." Tracy scrunched up her face while saying in a low voice, "Stomach pains. Digestive issues. When she'd finished her bottled water, she noticed that there was a white substance at the bottom of the bottle. She asked me if it would be possible to find out what it was. I took a sample of the substance to Tad, and he ran a chemical test. It ended up being a very strong laxative. Heather was thoroughly convinced Maddie had done it, but Maddie swore that it wasn't her. I believed her. Heather's friends didn't, of course. I've always wondered who did do that. Now, after what happened today … I wonder."

"Was Elizabeth competing against Heather at the competition?" J.J. asked.

"No," Tracy said. "But Maddie was, and Elizabeth had a thing for Maddie."

"What kind of thing?" Sheriff Sawyer asked with an arched eyebrow.

"Not sexual," Tracy said. "I think she considered Maddie a close friend—like best friends. Maybe Maddie was her only friend. We'd noticed that she spent a lot of time hanging around Maddie and Maddie was very nice to her. Now, I'm thinking she tried to sabotage Heather out of loyalty to her."

"Which would give her extra reason to be jealous when Madison and Heather reconnected and became besties," Poppy said. "Elizabeth put a lot of work in helping Madison set up her own dance studio."

"One could see it as Madison using Elizabeth's loyalty to sabotage Heather," Sheriff Sawyer said. "Now, years later, she uses her again to help her set up her business. Is it possible that Madison manipulated Elizabeth to do her dirty work?"

"Maddie didn't need to sabotage Heather," Tracy said. "Maddie was always a couple of steps ahead of her in competition."

"That's not how Maddie operates," J.J. said with a shake of his head. "Maddie has been gone for how many years? Even if Elizabeth sabotaged Heather back in high school, wouldn't you think she'd moved on since then? Why now, after all these years, would she feel compelled to kidnap Maddie?"

"Maybe she doesn't want to move on," Joshua said. "Look at her life. She got pregnant right out of high school. She gets married and has two kids. She's trapped in what may be an unhappy marriage—"

"Unhappy enough to cheat on Aaron," J.J. said.

"Cheat on Aaron?" Joshua asked.

"Remember I told you that she claimed to be Maddie's alibi," J.J. said, "because she had lied to Aaron when in reality she was out with another man."

"When she provided a phony alibi for Madison, she also provided a phony alibi for herself," Joshua said. "Cameron and I have reason to believe Elizabeth was the one who'd murdered John Davis."

"Why would Elizabeth kill John Davis?" Hunter asked. "Just because she's unhappy with her life? That's not his fault."

"I don't think she'd even met him," Tracy said.

"What makes you think she killed him?" J.J. asked.

"Elizabeth arrived at the hospital after we'd broken the news to Kathleen and Sherry about Davis's bigamy. They were in the ladies' room and Elizabeth asked Madison if the same killer who'd murdered her father had come after her mother. At that point, the only way Elizabeth could have known that Shawn Whitaker was dead was if she had been involved in his murder."

"She's a very disturbed girl," Sheriff Sawyer said. "Cameron called a bit ago. The pizza place on the corner next to the dance studio has security cameras outside to catch kids up to mischief after closing. Heather Davis's vehicle was right there in the shot. They caught Elizabeth loosening the lug nuts on her tires."

Stunned, Tracy shook her head. "Abduction. Attempted murder. Actual murder. I never would have dreamed Elizabeth would have been capable of something like that."

"We're meeting Cameron out at the Collins place," Sheriff Sawyer said. "I imagine you want to ride along, Josh."

"Just try to stop me."

CHAPTER TWENTY-EIGHT

The Collins home was a rundown colonial in New Manchester, a crossroads between Chester and New Cumberland. Most of the tiny community's residents lived on what amounted to three blocks. The young family's apartment was built above Aaron's parents' detached garage.

Joshua rode with the sheriff while Hunter led the way in his police cruiser.

"I've got a question," Joshua said while the sheriff raced along the rural country roads.

"We've all got questions," Sheriff Sawyer said. "What one do you want to discuss now?"

"Davis's body was dumped at the Newhart farm in Hookstown." Continuing, Joshua murmured, "The Newharts are Sherry Whitaker's parents. That connection is to the Whitaker family. The murder weapon was planted in Derek's trailer. That dot connects to the Davis family."

"I thought you guys had been all over this already," the sheriff said. "Whoever killed Davis knew about his double life and both families."

"And Elizabeth danced with both Heather and Madison," Joshua said with a nod of his head. "She worked at Madison's dance studio. Elizabeth could have learned through lurking around about Madison and Heather's secret. My question is this. How did Elizabeth move John Davis's body from that apartment in Calcutta to the farm in Hookstown? She's not that strong."

Sheriff Sawyer shot a glance in Joshua's direction.

"Why plant the knife in Derek's trailer and dump the body in Hookstown?" Joshua tapped his chin with his finger while the answer came to him. "Someone else moved the body."

"The apartment manager?"

"The Bayles knew Davis had a double life, but they didn't know any specifics," Joshua said with a shake of his head. "Cameron told me that Ross Bayles wasn't even aware that Bishop Moore had other identities. Now, J.J. mentioned that Aaron was setting up the computers and networking at the studio. The Collins used to be neighbors with Derek and Lindsay—"

"Until they got evicted," Sheriff Sawyer said. "Aaron has a lot of trouble holding a job. He thinks he's smarter than he really is."

"I think Aaron dumped the body and cleaned up the crime scene," Joshua said.

"Why?"

"The same reason he claimed to have picked up Elizabeth at Chester Park the night of the accident. To protect his wife. Whoever killed Davis had to have been covered in blood. How could he not have known what she'd done when she came home that night?"

Having tasked Tony with taking Sherry Whitaker home in case Madison called, Cameron waited in the parking lot of an abandoned pizza place located in the turn-off to New Manchester. Upon seeing the two police cruisers, she pulled out and led them one hundred yards down the street before parking in front of the house with wire fencing marking the Collins lot.

"We need to send the kids over to their grandparents before we talk to Aaron," Joshua told Cameron when she climbed out of her cruiser.

"Did Sawyer tell you that we have security video of Elizabeth tampering with Heather's tires?" Cameron asked him. "First, she tried to kill Heather and now she snatched Madison. I have a bad feeling about what she may do to her."

Sheriff Sawyer jerked his chin in the direction of the Collins' front stoop. Waiting behind the storm door, Aaron's mother and two small children, all dressed in pajamas and bathrobes, stared at the collection of law enforcement with curiosity filling their faces.

"This is your gig, Gates," Sheriff Sawyer said.

Cameron took out her police shield and made her way up the walkway to the door. "I'm Lieutenant Cameron Gates with the Pennsylvania State Police. We need to talk to your daughter-in-law Elizabeth. Is she here?"

"She's at work," the elderly woman said. "That's why I'm taking care of the grandkids. She teaches dance out in Beaver Falls. She's working for a big choreographer from Broadway."

Cameron exchanged looks of concern with Joshua. Someone had been telling lies. Was Elizabeth's lies a sign of deception or delusion?

"What about Aaron?" Joshua asked. "Is he here?"

She tossed her head in the direction of the garage. "He's over there. He claims he can't take care of the kids because he's got work to do." She scoffed. "If that's what you want to call it. Every time I look over his shoulder, he's playing a game."

Hunter was peering through the garage door windows when Cameron and Joshua rounded the corner of the house. "Looks like someone here has an old SUV. Didn't you say you have impressions for the vehicle that dumped Davis's body?"

Cameron looked through the window at the full-sized SUV. "That will work."

His hand on his service weapon, Hunter led the way up the narrow steps to the apartment door. The steps and landing at the top were only wide enough to serve their purpose and nothing more. In a line along the stairs, they waited while Hunter pounded on the door.

"Aaron Collins, Hunter Gardner with the Hancock County Sheriff's Department. We're here with a detective from the Pennsylvania State Police. We'd like to talk to you, if we may."

There was silence.

"He certainly had to hear that," Cameron said.

Hunter pressed his face close to the window in the door. "I can see him on the sofa."

"And what's he doing on that sofa?" Cameron asked.

"He's not moving." Hunter wrested the doorknob. It was locked. Once again, he pounded on the door. "Collins! Can you hear me?"

"Something's wrong," Cameron said.

Hunter stepped back and kicked in the door. They spilled into the apartment. While Hunter and Joshua searched the apartment for any sign of Elizabeth, which took five seconds, Cameron and Sheriff Sawyer descended on Aaron, who was sprawled out on the worn sofa with a gaming keyboard resting on his stomach. An oversized computer monitor was set up at the end of the coffee table, positioned for Aaron to see from the sofa. A huge plastic drinking glass rested on the floor next to his hand.

Sheriff Sawyer searched for a pulse on Aaron's flabby neck. "He's alive!" he told Hunter who was calling for an emergency crew. "It's faint, but I've got a pulse."

Cameron sniffed the drink. It was a flavored energy drink. Taking the container close to the lamp, she peeled off the cap and looked inside. She swirled the inch of drink around and studied the bottom. She could see some granular substance at the bottom. "I think she poisoned him."

"We're dealing with a very dangerous woman," Sheriff Sawyer said.

"I hope we find Madison in time," Joshua said.

CHAPTER TWENTY-NINE

Cameron was grateful for Joshua's presence in dealing with Martha Collins while the emergency crews worked on her son to rush him to the hospital. They took the cup with them. Hopefully, the staff in the emergency room would be able to determine with what he had been poisoned.

During her career, Cameron recognized her faults. One was becoming so focused on solving a case that she easily lost patience with potential witnesses who might not be fast enough to help her reach its conclusion.

Such was the case with Martha Collins. She was naturally distraught to see her son taken away by ambulance. With Aaron incapacitated, his mother appeared to be their last hope in figuring out what had been going on inside Elizabeth's head.

Quickly sending the children to bed with assurances that their father was going to be okay and their mother would be home soon, Martha poured a glass of wine to calm her nerves and sat with Joshua, Cameron, and Sheriff Sawyer in the living room that was so small that Sheriff Sawyer was forced to remain standing by the door.

"Elizabeth should be home by now." Martha checked the time on a clock on the end table. "I guess she and Madison decided to go out to unwind." She took a sip of her drink. "That's what they do in show business, you know."

"So I've heard," Joshua said. "I guess since Elizabeth has been working with Madison, she's been a big influence on her."

"It started with the hair." Martha rolled her eyes.

"What about the hair?" Cameron asked.

"Elizabeth had what you'd call a dishwater blond, dark blond, hair." Martha screwed up her face. "I admit, it wasn't a nice color—but it was natural. But then, as soon as she started working with Madison, she decided to start bleaching it. Then, she started wearing those skimpy dance clothes." She rolled her eyes. "All the time! Even when she's not at the dance studio, she's prancing around here in those tights and leotards." She covered her mouth with a giggle. "I think she looks like a hooker. But don't tell Aaron that."

"Are you saying all this happened right after she started working at the dance studio?" Sheriff Sawyer asked.

Martha nodded her head. "It hasn't been easy—with her suddenly working every day. Aaron has no patience for the kids, so I end up with them all the time." She offered a small grin. "But she's happy, and Elizabeth has been so unhappy for so long." With a quick glance in the direction of the children's bedroom, she said in a harsh whisper, "We were quite worried about her."

"Why were you worried?" Joshua asked.

"She was …" Martha seemed to reconsider divulging that piece of information.

"What?" Cameron snapped. "Elizabeth was what?"

Startled, Martha jumped back.

Joshua lifted his hand in a signal for Cameron to stand down. It was a slight gesture that only she noticed. "Martha, it's important that we find Elizabeth. She may be in trouble."

"Have you called Madison?" Martha sighed. "Elizabeth was so depressed that we were afraid she might hurt herself and even the children. And then, it was the end of summer. She came home from shopping out at Beaver Valley Mall and her face just glowed—all because she had run into Madison Whitaker, her best friend from school. Madison had danced on Broadway and knew all of these famous people, but she gave it all up to come back home. She asked Elizabeth to help her open up her dance studio. I hadn't seen Elizabeth that happy in years."

Joshua got up and gestured for Cameron to follow him out onto the front stoop. "Have you checked the dance studio in Beaver Falls?"

"That's where Elizabeth is happy." Cameron took out her phone to call for a uniformed officer to check the dance studio. "It's the thing that connects her and Madison."

Joshua stepped back inside where Sheriff Sawyer had continued the conversation.

"Oh yeah, Elizabeth got so messed up last Friday when she went out with Madison," Martha was saying. "I heard her car come flying in after ten o'clock. The headlights woke me up when she pulled into the driveway. She went running up the stairs—clap, clap, clap, clap, clap! I was just about to go back to sleep when I heard their door slam and stomp, stomp, stomp, stomp! Aaron went peeling out in the SUV."

"Where did he go?" Joshua asked.

Martha shrugged her shoulder and took a sip of her wine. "He and Elizabeth had a fight because she came home so drunk. I assume he went to a friend's house because Elizabeth locked him out of the bedroom. She's done that before. Rather than argue, Aaron will go to a friend's place and they'll play games until she cools off."

"What time did Aaron come back home that night?" Cameron asked.

Martha rolled her eyes. "I heard the SUV pull in. It was way after midnight. Maybe one o'clock?"

Joshua and Cameron exchanged glances.

"Do you mind if we take a look at your son's SUV?" Cameron asked.

"It's in the garage," Martha said with a wave of her hand.

The Collins' SUV was a ten-year-old model. When Cameron opened the back, she groaned upon finding that it had been recently cleaned.

"Do you really think Aaron is savvy enough to have gotten rid of every bit of evidence," Hunter said in Cameron's ear.

She turned to him to find that the deputy was holding a forensics kit in his hand. "Is that yours?"

Hunter knelt and opened the plastic case. "It was a gift."

"All Josh ever gave me was a pair of handcuffs," she said with a wicked grin.

Hunter opened his mouth to reply but thought better of it upon seeing the arch of his father-in-law's eyebrow. Rising to his feet, he held a bottle of luminol in one hand and a cotton swab with a long stick in the other. "Let's see if Aaron got all of the nooks and crannies."

While Joshua, Sheriff Sawyer, and Hunter explored the dark crevices of Aaron's SUV, Cameron's phone vibrated to signal a phone call. She saw that it was the Pennsylvania State Police dispatch. "Tell me that they found Madison at the dance studio."

"Sorry, Lieutenant," the dispatch officer replied. "All dark. The uniform shone the light through the windows and went all around. No sign of anyone inside and no sign of a break in."

"Rats!"

"Also, children's services gave me a phone number to pass on to you for a Naomi Fletcher. She was Elizabeth's foster mother. They've spoken to her and she would be willing to talk to you about Elizabeth. They said she might be helpful."

The men let out a whoop behind Cameron. She turned around to see Hunter holding the cotton swab up over his head while doing a dance.

"We got human blood," Sheriff Sawyer said. "Lots of it in the cracks."

"We've got the vehicle used to transport Davis to the dump site," Joshua said.

"Now all we need is the killer," Cameron said.

Chapter Thirty

Crime doesn't care how late it is. When a life is on the line, there will be a knock on the door no matter what the hour.

Such was the case for Naomi Fletcher of Hookstown, Pennsylvania. Instead of calling her, Cameron and Joshua drove to her small Cape Cod home on Old Mill Creek Road and rang the doorbell. It was close to midnight, but there was a light on in the living room and they could hear a movie playing on the television.

A teenaged boy dressed in a bathrobe over sweatpants answered the door. Upon seeing Cameron's detective's shield, his mouth dropped open. "Naomi!" he called up the stairs from over his shoulder. "The cops are here!" He turned back to Cameron and Joshua. "Are you here about Rickie?"

"Who's Rickie?" Cameron asked.

"No one."

A woman with long gray hair grabbed the open door. "Samson, why didn't you invite them inside?" she asked the teenager while ushering them into the living room. "Turn off the television and pick up your stuff so they have some place to sit down."

Samson picked up a pizza box, clothing, and other pieces of clutter while Naomi rattled on. "I didn't expect you to come out so quickly. I guess I should have since the detective who called said it was important." Suddenly realizing that she was also in her bathrobe, she tied the belt to conceal her flannel nightgown and smoothed her hair. "I guess Elizabeth got herself into trouble."

She told Samson, who had finished picking up his things, to allow them to talk alone. "You should go to bed anyway. It's late."

He hugged Naomi and offered the guests a pleasant smile before going up the stairs.

"Samson is a good kid," Naomi said in a soft voice while offering them a seat. "Smart as a whip. Unfortunately, his father is a deadbeat and his mother fell into some really hard times. They lost their house and ended up homeless. She's in a shelter."

"That's too bad," Joshua said.

"Samson missed four months of school because they were living in a car," Naomi said. "Then it got too cold and Samson's mother got pneumonia. He thought she was going to die. He took her into the hospital, and he ended up in the system. As soon as I got him back into school, he got caught up like that." She snapped her fingers with a proud grin. "With luck, we'll find a place for them to live and get her a job, and they can be on their way again."

"There's always hope," Joshua said.

Anxious to move onto their reason for being there, Cameron said, "Tell us about Elizabeth Gallagher."

"She was a strange one," Naomi said with a heavy sigh. "I don't know anything about her parents. No one could locate them. That's why no one could ever adopt her. Children's services couldn't find anyone to relinquish parental rights. Her parents were either missing or they'd abandoned the kids."

"Kids?" Cameron asked. "Elizabeth had siblings?"

"She had an older sister," Naomi said. "I'd never met her. They told me that she had run away from the foster home she had been placed in a long time ago. Elizabeth had been in several other home before I got her. She had a problem with stealing, which unfortunately many foster parents didn't want to deal with." She cocked her head at them. "What is this about?"

"We believe Elizabeth abducted Madison Whitaker," Joshua said. "They took lessons together at Miss Charlotte's Dance Studio."

"I remember Madison," Naomi said. "She was always very kind to Elizabeth. Madison was beautiful and very talented. Everyone at the dance studio adored her, but she wasn't snobbish about it. When she would talk to Elizabeth—that would make her day. Madison would just say hello, but it would mean so much more to her. She idolized her." She cringed. "Elizabeth would read things into their friendship that wasn't there."

"What kinds of things?" Cameron asked.

"Elizabeth thought she was going to New York with Madison." Naomi let out a sigh filled with sadness. "I had to explain to her that she wasn't going. She insisted that Madison had said they were. Then one day, Madison was gone. Elizabeth was broken hearted. Next thing I knew, she was pregnant and marrying Aaron." She lowered her voice. "I always suspected she got pregnant on purpose because she was afraid of being alone. I tried to talk to her about it, but she got mad and ran off with Aaron and I haven't talked to her since."

"Then I guess you don't know anything about her relationship with Lindsay Davis," Joshua asked. "Her married name was Ellison."

"Heather Davis's little sister," Naomi said with a nod of her head. "I heard they got really close after they both had babies and ended up being neighbors. One of my former foster kids ended up living not far from them. Sometimes, she'd end up at the playground with her kids while Lindsay and Elizabeth were there. They'd talk." She frowned. "Elizabeth was so jealous of Heather's relationship with Lindsay that she couldn't see straight. It was like she couldn't understand that there was a connection between real siblings that friendship can't trump."

"Then if Lindsay and Heather were fighting, Elizabeth would have a reason to feed that fight to break them up," Joshua said.

"Jealousy."

"She was looking for someone to fill the void left by her sister running away," Cameron said.

"Whose idea was it to sign Elizabeth up for dancing lessons?" Joshua asked.

"Hers," Naomi said. "I try to find out what my kids enjoy and get them into something. Being involved, finding out what they're good at. Through that, they meet others who share the same interest and make friends. That all contributes to making them feel like they belong. The first time we drove pass Miss Charlotte's Dance Studio, Elizabeth was instantly drawn to it." She sighed. "I think the only time she was happy was when she was in that studio. It was like she'd be in another world when she was dancing."

Cameron uttered a gasp. "We looked at the wrong dance studio!"

Joshua grasped her hand and pulled her to her feet. "Miss Charlotte's."

"Where's Miss Charlotte's Dance Studio?" Cameron asked Naomi.

"It's a half a mile down the road," Joshua said. "I know right where it's at."

LAUREN CARR

"Miss Charlotte sold it when she retired." Naomi followed them out the door. "A hairdresser bought it, but she went out of business and the bank foreclosed on it." She called to them from the porch, "It's abandoned now."

Cameron was on her phone calling for the dispatcher to send uniformed officers to assist in searching the deserted studio.

"We're only a couple of minutes away." Joshua was checking his semi-automatic in the holster on his belt and his back-up weapon, a twenty-two caliber Ruger, which he carried in his jacket pocket. "It's down by Laughlin's Corner."

"We drove right past it on the way to Naomi's," Cameron said. "I didn't see any lights on, but then, I wasn't looking for any." She turned the cruiser out onto the street.

"The place was foreclosed on. There's no electricity."

"Oh, I pray she's all right," she muttered. "Elizabeth's had her for six hours now."

As they approached the traffic light marking Laughlin's Corner, Cameron slowed the cruiser down. The darkness was pierced by the traffic light and the convenience store on the corner. Beyond the store, further off the road, Cameron could barely make out the darkened shape of a small building. "I never even noticed that there before."

"That's because you never took dance." Joshua pointed at a dark shape at the far end of the parking lot. "Someone's parked at the back door."

It was the same car that had tried to run Cameron down. Parked behind the convenience store, it was not visible from the road.

Cameron cut the lights on her cruiser and drove around the building. Together, they looked for any sign of light or activity inside.

"See anything?" she asked.

"They're here."

Cameron rolled the cruiser to a stop next to a tree and picnic table—as far from the building as possible, but close enough to see what was going on. She called into emergency dispatch to report finding Elizabeth's car.

"ETA five minutes," dispatch reported.

"Where are they coming from? Pittsburgh?" she asked as Joshua slipped out of the cruiser and hurried toward the rear door of the building. "Get back here."

After being assured by the dispatcher that backup was on its way, Cameron scurried across the lot to where Joshua was braced against the outer wall next to the door.

"What are you—"

Joshua put his finger to his lips and gestured for her to listen.

Cameron pressed her ear to the door. The rhythmic beat of the music made the door seem to vibrate. They could practically feel the pulse of the tune against their backs through the wall.

"I guess Elizabeth failed Evading the Police 101," Cameron whispered while unholstering her weapon. She discovered that the hook and eye plate and padlock that the bank had screwed onto the door and door frame to secure the building had been removed and tossed to the ground.

Joshua took out his gun and held it behind his back. "This door opens to the storeroom. Six feet across the storeroom is the doorway to the studio on the other side. The hair salon may have kept the mirrored walls."

"Which means she'll be able to see us coming," Cameron said.

"Exactly. There's also a basement. That's where Miss Charlotte used to keep her costumes. Doubt if they're there now. The stairs are a few feet to your right once you go in." Joshua placed his hand on the doorknob. Slowly, he turned it. The knob twisted, clicked, and swung open.

Aiming her gun to the floor, Cameron slipped in and braced her body against the wall. She took her pen light from her jacket pocket and held it low to get a sense of her surroundings. She discovered that only a foot from her was the open doorway to the basement stairs.

While the music was loud enough to hurt her eardrums, Cameron was grateful for it to cover up any noise they made.

Keeping low, Joshua slipped across the storeroom to the closed door leading into the studio and pressed flat against the wall. Cameron went over to take a position on the other side of the doorframe. Moving slowly, she reached for the doorknob and opened the door ever so slightly.

The music seemed to burst through the opening to box their ears. They could hear quick movement to the beat inside the studio.

Joshua pressed an eye against the opening and peered into the darkened room. With hand gestures, he told Cameron that Madison was in the corner on the other side of the studio.

"What's Elizabeth doing?" Cameron whispered.

With wide eyes, Joshua wiggled his fingers to indicate that she was dancing.

"Dancing?" It came out as a squawk.

The song coming to an end, Elizabeth's voice seemed to bounce off the rafters. "What did you think of that, Maddie? Tell me that you're having fun, Maddie!"

Receiving no answer, Elizabeth's question turned into a demand. "Tell me, Madison!"

"It was great. I've always thought you were a great dancer, Elizabeth." Madison sounded exhausted and frightened. "Don't you want to go home now? Your family's going to get worried."

"Stop saying that! *You* are my family." Elizabeth grabbed a fistful of Madison's hair. "I've done everything for you. When you hurt, I hurt. When you cry, I cry. When that worthless piece of garbage you called a father hurt you, I paid him back for you."

"You killed my daddy?"

"I did that for you!"

Madison uttered a cry of gut-wrenching remorse. "No!"

"He betrayed you! He made you cry! I couldn't let him get away with that!"

"You bitch!"

"Bitch? Bitch!" Elizabeth slapped her. "I'm your sister! I killed for you and that's how you thank me!"

"Where's our backup?" Cameron asked with a hiss.

"We need to go in." Joshua grabbed Cameron's arm and whispered into her ear. "I'm going to swing around and see if I can come in through the front door. You stay here. Distract her if you have to." He slipped out the back door.

Cameron opened the door ever so slightly to look inside.

Elizabeth was dressed in tights and leotards and dance shoes. Her bleached hair was held back with a headband. Madison sat in a straight back chair. Through a dim beam of light from a street light, Cameron could see that she was taped to the chair.

After finding another song on her phone, Elizabeth proceeded to leap and twirl and dance about the dimly-lit cluttered studio.

The floor to ceiling mirrors were filthy from lack of care, but Elizabeth didn't notice. She had escaped to a time when it had been a place of dreams—when she was young and her future was full of possibilities for acceptance and love.

Elizabeth was immersed in her dance when Cameron saw a slight movement behind where Madison was bound to the chair.

Just a little bit more.

Elizabeth went into a spin.

Keeping low, Joshua crept up behind Madison's chair. He took a knife from his pocket and placed his hand on hers.

Startled, Madison shrieked.

Elizabeth teetered and fell.

Joshua sliced through the tape holding one of Madison's arms to free her.

"No!" Elizabeth screamed above the music while holding out her arms to them. "Don't take my sister!"

"Police!" Her weapon drawn, Cameron sprung from the store room. "Don't move, Elizabeth!"

Elizabeth threw up her legs to kick the gun out of Cameron's hand. The weapon slid across the floor. Elizabeth then swiped Cameron's legs out from under her. Cameron hit the floor with a thud. Elizabeth pounced on her.

Seeing Elizabeth attacking Cameron like a crazed maniac, Joshua froze.

"Please don't leave me!" Madison grabbed him with her free hand.

"Get Madison out of here!" Cameron ordered while delivering a punch to Elizabeth's face, which barely seemed to faze her.

Joshua continued to slice through the tape holding Madison as fast as he could.

"You have no right taking my sister from me!" Elizabeth went after Cameron with everything she had—nails, fists, kicks. Cameron tried to fight her off as best she could while reaching for her backup weapon on her ankle.

Once Madison was free, Joshua pulled her out of the chair. Too terrified to move, she threw both arms around him and held on while he practically carried her outside.

Two cruisers pulled into the parking lot as he went out. A uniformed officer spilled out with his weapon drawn. "Hold it right there!"

Straddling Cameron, Elizabeth had both hands around her neck. "How dare you take my sister from me. Can't you see we're a pair? We belong together. No one can take my sister from me."

It took every ounce of strength for Cameron to suck in every bit of breath to stay conscious. With one arm, she fought to break Elizabeth's hold on her throat while stretching her other arm for her ankle. *Just a fraction of an inch more.*

Elizabeth's face swirled above her. Her expression was filled with complete insanity.

Consciousness slipping away, Cameron dropped her arm from her leg. The cold touch of metal against her forearm sent a jolt up her arm and to her brain.

The burst of gunfire drowned out the rock chorus of the song bursting from Elizabeth's phone.

Joshua pushed through the two uniformed officers leading the way inside. He found Elizabeth on top of Cameron in the middle of the floor. They were motionless. Cameron's service weapon lay next to them.

"Cameron!" He ran across the floor and shoved Elizabeth off his wife. There was so much blood on them, that he couldn't tell who shot who. "Cam?" He pressed his fingers against her throat.

The touch of his hand made Cameron jump up with a loud gasp. Her eyes flew open. She grabbed his arm as if intent to break it. He took her into a tight hug while she coughed and gasped for oxygen to fill her lungs.

"You scared me to death," he breathed into her ear.

"I scared you?" she gasped out. "I scared me."

Standing above them, the ranking uniformed officer called in the police shooting.

It wasn't until they had erected lights in the studio to examine the scene that the significance of Elizabeth's final dance struck home.

Under the brilliant spotlight, she lay sprawled out in the middle of the dance studio floor dressed in her bright blue leotards and dance shoes. One arm lay across her blood-soaked mid-section, while the other hand landed above her head. One leg was straight, while the other leg was crossed at the ankle.

Her blue eyes and mouth were open wide—an expression of ecstasy in the ballerina's fatal last dance.

Unsteady on her legs, Cameron knelt to study the half-heart necklace around her neck. It was the first time she had a chance to read the inscription on the heart:

Forever My Sister. Always My Friend.

CHAPTER THIRTY-ONE

"Whose cars are those?" Madison's voice went up an octave when Joshua pulled Cameron's cruiser into the Whitaker driveway. It was the middle of the night before they could take Madison home to where her mother had been waiting for word about her daughter.

Cameron recognized Tony's SUV. She also recognized Kathleen Davis's elegant vehicle. "What is Kathleen Davis doing here?" she asked in a raspy voice. Her throat was sore from being strangled.

"She killed Mom!" Madison threw open the car door before Cameron could come to a complete stop.

"I'm sure Tony wouldn't let that happen," Cameron said.

"Maybe she killed him, too," Joshua said.

The kitchen was filled with loud girlish laughter. Sherry, Kathleen, and Tony sat around the kitchen table. Each one had a margarita glass in front of them and a puppy in their arms. Kathleen wore a housecoat, plus an apron on top of that, to protect herself against puppy drool and dog hair.

"Then John told the police officer that I was choking and that he was doing the Heimlich maneuver, to which the officer replied," Kathleen laughed so hard, she could barely finish. "'What is she choking on? Your tongue?'"

They bent over with laughter. Even Sherry's pack of dogs and pups seemed to be joining in the merriment.

"I guess the wives are getting along," Joshua said.

"Oh, yeah, we've been getting along great," Sherry said while taking the last sip of her margarita. Seeing Madison, she jumped to her feet. "Maddie! You're okay!" Still clutching the pup, she hurried across the kitchen to hug her daughter.

"They found her!" Kathleen flew out of the chair to join in the hug.

"I'm so happy!" To their surprise, Tony also stood to join in the group hug.

Puzzled, Madison looked over her mother's shoulder to Cameron, who picked up the empty pitcher that had held margaritas.

"I guess you two are okay with Dad's shenanigans," Madison said.

"Well," Kathleen said, "the news was an awful shock to say the least."

"To say the least," Sherry said.

"But then, between Heather's being in intensive care and you getting abducted, we both needed someone to lean on. I wouldn't have made it through the last several hours of waiting, if it hadn't been for your mother." Kathleen took Sherry's hand. "I can see what it is about her that made my husband run off to commit bigamy."

"Oh, you're too kind, Kathleen," Sherry said. "You were the strong woman behind the man, and Shawn respected that. He knew he needed you. It was your strength that got me through this night. Why, I wouldn't have made it if I didn't have you to listen to me rattle on and on."

"I was rattling more than you," Kathleen said while stroking the puppy, who was licking her jaw.

"We were all rattling," Tony said.

"The doctor called," Kathleen said, "and if Heather continues like she has been, he'll be able to bring her out of the coma tomorrow morning." She smiled at Madison. "Maddie, I know she'll want you there."

"I guess you arrested Elizabeth?" Sherry asked Cameron.

"She's dead," Cameron said.

"You were right, Mom," Madison said. "She was crazier than a fruit bat. She thought I was her sister."

"Did your father have a third wife?" Sherry asked.

"I don't see where he would have had the energy," Tony said.

"Mom, she killed Dad," Madison said with a sob.

The three women once more went into a group hug.

"Well," Sherry sniffed, "Shawn or John, depending on who he is to you, may be gone, but one good thing did come out of this. We've all found each other—and I have a feeling your father is looking down on us with a big grin on his face."

Exhausted, Joshua and Cameron left, with Tony directly behind them on the way out the door.

"We'll drive you home," Cameron ordered Tony.

"They insisted."

"You're on duty," she said.

"Are you going to write me up?"

"I should, but I'm tired. Get in the car."

Tony slid into the back seat of Cameron's cruiser. Joshua got behind the wheel.

"I found out what it is about Davis that had those two women falling all over him," Tony said. "I mean, let's face it. The guy wasn't any Brad Pitt in the looks department, and they were ga-ga over him."

"What was it?" Joshua asked.

"He had sex with them every night."

Joshua hit the brakes. "Every night?" He looked over at Cameron who was looking him up and down.

Tony hiccupped.

"I'm sure they were just exaggerating." Joshua pressed his foot back on the accelerator.

"That's what I thought until they started comparing notes," Tony said.

"Notes?" Cameron asked.

"We're talking glorious details. From what those two were saying, John Davis could have taught Hugh Hefner a thing or two."

"I'm sure it wasn't every night," Joshua said with a shake of his head.

"Josh," Cameron said, "why don't—"

"We're not going to talk about it."

Tony grabbed the back of Joshua's seat. "Every single night, I tell you. Whichever wife he was with at the time."

"Nobody is that amorous," Joshua said.

"He was married to Kathleen Davis for over thirty years and she said he never missed a night when he was home." Tony pounded Joshua's seat. "Not even food poisoning could stop him."

"Now I'm depressed," Joshua said.

"I thought we weren't going to talk about this," Cameron said.

Sheriff Sawyer woke Joshua up the next morning with the news that Aaron Collins had not only survived the night, but that he had also regained consciousness. A chemical analysis of his drink revealed that it contained an overdose of over-the-counter sleeping pills. The doctor suggested that the only thing that kept Aaron alive was a combination of the caffeine in his energy drink to counter the sedative and his large size.

Aaron broke down upon learning the news of his wife's death.

Sheriff Sawyer, Joshua, and Cameron exchanged glances of sympathy while the young man, who was not quite twenty-five, sobbed upon hearing the news that the mother of his children was dead.

"We know this is a very difficult time for you," Joshua held out a tissue box to him. "but we do have to ask you some important questions. We need to make sense of this."

Aaron took several tissues and dabbed his tear-filled eyes. "I guess you've figured out that Elizabeth was the one who put the sleeping pills in my energy drink."

"Why would she try to kill you?" Cameron asked.

"We had a fight."

"Every couple fights," Cameron said, "but they don't all try to kill each other."

Aaron hung his head. "Elizabeth had issues."

"Elizabeth was a killer," Cameron said. "She murdered Madison's father."

"I thought he was Heather's father," Aaron said.

"He was also Madison's father," Joshua said.

"Last week, Elizabeth told me that she had killed Heather's dad because Maddie was upset because he was carrying on with her mother," Aaron said. "Then, a couple of days ago, she came home saying that she'd overheard Maddie and Heather talking. Turns out she'd murdered Maddie's dad and he was cheating on her mother with Heather's mom. I thought she'd killed a second man." He looked up at them. "Who did she kill?"

"It's complicated," Sheriff Sawyer said.

"You moved the body, didn't you, Aaron?" Joshua said.

"We matched tracks left at the dump site to your SUV," Cameron said. "We also found blood in the rear compartment—enough to run DNA tests."

Aaron rose his eyes to Cameron's. Slowly, he dragged his gaze to Joshua's.

"Elizabeth wasn't strong enough to move a grown man," Cameron said. "Davis had been stabbed thirty-two times. She must have been covered in blood when she got home that night. She told you what she'd done, so you went to the apartment and found John Davis's body."

"Your first thought was to protect Elizabeth. So you moved the body and cleaned up the scene in hopes of destroying any evidence that she had been there," Joshua said.

"She was my wife," Aaron said. "It was my job to protect her. I knew I couldn't support her like she wanted to be supported, but I could do what I could to protect her."

"Even when it's murder?" Sheriff Sawyer asked.

"She was sick," Aaron said with a shrug of his shoulders.

"Then she needed help," Cameron said. "Not having her crimes covered up. Did Elizabeth tell you how the murder had happened?"

Aaron wiped his nose. "Somehow, Madison had become friends with Heather Davis. Those two hated each other back when they were competing in dance. Well, suddenly, out of the blue they were friends and that drove Elizabeth crazy—especially since she blamed Heather for Lindsay getting killed. She felt like Heather was muscling in on her position at the dance studio."

"What was her position at the dance studio?" Cameron asked.

"She told me that Madison hired her to manage the place so that she'd be free to teach dance," Aaron said. "But then I saw when I was setting up the computers at the place that really Elizabeth was just a receptionist. She did some social media stuff, but not much else. But if you had asked her, she'd make like it was a lot more. When she told Mom that she was teaching dance, I thought she was just trying to sound more important than she really was."

"But it was more than that," Cameron said.

"She bleached her hair to make it the same color as Madison's and got all these dance clothes like what Madison wore. I thought she just admired Madison and wanted to be like her," Aaron said. "Then, one day last week, she went into the studio where a class was getting ready and started to lead them on the warmup. Madison was really upset about that when she walked in and saw it."

"Elizabeth was delusional," Joshua said.

"When she found out that Madison and Heather were going out together that Friday night, she went nuts," Aaron said. "Madison had left early—leaving Elizabeth at the studio. Elizabeth closed up the studio early and followed her."

"We have witnesses who identified her from a picture at the bar where Madison had met Heather," Cameron said. "She hid at a corner table to watch them."

"Elizabeth told me that Heather's father was having an affair with Madison's mom," Aaron said. "Or maybe it was the other way around. They found Madison's dad cheating with Heather's mom? Whatever? They all got into a huge fight. Madison was hysterical when they left. Elizabeth went nuts because he had hurt her. So, she knocked on the door. He answered and she confronted him about upsetting Madison. She said he didn't even know who she was—which got her even madder." He shook his head. "She told me that he should have known who she was—because she was Madison's sister. Totally weird."

"After killing who she thought was Heather's father," Cameron said, "Elizabeth tried to frame Derek because she knew he had issues with the Davis family. Why did you dump his body out at the Newhart farm?"

"Because it was out in the sticks," Aaron said. "We'd gone out there for Madison's Christmas party. It was out in the middle of nowhere and since it was late at night, I figured it might take a while for anyone to find the body. I had wrapped it up in a comforter and doused it in gasoline. I figured it'd burn up into ashes and no one would know who it was."

Cameron and Joshua exchanged glances.

"Tell us about the necklace that Elizabeth wore," Cameron said.

"What about it?" Aaron shrugged his shoulders. "Lindsay gave that to her."

"Why would Lindsay give that to Elizabeth?" Cameron asked. "It's a sister's necklace. Heather had given it to Lindsay."

Aaron shook his head. "Elizabeth told me that Lindsay gave it to her that night she died because she had fired Heather."

"You can't fire your family," Joshua said.

Aaron hung his head.

Joshua leaned over to catch his eye. "Elizabeth was driving the night of the accident, wasn't she?"

Aaron nodded his head. "She had walked home from the accident. She was wasted. She said it was Lindsay's fault."

"But Elizabeth was driving."

"How'd you know—"

"Accident re-construction," Joshua said. "Lindsay's injuries indicate that she was struck by the rear passenger fender. How could it be Lindsay's fault if Elizabeth was driving?"

"Lindsay had given the necklace to Elizabeth because she was fighting with Heather. But on the way home, Lindsay—I guess she started sobering up or something. She changed her mind. She wanted the necklace back and Elizabeth said no. They got into a fight. Elizabeth said Lindsay tried to take it off her neck—while she was driving—and that's how the accident happened."

"And after the accident, Elizabeth never offered to give the necklace back to Heather?" Cameron asked.

"Why would she?" Aaron asked. "She never took it off. She loved that necklace. She said that Lindsay had told her that the necklace made them sisters forever. Nothing could ever come between them."

"Even death," Joshua said.

"I guess that proves you can overthink things." Cameron looked out the side window of Joshua's SUV at the Ohio River while he drove across the bridge to take them home. With the murders solved and Heather on her way to recovery, she was ready for a few days off.

Joshua smiled softly. "Aaron had no intention of planting any false leads when he dumped Davis's body at the Newhart farm. He didn't even know Davis was connected to them. He just figured it was a good place to dump a body far away from where Elizabeth would be implicated."

Cameron uttered a deep sigh. She felt as if she would fall instantly into a deep sleep if she closed her eyes. "All we have to do now is finish renovating that mansion, open a fancy restaurant, and plan a wedding."

Reminded of the wedding, Joshua said, "And find a wedding gown with gold lace overlay."

"Okay, Valerie, where did I put it?" His hands on his hips, Joshua stood in the middle of the store room in the basement of their home and looked up and down—from the floor to the ceiling—taking stock of every object on the shelves.

Cameron's reminder of the upcoming wedding brought home the dilemma of Poppy's wedding gown. A wedding gown with a gold lace overlay.

"I've never seen a gown like that. Have you?" Tracy had asked.

As a matter of fact, he had.

Cameron had gone upstairs to bed and fallen fast asleep as soon as they got home. Joshua couldn't sleep until he took care of this matter.

"Where is it, Valerie?" Joshua asked his late wife—the mother of his five older children. "Poppy wouldn't have gotten that idea in her mind if you didn't plant it there. If you want her to wear your gown, you need to tell me where it is."

Abruptly, there was a rattle from a far corner in the room. A pile of board games tumbled to the floor. Monopoly money floated and game pieces scattered. Joshua saw the top corner of a large ivory box encased in thick plastic standing upright against the wall.

"That's my girl." Joshua moved the remaining boxes blocking his access to the box and pulled it out. Almost three decades after the gown had been cleaned, preserved, boxed, and stored in plastic, it was still in good shape—or so he guessed. He wasn't going to unseal it to check. He was going to leave that up to the bride.

It was a miracle that it hadn't been lost long ago. During his career in the Navy, the gown had made every move with the Thornton family at Valerie's insistence. Even after Valerie had passed away, Joshua had it shipped to his family home in Chester.

It was what she wanted.

Now, he knew why.

He plopped the box in the front seat of his SUV and hurried out to J.J.'s farm. Per usual, Ollie and Charley raced out to greet him. This time, Charley rode on Ollie's back.

Izzy, who had spent the night at the farm while Joshua and Cameron pursued Elizabeth, appeared in the barn door. "You're not taking me home now, are you?" Her face was filled with disappointment. "The vet just cleared Pilgrim to be let out with the other horses. Poppy and I are going to introduce them."

"I came to see Poppy."

"What about?" J.J. had stepped out onto the porch upon seeing the SUV.

"It's a secret," Joshua said with a sly grin.

With the barnyard between them, Poppy and J.J. exchanged puzzled glances.

Joshua extracted the oversized box from the seat and handed it to her. "Is this your dream gown?" he asked her in a low voice.

Curious, Izzy had trotted up behind her and sneaked a look at the box.

Poppy cocked her head at him. A slim grin crossed her lips. She carried the box into the barn with Joshua and Izzy behind her. When J.J. started to follow, Izzy yelled back at him. "Don't you come in here!"

Poppy set the box on a work bench and cut a slit in the heavy plastic.

The wonderful scent of fresh flowers floated from inside the box. It was the scent of Valerie's favorite perfume.

Poppy slipped the box from the plastic and carefully opened it.

The gown was not stark white, but not ivory either. It was an eggshell white—with a delicate golden lace overlay over the entire gown.

"Is that—" Izzy looked up at Joshua. "Where did you find it?"

"Valerie wore it on our wedding day," Joshua said. "Her grandmother was a seamstress. She never had much money. She designed this gown and made it by hand as her wedding gift to us. Valerie loved it so much that she insisted on preserving and saving it to pass down to our daughters. Tracy insisted on having her own gown and Sarah—" He shrugged his shoulders. "She's so independent—if she ever gets married—it will be at the justice of the peace after a night of heavy drinking."

"I'm never getting married either." Izzy patted Poppy on the shoulder. "That leaves you."

"Is this your dream gown, Poppy?" Joshua asked.

Tears filled Poppy's eyes as she fingered the gown's delicate material. She nodded her head.

"I guess this is Valerie's way of giving her blessing on your marriage." Joshua kissed her on the forehead.

After reminding Izzy that he would pick her up later, he turned to leave only to find Poppy's hand on his arm. He looked down at her.

"Josh …" She swallowed and started again. "Would you mind giving me away at our wedding … Dad?"

He hugged her tight. "I'd be honored."

Epilogue

Even Mother Nature blessed the Ashburn-Thornton wedding with a beautiful spring day. During the week leading up to the big day, the lilies had sprouted in the gardens surrounding the Russell Ridge Inn to add to those supplied by the florist for the outdoor ceremony.

Every able-bodied member of the family, and more than a few friends, joined in working on the mansion to get it ready for the grand opening. There was nothing like the stress of getting every inspection, from building to health department, approved in time. The last inspection was approved with one day to spare.

It was time to focus on the wedding.

The plan was for an elegant garden wedding in the afternoon followed by a sit-down dinner reception. In addition to the formal dining rooms, the inn also boasted a cellar pub with a dance floor. A local band had been hired to play music after dinner and late into the evening.

Family and friends spilled into town. The Thornton home on Rock Springs Boulevard was filled with grown children. Sarah had brought along Tristan Faraday, her boyfriend, who happened to be her sister's-in-law brother. Joshua loved intimidating the young man.

Best man Murphy and his wife, Jessica, a bridesmaid, had accepted J.J.'s invitation to stay at his home. Since Charley intimidated their sheltie Spencer, they had left the dog at Joshua and Cameron's home. Staying with J.J. gave the twin brothers a chance to catch up the night before the wedding, which they did way into the early morning hours.

In the morning, Jessica found them asleep in the living room. She gave her husband a quick kiss good-bye and hurried out to meet the bridesmaids and the bride at the inn for brunch. Afterwards, the ladies were going to spend the hours leading up to the ceremony getting pampered with makeovers.

Careful not to trip over J.J.'s and Poppy's suitcases stacked in the foyer, she stepped outside to be greeted with a boisterous crow from Charley, who was perched on the porch rail. It wouldn't have been so bad if the huge rooster hadn't scared the daylights out of her.

"I have a feeling you're not in Great Falls anymore, Jessie." Jessica muttered to herself before noticing Poppy's truck parked next to the barn.

The horses were out in the pastures—a clue that they had been fed.

"What is she—" With a sense of duty, she trotted across the barnyard, while being mindful of stepping in any canine, lamb, or horse landmines.

At the rehearsal dinner, J.J. had assured Poppy that he and Murphy would take care of the morning chores so that she could sleep in and enjoy being queen for the day.

"I'm queen every day," Poppy quipped back.

"That you are," J.J. bestowed a kiss on her hand.

Ollie met Jessica at the barn door and led the way to a corner stall, where she found Poppy speaking softly to Pilgrim.

They had introduced Jessica and Murphy to the horse the day before.

"Poppy, what are you doing here? J.J. and Murphy said they'd do your chores."

"I had a bad feeling this morning." Poppy went around to the side of the horse and placed her hands on her pregnant stomach. "Good thing I came out. She's in labor."

"Labor! What do you mean she's in labor?"

"She's going to have her colt. I don't know how well she'll do. We don't know anything about her. If she's had a colt before? If she'll have difficulty?"

"Poppy, you are not going to postpone this wedding because a *horse* has gone into labor."

"But I can't just leave her," Poppy said. "What if she runs into trouble?"

Jessica stepped into the stall, took Poppy by the arm, and tugged on it the lead her out. "Poppy, horses have been giving birth for thousands of years before humans decided to stick their noses into their business. They have all done fine without us."

With a worried look back at the horse, Poppy objected, "But—"

"I'll text Murphy to keep an eye on her."

Reluctant to leave, Poppy whispered one last word of encouragement to Pilgrim before allowing Jessica to usher her out. "The guys are going to be here all morning. They'll take care of her." In the barnyard, she yanked open the door to Poppy's truck. "Now get in that truck and follow me to the Inn. This is your wedding day!"

"Where's J.J.?" Tristan Faraday asked Murphy after finding him in the kitchen making a green power smoothie.

Sarah Thornton had dropped him off on her way to the Inn. Since the tall lanky young man had only drunk one pot of coffee that morning, he decided to make another for himself and the rest of the groomsmen, who were expected any minute.

"He's checking on a pregnant mare, who decided to go into labor," Murphy said while slicing a banana into the blender. "Poppy's worried about her." He pointed the paring knife in the general direction of the foyer. "That luggage is theirs for the honeymoon. We can go ahead and put it in J.J.'s truck so that they can be ready to hit the road after the reception."

"Poppy still doesn't know where they're going?" Tristan asked with a sly grin.

"J.J. had to give her a clue because she didn't know what to pack," Murphy said. "So, he had to tell her to pack for warm weather. Since she needed to get a passport, she knows that they're leaving the country."

"Ah, Poppy is going to have a ball," Tristan said. "Two nights in a bridal suite at the Spencer Inn—wedding present from Dad. Then, a ten-day Mexican cruise."

A sly grin crossed Murphy's face. He looked out the window to make sure J.J. wouldn't walk in on them. "For our wedding present, Jessica and I upgraded J.J.'s cruise reservations to a deluxe suite. He's going to arrive thinking they're getting a regular room. Wait until they get led to a suite!" With a laugh, they bumped fists.

Hearing a vehicle pull up to the house, they went out to greet either Hunter or their father and Donny. Instead, they found Tad MacMillan getting out of his SUV. An exceedingly thin young man in an ill-fitting suit slid from the passenger seat.

"I'm delivering a breakfast casserole and pastry tray from Tracy," Tad said.

Tristan's eyes lit up. "Food!" A flash of concern crossed his face. "Did she include cheese danish?"

Tad placed a tray in Tristan's arms. "Homemade. She put a post-it with your name on one."

"Should I be scared? She did say she was going to get even with me for that incident at Christmas."

Tad arched an eyebrow. One corner of his mouth curled upward. With a shrug of his shoulders, he carried the food container inside.

"She wouldn't." Tristan turned to Murphy. "Would she?"

"She did ask me to pick up a case of rat poison on the way out yesterday," Murphy said while regarding Tad's passenger who was climbing from the vehicle.

Like a man on his way to the gallows, Tristan went inside the house.

J.J. stepped out of the barn and started to make his way across the barnyard.

"Tad had asked me to help him," the young man told Murphy, who peered him with curiosity. He looked familiar, but Murphy wasn't sure how he knew him. "He says the saying that idle hands are the devil's playground is true."

"That is true," Murphy said.

"Congratulations on your wedding. And I mean that."

Murphy started to explain that he was not J.J. when abruptly the young man threw his arms around him and gave him a tight hug. "You saved my life!" He proceeded to sob.

"Should I leave the two of you alone?" J.J. whispered to Murphy.

"I think this belongs to you." Murphy peeled the emotional man's arms from where they held him and deposited them on J.J.'s shoulders.

"I owe you my life!" He tightened his grip and cried into J.J.'s shoulder.

"Who is this guy?" Murphy asked.

J.J. shook his head. "I didn't get a clear look at him."

"Whoever he is, his tears of gratitude are leaving water marks on your shirt."

"You're welcome for my saving your life." J.J. pulled out of the embrace. "I think you've thanked me enough, whoever you are."

"I'm Derek. Derek Ellison." He sniffed and wiped the tears from his cheeks. "You defended me when everyone— and I mean *everyone*—thought I'd killed my father-in-law. John Davis. Everyone told me to cop a plea. But you believed in my innocence."

"Derek Ellison." Murphy folded his arms. "The same Derek Ellison who stabbed a friend of ours back at Oak Glen."

"That would be me. I'm really sorry about that. Between the drugs and alcohol, I just couldn't think straight."

"Derek?" J.J. looked the young man up and down. He was bathed, shaven, and dressed in fairly nice clothes. He looked nothing like the Derek Ellison he had defended months earlier. "What happened to you?"

"I've been clean and sober for sixty-two days," Derek said. "Got out of rehab two weeks ago. I've moved in with Mom. Going to Narcotics Anonymous every day. Tad is working on getting me a sponsor. Going back to school and looking for a job. Kathleen says that if I make it to the six-month mark, she'll let me have supervised visitations with Luke." With a grin, he leaned in to whisper. "But I'll get to see him today. She's letting me sit with them at the wedding. John's other wife talked her into it. Sherry says everyone deserves a second chance." He patted J.J. on the back. "I owe it all to this guy."

"I guess things are working out then," J.J. said. "I mean, after it came out about John Davis's …" He didn't quite know what to call it.

"'Bigamy," Murphy said. "He was a bigamist."

"You'd think that the fur would be flying," Derek said. "But it's not. Those women have become besties. Kathleen and Sherry are like this." He held up his crossed fingers. "I guess it's helping. Kathleen was really OCD, but she's loosened up since she met Sherry, who's actually pretty cool. Sherry is teaching Kathleen and Luke how to control that dog John gave him and she babysits Luke when Kathleen is working late. Luke adores Sherry and all of those dogs."

"And Heather's recovered from the accident?" Murphy asked.

"Did you hear about her quitting her job?"

"She quit her job?" J.J. asked. "She had a good job with a big company out in Robinson."

"Said she didn't like it, and life's too short to spend it doing something you don't like," Derek said. "She and Madison are partners at the dance studio. You'd never believe those two used to be at each other's throats."

"Really?" Murphy shot a sly grin in J.J.'s direction. "I don't remember that. Do you, J.J.?"

J.J. jabbed Murphy in the ribs.

"It's like they didn't lose a husband and father, but they extended their family big-time."

"That's what it sounds like," J.J. said.

"You know what Dad always told us," Murphy said.

"What did Mr. Thornton say?" Derek asked.

"As long as you have your family," J.J. said. "you have everything. Without it, you have nothing."

"Is he still not ready?" Dressed in his tux, Joshua rushed from J.J.'s master suite and across the hall to the guest room where Hunter was helping Donny Thornton tie his bowtie. Joshua pointed to where J.J.'s tuxedo was still sealed in the garment bag.

"I thought he would have been back from the barn long ago," Hunter said.

"The horse is having problems," Donny said. "Tristan went out a bit ago to check on them."

"They're still fussing over that horse?" Joshua asked.

"Poppy has been calling every hour checking on her," Hunter said. "Tracy and Jessica had to talk her out of running over here to deliver the colt herself."

"Horses have been having colts without any help for thousands of years." Joshua spun around and ran down the stairs. "Murphy is the best man! If he was doing his job he'd hog-tie J.J. and bring him up here and throw him in the shower."

Hunter and Donny followed Joshua out the door. Charley crowed and jumped down from the porch railing to lead them to the barn.

His face pale, Tristan Faraday met them at the door.

"Where's J.J.?"

"He's got—" Tristan pointed toward the stall.

Joshua pushed him aside and went to where Ollie and Gulliver gazed wide-eyed into the corner stall.

"You don't want to see," Tristan told Hunter and Donny.

Taking Tristan's advice, Donny turned around and went back outside—only to find Charley glaring at him. "That rooster never did like me." He backed up against the side of the barn.

Tristan joined him. "He doesn't like me either."

"What should we do?" Hunter asked.

"There's a case of beer left over from rehearsal dinner," Tristan said.

"Sounds good to me."

They turned to find Charley blocking the path to the house.

"I guess he wants us to go help," Donny said.

Lying on her side, Pilgrim was in agony. Murphy tugged on the colt's front legs. J.J. had his hand inside the horse when Joshua and Hunter found them.

"What are you doing?" Joshua demanded to know.

Unable to look, Hunter turned away.

"The colt is stuck. If we don't help her, both her and the baby are going to die." He grunted and tugged on the colt. "Okay, I turned the head. Its snout is right here. We should be able to get it out if we pull really hard this time." He patted the mare's rump. "Come on, girl. You're almost there."

Forgetting his rented tux, Joshua dropped next to J.J. and grabbed the colt's slimy white leg. Hunter went around to help Murphy.

"Count of three," J.J. said. "One. Two. Three!"

They pulled on the two legs as hard as they could. Even Pilgrim seemed to push from her end. A white head with brown ears appeared.

"Again!" J.J. said. "Once the shoulder is out, then she'll be home free!"

They tightened their grip on the legs and pulled again—refusing to let up until both shoulders emerged. From there, the rest of the colt tumbled out.

Like the sudden winner in a game of tug of war, J.J. fell back onto his rump. The newborn horse landed in his lap.

Pilgrim uttered a deep sigh of relief.

"Ewww!" Tristan said.

Donny covered his mouth and turned away.

Murphy was impressed. "Dude, did they teach you about equine midwifery in law school?" He stroked the slimy newborn colt, who struggled to climb to his feet.

"He's a handsome guy." Joshua patted Pilgrim who climbed to her feet to inspect her new baby. "How did you know how to help her?"

"I saw Poppy help another one of our mares last year when she was having the same problem," J.J. said.

"He looks like he's wearing a hat." Hunter stroked one of the colt's brown ears.

"I don't know about you guys," Tristan said, "but I don't recall agreeing to act as a midwife when I signed up to be in this wedding."

"Smile!" Donny yelled from the stall door while focusing his cell phone on them.

The men gathered around J.J. who proudly held the white colt with brown ears. Donny snapped the picture just as the mother's and son's snouts met in a kiss.

There wasn't a dry eye in the rooms on the upper floor of the inn when Poppy emerged in her bridal gown. The form fitting gown hugged her slender frame down to her knees before flaring out. In addition to the gold lace overlay, the gown featured a detachable six-foot long train made of a sheer golden material that was hooked low on the waist, around to the front to create the illusion of a full skirt.

"That is the most beautiful gown I have ever seen in my life," Tracy blubbered, "and I've seen a lot of wedding gowns."

"I'd say. She dragged me up and down the coast looking for that perfect gown. Here it was at home in the basement." Sarah reminded Tracy, "You didn't think it was that beautiful in Mom and Dad's wedding pictures."

"I knew it was beautiful. Dad told me that he had it and that Mom wanted me to wear it." Tracy frowned. "I just wanted my own gown."

"And where is your own gown now?" Jessica asked.

"Preserved and stored in a closet for my daughter to wear," Tracy said.

"A daughter who will be wanting *her* own gown," Jessica said with a smile.

With no mother of the bride, it had become increasingly apparent during the wedding planning that Cameron was filling the role of both mother of the bride and groom. In keeping with the theme color for the wedding, she wore a tea-length lilac sleeveless tunic dress with a silky long-sleeve overlay.

Rushing into the room, Cameron relayed a message from Joshua. "You're not going to believe this. The good news is that Joshua is on his way over now. The bad news is that he's had to change into the suit he wore at the rehearsal dinner because he ruined his tux. The good news is that Pilgrim had her baby, which is how Joshua and Hunter ruined their tuxedoes. The bad news is that the groom and the groomsmen will be about a half hour late because they're too busy taking selfies with the horses to get ready. The good news is that the mother and colt are doing well."

The stylist was completing the finishing touches to the bride's French twist with tendrils falling around her face, when Poppy rushed out of her reach to grab her phone from the dressing table to check for a text from J.J. "It's a boy! Oh, he's beautiful!"

Izzy read a post on her phone. "Donny just posted a video of him having his first meal."

Poppy grabbed the phone from Izzy's hand. "That's a medicine hat horse." She smiled. "That's good luck. In the Native American legend, any tribe or ranch that has a medicine hat horse is blessed. They were so valuable because of the legend that people used to steal them."

The stylist, who was chasing the bride with a comb and brush, let out a breath filled with exasperation. "Hold still. We only need to make a few more adjustments."

Excited about the new colt, Poppy insisted on glancing at each picture being sent to the bridemaids.

"What's a medicine hat horse?" Jessica asked around a giggle of a selfie of Murphy and the colt.

"It's a white horse with a brown or black hat." Poppy pointed out the brown ears. "See how they look like a Native American headdress. Like medicine men used to wear back in the wild west."

There was a knock on the door. "The groom is on his way. Is the bride ready?" Joshua asked.

"Are we ready?" Cameron asked.

Hurriedly, the bridesmaid gathered their bouquets. The stylist made one last adjustment to the tendrils that framed Poppy's face.

Cameron opened the door.

Joshua stepped inside and stopped.

Speechless, he stared at Poppy. Memories of his wedding day filled his mind. Poppy did not physically resemble his first wife. Maybe that was why he had never noticed it before. The generosity, the compassion, the love—that was so much like Valerie. He had seen it but he hadn't seen it—until she stood before him wearing that gown.

No wonder Valerie wanted her to wear it.

"Are you okay?" Cameron whispered softly in his ear.

Joshua started. "Yes." He swallowed. "I'd forgotten how beautiful that gown was."

"J.J. is going to faint," Izzy said.

"If he faints, I'll never let him forget about it," Sarah said.

"We need to get a move on," Tracy said. "The ice sculptures are melting."

"The verandah on the other side of the mansion provides a perfect view of the garden. I'll go stake it out and send word over when the men arrive." Cameron gave both Izzy and Poppy kisses.

She pinched Joshua on the butt. "I'll see you later, handsome," she whispered before kissing him on the cheek on her way out the door.

The bridesmaids followed her out to check out the guests waiting in the garden. Exhausted from chasing the bride, the stylist gathered her materials and left. Joshua heard her muttering under her breath as she passed him on her way out the door.

Alone in the room, Joshua gestured at his suit. "My tux got ruined during colt birth."

"Cam mentioned that." With a soft smile, Poppy took his hand. "You look very handsome."

"Hunter's tux got ruined, too. Luckily, he still fits into his dress uni—"

She pressed her fingers against his lips. "All I care about is that J.J. is there at the altar. You can all be dressed in your birthday suits, as far as I care."

He laughed. "That would make this one wedding to remember."

She looked down at the video of the horse and her colt. "Thank you for taking care of Pilgrim."

"We couldn't exactly let her die on your wedding day, could we?" He peered into her eyes. They looked like two pools of emeralds. "Are you nervous?"

"Excited." She set the phone on the dressing table. "I'm sure J.J told you that ever since I left Montana, I never stayed any place more than a few months. I didn't allow myself to get close to anyone. Gulliver was all the family I needed."

"It's been more than a year, and you're still here," Joshua said. "And now you're getting married."

"I didn't intend for this to happen. It just—" She wiped away a tear threatening to mess up her makeup. "One day, it hit me. I'd gone and fallen in love without even knowing it was happening." She sniffed. "Now, you're all stuck with me."

"And you're stuck with us. But that's okay. With family, you have everything."

With a sniff, she turned to check her make-up in the mirror one last time. As she looked in the mirror, she saw a lovely woman with long blond hair behind Joshua.

It was the same woman she had seen in her dream.

Valerie brought her hand to her lips and blew Poppy a kiss. Then, with a wink, she faded away.

Two Weeks Later

"You're scaring me." Poppy had to restrain herself to keep from lifting the blindfold up and over her head to see where Joshua Thornton was taking them.

Joshua and Izzy had picked them up at the airport after their cruise. Cameron couldn't meet them because of an appointment.

Izzy wore a wicked grin on her face. "We have a surprise for you," she whispered into Poppy's ear while greeting her with a hug.

"What?" Poppy asked.

Izzy pursed her lips together and made a motion of turning a key. She wasn't talking.

With wide eyes, J.J. shrugged his shoulders in a broad gesture.

Conversation during the ride home was merry. The wedding had been beautiful. The guests had been impressed with the Russell Ridge Inn. Tracy had managed to get a full-page spread in the newspaper about its opening. Of course, the posts to social media from wedding guests raving about Russell Ridge Inn as being the place for gourmet food or an elegant fairy-tale garden wedding didn't hurt either. The farm-to-table restaurant was booked full for dining and special events—including weddings and receptions through the summer.

The honeymoon could not have been more perfect. With the surprise upgrade to a deluxe suite on the cruise, J.J. and Poppy were indeed treated like royalty. After months of rushing about for the wedding and restaurant opening, they enjoyed ten days of one-on-one time for intimacy, pampering, and complete relaxation.

Unbeknownst to the newlyweds, a star had been born on their wedding day in the form of the medicine hat colt, who J.J. had named Chief. Donny's pictures and videos had gone viral on social media.

As they got closer to home, Izzy turned around in her seat and held out a blindfold to Poppy. "Put this on."

Poppy looked at J.J., who shrugged his shoulders again. She took the blindfold. "Why doesn't J.J. have to put one on?"

"Because we only have one," Izzy said with a giggle.

Poppy slipped the blindfold over her eyes. J.J. draped his arm across her shoulders. She could feel his lips close to her ear.

"You're not going to believe this," he whispered.

"You already gave me my wedding present." She squeezed his hands.

"This isn't from me."

She could feel the vehicle rock back and forth as it turned onto a rough road. It slowed down while making its way up a steep hill. "We're going further away from civilization."

"I thought you didn't like civilization," Joshua said.

Finally, the SUV came to a halt. Poppy heard a loud whinny followed by many voices.

"She's here!" she heard Cameron call out.

J.J. grasped her hand when she reached for the blindfold. "Not yet! I want your surprise to be the first thing you see."

He helped her out of the back seat of the SUV. J.J. and Izzy each took one arm to guide her. She could sense several people around her and heard whinnies from more than one horse.

What is going on? We can't be home. That driveway is paved. Where are we?

Finally, they came to a halt.

Izzy was giggling like a maniac.

J.J. grabbed one corner of the blindfold. "Okay now—"

"Wait a minute!" a voice that Poppy recognized as Heather Davis's interrupted with a scream. "I need to record her reaction for the website!"

"Well, hurry up. We can't hold her here forever," J.J. said.

There was hurried movement.

Izzy grabbed the other corner of the blindfold. "Now?"

"Heather, are we good?" J.J. asked with a note of annoyance in his tone. After a beat, he told Izzy, "Let 'er rip."

The blindfold was pulled up and over Poppy's head.

The bright sun blinded her so that all she could see were shadows of people moving about. She then made out J.J.'s arm pointing at an upward angle. As her vision cleared, she saw that she was standing before an old barn.

She quickly realized that they had taken her to the old dairy farm.

Russell Ridge Farm and Orchards had been founded by the Russell family several generations earlier. As smaller farms around it had been bought and added onto the original farm, it had grown. When the dairy farm outgrew the original, a larger, more modern barn had been built on the other side of the property and the cattle moved. Like the Russell mansion, the original barn had been abandoned and forgotten.

Not any more.

The old barn had been rebuilt with a shiny red roof and bright white siding. The paddocks had sturdy fencing. The overgrown fields had been mowed.

Chief and Pilgrim trotted around one of the paddocks. Pilgrim was fighting to keep Chief nearby. This was not an easy task because he was chasing Ollie, who had somehow gotten inside the paddock. The two youngsters were enjoying a game of chase.

"I don't understand." Poppy gazed at Heather Davis who stood a couple of feet away with her phone recording her reaction, which was confusion.

"It's your own ranch," Cameron said with a sly grin.

Poppy turned to J.J. "You've decided to get me my own place? It's because I got red hair in your hairbrush, isn't it?"

"It's a rescue ranch for horses." Izzy's chest puffed out with pride. "It was my idea."

"Actually, you gave us the germ of the idea, Poppy," Joshua said. "Because of Donny's post to social media, people kept asking about Chief—especially when they found out how you had saved his mother from the slaughterhouse."

The farm foreman said, "We had folks stopping by here every day to see the little fellow. Many wanted to make donations to help take care of him and his mother."

"So many people wanted to know what was happening with Chief that I set up an Instagram page for him and start posting pictures and videos of him," Izzy said. "When I posted his story, he got *thousands* of followers overnight and a lot of them asked if they could make donations, too." She tapped her temple. "That was when I got my idea."

"Start a ranch for rescued horses," Poppy said in a soft voice.

"They called me on the ship to ask if there was any place on the farm for us to keep the horses." J.J. looked at the barn. "I remembered the original dairy farm. Dad set the rescue ranch up as a non-profit foundation."

"Donations are already pouring into the website that I set up," Heather said.

"The building supply company in town donated their materials to rebuild the barn and fences," Joshua said. "The feed store will give us a non-profit discount on food and anything else we need for the horses."

"Donated materials and discount on feed?" Poppy let out a gasp. "I don't believe it."

Cameron wrapped her arms around Joshua. "Josh and I can be very persuasive."

"Many of the farmhands and their families jumped right in to donate their time and labor to get the place ready to take in horses." The foreman jerked a thumb in the direction of the barn. "We got all of this done in just one week."

"Unfortunately, we discovered Maddie doesn't know the first thing about hammering a nail." Heather Davis winked at her half-sister, who was playing with Luke and Munster on what resembled an obstacle course.

"If it wasn't for me, we wouldn't have dates for line dancing tonight," Madison said while gesturing for Munster to run through a long tube.

"She's right," Heather said. "She may not know how to hammer a nail, but her and Sherry sure know how to transform a dog. Turns out, Dad did get Munster from Sherry. He turned into a menace because he was bored. We're alleviating his boredom with agility training. Sherry thinks we've got a shot at a trophy."

"We had to set up a course to keep him and Luke from chasing Chief," Cameron said. "We had a lot of work to do in a short amount of time."

"We've already got two horses in the barn. They arrived yesterday from a hoarder situation." Poppy saw Rod, their vet, among the crowd. "I'm volunteering my services. The foundation will pay for medicine and supplies."

"Once the horses are healthy and able, we'll find forever homes for them. Those that can't be adopted, we'll keep." J.J.

peered into her eyes. "Poppy, say something. What do you think?"

"I think ..." Her eyes narrowed as she took in the collection of volunteers and hard work accomplished in only one week—all to save beautiful innocent animals like Chief and Pilgrim. "I think we're going to need a bigger horse trailer."

J.J. turned her around to face the barn. "Did you see the sign?"

She followed the invisible line from his index finger to the sign hanging above the barn door. In block letters it read:

Poppy Ashurn-Thornton's Rescue Ranch
"Where there is love, there's always room for one more."

The End

About the Author

Lauren Carr

Lauren Carr is the international best-selling author of the Thorny Rose, Lovers in Crime, Mac Faraday, and Chris Matheson Cold Case Mysteries—over twenty titles across four fast-paced mystery series filled with twists and turns!

Book reviewers and readers alike rave about how Lauren Carr seamlessly crosses genres to include mystery, suspense, crime fiction, police procedurals, romance, and humor.

Lauren is a popular speaker who has made appearances at schools, youth groups, and on author panels at conventions. She lives with her husband and two German Shepherds, including the real Sterling, on a mountain in Harpers Ferry, WV.

Visit Lauren Carr's website at www.mysterylady.net to learn more about Lauren and her upcoming mysteries.

Check Out Lauren Carr's Mysteries!

All of Lauren Carr's books are stand alone. However for those readers wanting to start at the beginning, here is the list of Lauren Carr's mysteries. The number next to the book title is the actual order in which the book was released.

Joshua Thornton Mysteries

Fans of the *Lovers in Crime Mysteries* may wish to read these two books which feature Joshua Thornton years before meeting Detective Cameron Gates. Also in these mysteries, readers will meet Joshua Thornton's five children before they had flown the nest.

1) A Small Case of Murder
2) A Reunion to Die For

Mac Faraday Mysteries

3) It's Murder, My Son
4) Old Loves Die Hard
5) Shades of Murder   (*introduces the Lovers in Crime: Joshua Thornton & Cameron Gates*)
7) Blast from the Past
8) The Murders at Astaire Castle
9) The Lady Who Cried Murder   (*The Lovers in Crime make a guest appearance in this Mac Faraday Mystery*)
10) Twelve to Murder
12) A Wedding and a Killing
13) Three Days to Forever
15) Open Season for Murder
!6) Cancelled Vows

ATTENTION BOOK CLUB-BERS!

Want to add some excitement to your next book club meeting? Are you curious about Lauren Carr's theme's regarding mystery and family? Do you wonder where she picks up her inspiration for such interesting characters? What does she have planned next for the Thornton family? Well, now is your chance to ask this international best-selling mystery writer, in person, you and your book club.

That's right. Lauren Carr is available to personally meet with your book club to discuss *The Root of Murder* or any of her best-selling mystery novels.

Don't worry if your club is meeting on the other side of the continent. Lauren can pop in to answer your questions via webcam. But, if your club is close enough, Lauren would love to personally meet with your group. Who knows! She may even bring her muse Sterling along!

To invite Lauren Carr to your next book club meeting, visit www.mysterylady.net and fill out a request form with your club's details.

Coming Summer 2019!

The Geezer Squad Rides Again in:

THE LAST THING SHE SAID

A Chris Matheson Cold Case Mystery

Made in the USA
Columbia, SC
22 August 2019